REVENGE. BETRAYAL. DEATH.

HERA'S SCREAM

SHAUN GRIFFIN

BOOK TWO OF THE AMERICAN NOIR TRILOGY

To Jane, Kyle & Claire for all your support.

Special thanks to Monika for providing the Polish translation.

HERA'S
SCREAM

EVEN THOUGH I KNOW THE HOUR OF MY DEATH, I COULD ALTER NAUGHT, FOR THE NORNS HAVE WOVEN THE THREAD TIGHT INTO THE TAPESTRY OF LIFE.

–Old Norse verse.

1

N ick Kovic knew he was in trouble.

The cold eyes of the stranger standing in front of him confirmed it. He shifted painfully on the stool and eyed the cutthroat razor in the man's right hand. Nick flinched as he flicked the blood idly off the razor. The past three hours had been almost more than he could endure.

He remembered walking to his car the night before and opening the door, but he couldn't remember anything after that. He'd come round to find himself lying in his underwear on the cold concrete floor of a deserted warehouse. Plastic ties secured his hands behind his back. A man armed with a silenced 9mm automatic had appeared and instructed him to sit on the small stool. He had introduced himself as Goran, the brother of Dragan Millovic, the gang boss Nick had once worked for.

Goran had then questioned him about Dragan's death. Nick had told him everything, but Goran was convinced he knew more. He'd progressed to a more vigorous method to get what he considered the truth. He had been particularly creative with the cutthroat razor. But despite hours of torture, Nick could only repeat what he knew.

"Look, I've told you all I know, man," he croaked. "Dragan had a deal with some guy called Matthew."

"You have last name?"

"No. Your brother never said. Anyway, the deal must've turned sour, so Dragan was planning to kill Matthew and the other guy he was with."

"But you never meet this other one—his partner. Tell me, does Dragan ever meet with this one?"

Nick stared fearfully at Goran. He looked very different from his brother. Whereas Dragan had been overweight, Goran was wiry, the corded muscles of his chest and arms visible through the thin fabric of his long sleeve black top. Perhaps Dragan had been the same once but had allowed a debauched lifestyle to soften him. The trim physique, tailored outfit and close-cropped hair of this man signaled a rigorous self-discipline. Nick forced himself to look into Goran's eyes but found no answers in their cruel black depths. It was like looking into the soul of death itself. He swallowed hard.

"Like I keep saying, Matthew's partner didn't even know he was working for us, so there's no way Dragan would have met him."

"You mean, working for Dragan."

The razor flashed and Nick cried out.

"You said Matthew is working for us—you and Dragan. But Dragan is boss, not you," snarled Goran.

"Yes, sorry, that's what I meant. Matthew was working for Dragan."

"You say, Dragan pay this Matthew to kill other gangsters?"

"Yes, I mean, no. He was only going to pay him once the job was done."

"Yes or no? Which one is it? I think you are not sure."

The razor glinted wickedly.

"No! I mean, yes, I'm sure. He hadn't paid him yet, but he was going to pay him after the job."

"And what is job?"

"What?"

Nick screamed as the razor sliced into his flesh.

"I want to know, what is job?" pressed Goran, brandishing the cut-throat with menace.

Nick leaned back as far as the small stool would allow without toppling over. Blood flowed from each cut mixing with the rivulets of sweat that ran down his body. The gruesome blend dripped steadily onto the concrete floor.

"I told you! I don't know all the details. All I know is Dragan wanted someone to hit the da Silva gang. That's where Matthew and his buddy came in. Look, I don't know what went down between Dragan and them. Maybe there was a disagreement or something. Next thing I know, he's planning to rub out Matthew and the other guy. But the night the hit was meant to go down, I got arrested."

"Yes, you are arrested. Then Dragan go to this place with his men to kill Matthew and things go bad. Everyone die. Everyone except you," noted Goran with a jab of the cutthroat.

"I know how this looks, man, but I'm telling you the truth. First, I get pulled over for some outstanding parking tickets. Next I get pinched for some blow and get thrown in lock-up."

"Yes, you are in jail when my brother is killed. This is very convenient."

"Yes, I mean, no! No, it's not convenient. Look, I'm sorry it went down the way it did. I really am."

Goran stepped forward menacingly, his sneering face inches away. Nick saw himself reflected in the man's black eyes. "I think you lie."

"What? No! I'm telling you the God's honest truth, I swear!"

"You work for da Silva."

"No! I don't even know the man. Please."

"I think you tell da Silva where my brother is going. Maybe you help da Silva set trap. Maybe this Matthew is already dead and when my brother and his men come, da Silva and his people wait for them."

A flash of the razor produced another scream from Nick.

"Please, man, it's the truth. I told you I don't even know him!"

"That is what you say. Now make me believe," said Goran, lifting the razor.

"No, please, I'm begging you. Don't cut me no more."

"Make me believe."

"There was a police report!"

Goran stepped back and eyed his victim speculatively, the razor held loosely at his side.

"Police report?"

"Yeah, I heard from someone the report said there was shell casings lying everywhere, but the only bodies on the scene was Dragan and the rest of our guys. With all those shots fired, there should've been others."

"You have proof?"

"I told you. They didn't find any other bodies. And the shell casings was all from our guys. There was nothing from other weapons. Don't you see? It doesn't add up!"

"That is what you say," said Goran, waving the razor idly from side to side.

Nick shifted unsteadily on the stool. "Wait! Please, I can get you the report."

"You have copy?"

"No, not with me, but I can get it. I've got a contact."

"Give me contact details."

Goran's tone did not invite negotiation.

"Sure, okay."

Nick was relieved when his captor began cleaning the razor on an old cloth rag. He folded the blade closed. A phone call later, Goran appeared satisfied that he'd get the information he wanted.

"What now?" asked Nick.

He still couldn't read Goran's expression. Was the man going to let him go or not?

"I am going to tell you story," began Goran before pausing to ensure he had his captive's full attention.

Nick nodded passively.

"Dragan and me," said Goran, "we live with my mother in Kragujevac. My father, he dies in accident in factory. We struggle. My mother is working very long hours in same factory. Life is hard. Dragan and me, we join gang. Vlada is gang leader. Vlada is hard man. Everyone in gang does what he says. But Dragan is not scared of Vlada. He talks back to Vlada, tells him there is better way of doing things. This makes Vlada angry. One day, Vlada says Dragan is not respecting him. He gives Dragan choice. Take punishment or leave gang. Dragan chooses punishment. Punishment is always same—Vlada cut off small finger of left hand. But now Vlada looks to me. You cut off your brother's finger, he says. I do not want to do this, but Dragan says to me I must, so I do what my brother says."

Goran leaned forward and placed his hands on Nick's bare knees, his leering face inches from his victim.

"One night, we wait for Vlada. We take him to forest. Dragan has knife."

Goran smiled grimly. "Vlada dies slowly. We do not hide body because we want everyone to see Vlada is dead. We want everyone to know how he die. Now Dragan is gang leader. From that day, no one in Kragujevac fuck with us." He spoke the last words slowly, emphasizing each syllable. He stepped back from Nick.

"We square then?" asked Nick carefully.

Goran smiled. "Square? Sure."

He pulled the silenced pistol from his belt and fired. The bullet hit Nick in the forehead, jerking him back off the stool. Goran stepped forward and fired two more shots into the corpse. He stepped back to avoid the expanding pool of blood and bent down to retrieve the three shell casings. He looked about briefly to ensure he'd overlooked nothing then turned and walked back towards the warehouse door. He felt sure he was now one step closer to finding his brother's killers and that was one step closer to getting his revenge. A day. A month. A year. Time was of no consequence. In the end, the result was all that mattered.

2

Faith watched the naked threesome on the bed with disinterest.

A woman sat astride the man, her hips moving rhythmically. He appeared mesmerized, caught between his physical pleasure and the erotic vision of a second female stimulating the woman impaled on him. It was then that Faith realized she recognized the girl fucking the man. It was her. Was she having an out-of-body experience?

She wasn't sure, nor did she care. The only thing that mattered now was what came next, and the thought of it excited her. She felt an electric tingle stimulating each nerve of her body as she watched the man beneath her. The moment was near. He reached his orgasm. But his pleasure was cut short as the two women sank their fangs into his exposed flesh.

They ignored his screams as they continued to feed voraciously, draining the life blood from him. His soul was theirs.

She woke with a start, her heart pounding. Staring up at the ceiling, she slowly let her body relax. Had she been dreaming? For a moment, she almost believed she had. Almost. She turned her head to look into the sightless eyes of the dead man lying next to her and knew the truth of it.

She sat up and turned to look across the corpse to where Jennifer, her sister vampire, slept soundly. The sleep of the guiltless? Jennifer was the most recent of Anastasiya's converts. She noted how the virus had already transformed the girl, from the subtle enhancement of her musculature to the inevitable bleaching of her hair.

She looked down at her own blonde hair and tried to recall its original color. Dark brown? Auburn? She couldn't remember. That was part of the other Faith, a girl now lost in a past life. A girl weakened by human frailty and self-doubt.

But at least human.

She slid off the bed and walked over to the full-length mirror on the wall opposite to look at her reflection. Firm, full breasts perched upon a svelte, finely muscled body. So different from the skinny girl of before. Different and yet nothing more than a caricature. An image of a female the virus infecting her used to appeal to human males. She frowned.

Was that even possible? Could a virus, even an alien one, be sentient? And even if it were, how could it know what humans thought or what men found attractive? She didn't have the answer. Perhaps the simplest explanation was this was the way the genes of female homo sapiens responded to the virus infecting them.

But there was one difference between her and her vampire sisters. Faith leant closer to the mirror. The color of her eyes remained their original deep hazel rather than the ice blue of the other girls. Perhaps her eyes would still change color, but she doubted it. It had been a year since she'd undergone the transformation, when she and John had come to this place intent upon revenge.

John.

She closed her eyes and attempted to visualize him but found she couldn't. His face had become a featureless blur, blended with the countless faces of the men she had since fed upon.

Stop it! For better or worse, this is your life now.

She opened her eyes and regarded the pensive girl staring back in the mirror. Perhaps it was best not to remember. She turned away from her reflection and walked back to the foot of the four-poster bed to look at the dead man she and Jennifer had fed on only hours before.

Any empathy she might have once felt had long since been eroded by the necessity of her new life. Fresh human blood was her only source of food, and to survive she needed to feed. Humans were nothing more than cattle. That was the way Meredith put it. Every time she fed on them it became more difficult to see them as anything else.

Faith found the drive to copulate that accompanied her hunger a little disconcerting at times. In part, she supposed it was a product of the obvious need to entice the victim to a place of her choosing. But she felt it was something other than the alien virus that infected them. What then—the need to procreate? Was it that simple? The thought elicited a wry smile. Human or not, perhaps they were all still slaves to nature's fundamental drive.

Replicating within a new host may have satisfied the virus, but the vampire it inhabited also needed to ensure its genes survived. Reproduction required sex, plain and simple. Despite knowing that she could not deny the thrill of the hunt, she relished the tactile sensation of warm flesh, the metallic taste of warm blood, and the contentment of a hunger sated.

But a hunger that will return. Again and again.

Faith noted the familiar changes starting in the corpse — the once opaque flesh shifting to an odd translucence, allowing the observer to watch the corruption of the dead body, each blackened vein marking the passage of the virus. She reached down, picked up the red silk robe from the floor, and slipped it on.

A moment later, the door to the room opened. Faith watched as Anastasiya's manservant, Lotho, entered. He greeted her with a somber nod and walked silently over to the bed. The large man appeared not to notice the naked Jennifer as he reached over her to effortlessly lift the dead body from the bed. He slung the corpse over his shoulder and left the room. Faith knew what was to follow.

First, a shot would be delivered to the head with a cattle gun to destroy the brain. This ensured the infected corpse could not be resurrected by the virus. The corpse would then be allowed to deteriorate, the virus consuming all soft tissue until there was nothing but a desiccated shell. Lotho would then dismember the parchment-like remains and dispose of them in the basement furnace.

Human cattle.

Faith shuddered involuntarily. It was not the first time she had allowed herself to dwell on the eventual fate of the men brought to this place. She wondered again whether there was any alternative to the never-ending cycle. If there was, she had yet to think of it. The virus required the ingestion of fresh human blood, direct from the source. The volume required for each feed — at least a quart per vampire — meant having more than a few humans readily available. The logistics of keeping that many humans in captivity without detection appeared impractical to Faith. Besides, if Anastasiya, centuries old, had not yet thought of a way, then how could she divine a better alternative?

"Time to get up," she said, gently touching Jennifer on the shoulder.

Jennifer opened her eyes and gave a self-satisfied yawn as she stretched with a feline grace.

"I had the most incredible dream," she said.

"Let me guess. You're a wolf running through a forest. Your heart pounds with excitement the closer you get to your prey. You can smell its fear, though it remains out of sight. You increase your pace, your hunger driving you on."

Faith leant forward so that her face was inches from Jennifer's, and the pace of her voice quickened.

"You're now close enough to hear the labored panting of your prey as it tires, and then you know. You know it's a person you're hunting, and yet strangely that makes it even more exciting. The high you feel keeps building inside you 'till finally you chase your prey down and tear into its warm flesh."

She stood back up and noted the look of disappointment on Jennifer's face.

"All the girls have had similar dreams, Jen. Or variations of them."

"I wasn't saying it was anything more than that," said Jen.

She sat up, picked up her robe, and slipped it on with feigned nonchalance.

"What? Did you think you were unique?" said Faith, pretending to pout.

"You don't have to make fun of me."

Jennifer was the youngest of the acolytes — in both human and vampire terms. Anastasiya had turned her a few weeks before. Faith immediately regretted her flippant response, because she knew as well as any of them the highs and lows Jennifer would be feeling. Each kill brought a lingering remorse, a sobering counterpoint to the euphoria of omnipotence the virus afforded each of them. A lingering remorse she knew would fade all too soon.

Perhaps that was the reason Anastasiya chose young sex workers. Young women usually enslaved to either their drug habits, their pimps, or both. They would be loath to relinquish the power they now had over the very men who'd made their lives hell before. Perhaps Anastasiya herself had suffered similar abuse, though there was no way of knowing for sure. The woman continued to remain an enigma.

"Faith?"

Faith realized she'd been staring off into space. "Sorry, I didn't mean to drift off. Look, I'm not making fun of you." She placed a hand on Jen's shoulder and continued, "What you're experiencing is the same thing we've all been through. Maybe I lost sight of the fact that it's all still very new and exciting to you."

"Exciting, yes, I suppose. But sometimes I get scared."

Jen felt she could confide in Faith, a trust she extended to none of the others.

"Scared? Why?"

"I don't know. Maybe I'm worried that in the end there's going to be a price to pay. I mean, killing these men. It can't go on forever, can it? I know I should feel bad about it, and sometimes I still do, but most of the time..." She looked away.

"There's always a price to pay, Jen."

"Do you really believe that?"

"Isn't that the stuff of life?"

"Maybe it is, but it's not like we asked for this, is it?"

"Does that make us any less guilty?"

"You think we deserve what's coming to us?"

"Nobody deserves anything, Jen. Good or bad, things happen. That's what I'm talking about. And the price is total loyalty and obedience to Anastasiya. Not too bad a price considering the hell we've escaped."

"I suppose you're right," said Jen. "Look, I don't mean to sound negative. Sometimes things can get a bit overwhelming, you know? It's all so different from the way I was before. It gets confusing."

"You're not being negative. Anyway, it takes some time getting used to your new self. You know, comfortable in your own skin. Wait and see."

"I guess so."

"Come," said Faith, offering her hand to Jen. "We'd better get going. Class is in another hour."

"Thanks," said Jen, pulling herself up. "I can't say I'm looking forward to the morning lesson. All that philosophy and art bullshit. It feels like I'm back in school. I prefer the fight training we do in the afternoons."

Faith smiled. "If you think about it, we are in a type of school."

"Not like any school I've ever been to."

"True, but you're no longer like the average person, are you?"

They laughed and left the room arm in arm like two innocent schoolgirls. The dead looked on, hollow eyed wraiths screaming in silent agony.

◊ ◊ ◊

At about the same time, Anastasiya was in the large conservatory tending to her favorite pitcher plants. She enjoyed being in her small tropical Eden even though the morning sunlight that shone through the glass panels made her nauseous. She tolerated the daylight, but she preferred the night because that was when she hunted, and she enjoyed the hunt most of all.

There was something primeval and even exhilarating about going out into the city to choose her prey and then entice them back to her lair. Most times, she enjoyed the physical intimacy of sex with them, but occasionally she did not. Sometimes she chose men and other times women. Yet no matter how pleasurable the evening or who her prey was, it always ended in death. She was a killer, an apex predator whose victims numbered in the thousands.

The countless years lived had allowed her to experience the full range of emotions — at first remorseful regret, followed by self-loathing, and finally omnipotent contempt for the humans she fed upon. Perhaps in a way she had maintained some semblance of her sanity by coming to see herself as being above the humans she killed to sate her hunger. She was a god who lived amongst human cattle. And as with any god, she too had her disciples — her acolytes, the same yet different from her because besides human blood they also needed her blood to survive. The alien virus infecting them had failed to fully mutate their cells, which necessitated infusions of her blood to regenerate the virus.

In essence, this power over her acolytes made them her slaves, though most chose not to see themselves thus. From the very first of them she had chosen, it had always been so.

Until now. The girl, Faith, was different from the others. She did not need Anastasiya's blood to survive. Her body had successfully combined with the virus, though how and why was a mystery. Anastasiya had not revealed this truth to the girl, who still believed she was no different from the others.

Anastasiya ran her long fingers across the lush purple and red rims of the pitcher plants that hung from the trellis. She reflected that some of the plants appeared more adept at attracting prey despite appearing no different from their sisters. She wondered why this was and why the virus had chosen this girl amongst all the others she had infected over the years. Why this girl—visibly no different from the others—had fused so completely with the virus when others could not. Could it be the virus had no choice, being as much a pawn of nature as all living creatures appeared to be? Anastasiya frowned at the thought. *No!*

She would not countenance the idea. Accepting it would mean relinquishing her special place as the one first chosen. Of all humans, the alien virus had chosen to bond with her, mutating her as it too had mutated. She had become something other than human. She had become a god. What then of the girl? Had union with the virus made her a god too?

Anastasiya would not accept that. She was an anomaly, nothing more, proven by the fact that none of the others she had chosen since had managed full union. What did this mean? She was still not sure. Anastasiya had at first been intrigued, thinking perhaps the virus had chosen the girl as a challenge to her position as queen.

Yet though Faith had proven more resistant to Anastasiya's teachings, she had never challenged her leadership. At least, not to date. She had allowed Faith to live a year now, choosing to view her as a kind of experiment. A thing to be studied until a conclusion could be determined or the experiment finally terminated. A vampire's extended longevity allowed that luxury. There was always time enough.

She looked up at the light streaming through the glass panels of the conservatory with annoyance. The daylight was a necessary evil. She reflected that as much as her plants required the light to survive, she too needed human blood. But humans could be a threat too. She wondered again why she had chosen not to move the school elsewhere after this last attack. She had been in similar situations in past years and each time had chosen to disappear back into the shadows rather than risk exposure.

This strategy had served her well for two centuries. Why then had she chosen to stay this time, especially after having lost most of her acolytes and her love, Eden, in the fight? Was it because she was sure she had eliminated the threat? There was no way of knowing this for sure. Why then choose this course of action? A thought occurred to her then. Perhaps she had become tired of it all. Hiding in the shadows, always on her guard, always having to move when threatened with the possibility of discovery. Constantly having to reinvent herself.

Or had realizing that this cycle would never ever end finally driven a part of her to want to finish it all? She paused to consider the thought before rejecting it. Not even two hundred years and already self-doubt! She scowled.

To absurdalne, nie dam wygrać słabościom!

She had chosen to stay because moving would have been an acknowledgment that they and not she had true power, something she was not willing to concede. This time, the choice would be hers and hers alone to make.

Anastasiya turned from her plants and walked back through the lush vegetation towards the pond that dominated the conservatory. She stood a moment at the water's edge and looked down at her reflection in contemplation. Dipping a toe into the cool water, she watched her reflection dissolve in the widening circle of ripples. Gone forever? She waited.

The ripples subsided, and her reflection gazed up at her once more from the water's still surface. She dipped her toe in the water and watched her image disappear again then return as the water stilled. She smiled. For as long as she chose, she would remain.

With that thought, she stepped onto the first of the flat stones set beneath the water's surface and strode resolutely over the pond towards the conservatory's exit. Her acolytes would be waiting for her.

3

Anastasiya stood in front of her students. A large book was open upon an ornate book stand to her left. The double page spread showed a naked woman floating above the sea, her translucent flesh stark against the aquamarine and emerald hue of the water. Winged cherubs hovered above her supine form.

"*The Birth of Venus* by Alexandre Cabanel. Note the way the artist has portrayed her," she said, tracing her fingers along the contours of the nude figure. "See how her arm is extended back over her head, accentuating the curve of her breasts, with one leg drawn up seductively to cover the promise of her sex. The way her eyes appear almost shut suggests she has just awoken, but the sensuous curve of her mouth hints to something else. What do you think that is?"

She looked around expectantly, but none of the girls would venture an answer.

"She recognizes the viewer," she said. "He is her prospective lover. He is every man who looks at her portrait. She waits—virginal, prostate, and willing before him, the embodiment of all his desires."

She turned the page.

"*The Nymphaeum* by William Bouguereau. Note the pose of each nude. They are aware that they are on display. See how most choose to look away from the viewer. Even the few who look out from the painting do so with a demure expression. Why do you think this is?"

"They don't want to challenge the male viewer," answered Meredith confidently.

Her expression betrayed that she felt she was above the other girls in the class. It was a position granted by the fact she was the first among them that Anastasiya turned. She was also the only one to have experienced actual life-or-death combat.

"Yes, that is correct. If they were to look directly at him, it would not only destroy the illusion that they are there for his viewing pleasure but also that he has power over them."

Anastasiya turned the page.

"*Danae* by Alexandre Chantron. Again, we see the supine female form. The paleness of her flesh against the red of the curtain is meant to add to her allure. Again, she chooses to look away from the viewer, yet her expression betrays that she is aware she is being looked at."

"But being desired isn't a bad thing, is it?" said Jennifer, who had not meant to question her mistress. She had merely spoken her thoughts out loud.

"Isn't a bad thing?" repeated Meredith, mimicking Jen's voice. "What? Do you enjoy existing only for men's pleasure?"

She offered Jen a look of undisguised contempt. A few of the girls chuckled and glanced nervously at Anastasiya. But their mistress stood silently, her arms folded across her chest as she regarded the newest recruit with a cold, calculating glare.

"I don't think Jen meant it like that," said Faith.

"Oh? Well, what did she mean then?" Meredith fired back.

"I didn't hear her say anything about existing only for men's pleasure, Meredith. That was all you. Maybe if you let her explain, you would understand," said Faith.

"I understand plenty, girl, and I know what she meant, and so did everyone else here. Everyone except you."

"Maybe I'm the one who gets it and you're the one who doesn't. Ever think of that, girl?"

"Enough!" snapped Anastasiya.

She was aware of the animosity between the two but had done little to prevent it. She preferred a certain tension amongst her acolytes. It kept them on edge and avoided complacency—something they could ill afford in this world. Her latest convert, Jennifer, concerned her though. The virus allowed her to sense whether the genetics of a chosen female would adapt or not. It did not give her insight into their psychology. That ability—the skill to choose those women ideal for conversion—was something she'd developed herself. It was something she was proud of. She did not make mistakes. Was this the first? She looked pointedly at Jennifer.

"Well, girl? Explain yourself."

"I'm sorry, ma'am. What I meant to say is that being desired by someone isn't always bad," said Jen.

She looked around to the other girls for support. They looked away.

"You mean, because that desire is what allows us to lure our prey closer?" prompted Faith.

She'd never seen Anastasiya resort to anything more than a verbal rebuke but knew their mistress could be far more ruthless. Was her friend in danger of crossing some unseen line?

"Of course. Why, what did everyone think I meant?" said Jen, flashing Meredith an innocent smile.

"Why don't you tell me?" shot back Meredith acidly.

"I thought I did."

"Funny, your lips might've moved, but I swear I heard someone else."

"I'm no one's puppet," snapped Jen.

"Ladies, you will confine your argument to the lesson at hand," said Anastasiya.

The tension subsided as the girls turned to face her. Once she had their attention, she continued.

"This type of painting was very popular in the nineteenth century and was most often displayed in gentleman's clubs or the drawing rooms of rich men. These paintings were the exclusive property of men and as much as these paintings were their property, so too their women, for what rights did the females of that time have? No suffrage, little access to education, and excluded from most employment. Even a woman's property became that of her husband's the moment she was married. Women were viewed as the inferior of the species, a view supported by male scientists and philosophers of the time."

Anastasiya stepped over to the bookshelf against one wall and ran her fingers along the row of books until she located the one she wanted. She pulled it from the rack and opened it to a random page.

"I will provide you with a rough translation from the original German. In this passage, it is stated that a woman should be devoted only to matters of sex, in other words, to the acts of conceiving and reproduction. Her husband and children should complete her life. The male in contrast is more than a sexual being. That is to say, males are intended for higher pursuits, whilst females are allotted the role of brood mare."

She flicked through the pages and read another passage. She gave a wry smile and looked up at the girls.

"Women are illogical by nature and resent any guidance to correct that. The writer contends that because of this they might be regarded as logically insane."

She looked down and flicked past a few more pages.

"Only man can achieve the characteristics of personality and individuality, of ego and soul, and of will and character. Females by their nature cannot. In other words, they are less than human."

Anastasiya closed the book and returned it to its place.

"The book is called *Sex and Character* and was written by Otto Weininger. A troubled little man, as I recall."

Amused by the memory, she smiled.

"Many other books with a similar view litter these shelves. I have collected them for their comic value only."

Faith wanted to ask if any other books had been published at that time challenging this type of thinking. She could not believe all men had thought this way or that no woman of that time had spoken up. She wanted to ask but did not. Questioning would only serve to antagonize Anastasiya, and that was something she preferred to avoid. She understood the precariousness of her position. Still, the idea that the only access to learning was whatever Anastasiya allowed chafed at her. No cell phones. No internet. No electronic devices of any sort, in fact. Why, if not to control?

"You have a question, Faith?" asked Anastasiya.

"No, ma'am," said Faith, resolving to better mask her thoughts.

Anastasiya's brow arched in response. She walked back to where a second book stand stood and turned to her small audience.

"And why is it that men choose to view all women in this way?" She opened the large bound book on the stand.

"And when the woman saw that the tree was good for food, and that it was pleasant to the eyes, and a tree to be desired to make one wise, she took of the fruit thereof, and did eat."

She pointed to the painting on each page. Both depicted the classic *Fall of Man*.

"And what is it you see in these paintings? Do you only see what patriarchal society would want you to believe? Do you only see a naked Eve tempting Adam with forbidden fruit? Tempting him to original sin? Or do you see the truth? That it was woman who first had the power of knowledge and that it was woman who chose to share it with man. Note how Eve is positioned relative to Adam in these paintings. She is either level with him – his equal – or she is above him. In each, she extends her hand, offering the fruit of knowledge. Perhaps on some level, the male artists who painted these pictures during the Renaissance were aware of the truth. At this moment, it is she who holds the power. It is she who chooses to share that power. What has it gained us? Equality?"

Anastasiya laughed.

"Now you can understand why men prefer to see us as something inferior. It is because they do not have to acknowledge that we first held the power of true knowledge."

She stood silently to allow her acolytes to ponder what she had said.

"Think of the gift I have granted each of you and ask yourselves: Why is it men cannot achieve the same union? Why is it they are nothing more than our source of food? Why if not because it is they who are truly the inferior?"

She looked at the girls and gauged from their expressions an unquestioning acceptance. Even Faith appeared to agree, or at least offered no hint to the contrary. She looked at the clock and noted the time.

"That is all for today. You may return to your rooms. Fight training will be in one hour."

The girls rose quietly and waited for Anastasiya to exit the room.

Meredith was the first to leave after that, leading a clique of girls who had gravitated naturally towards her queen-bitch persona. In her previous life, her less than ideal trailer-park upbringing had assigned her the role of misfit in the social caste system that passed for high school. There, she was doomed to skulk on the sidelines and watch as the pretty, rich girls flaunted their popularity. But that life was past. In this life, she'd been first chosen by the countess and so naturally had been afforded a position of power. This was a position she reveled in, and she was determined to keep it. She shot Faith a look of contempt as she exited the door. The feeling was mutual. It had been Meredith's bite that had infected Faith. Usually this afforded a kind of natural bond between creator and creation. But not in this case, for the intention of Meredith's attack on Faith had been to kill, a fact both girls were only too aware of.

When the last of the acolytes had left, Faith turned to Jen.

"I'll help you with the chairs," she said.

As the new girl, Jennifer was expected to remain behind and pack away after each lesson.

"Thanks," said Jen, who proceeded to move the chairs to their usual place along the far wall.

"What did you really mean before by saying being desired wasn't all bad?" asked Faith as she closed one of the large books and lifted it from the stand.

"What?" responded Jen nervously.

"You said being desired wasn't all bad, but it sounded like you wanted to be more than desired. It sounded like you wanted to be loved and maybe looked after."

Faith walked over to the appropriate spot on the bookshelf and replaced the book. She turned and looked at her friend.

"Was it that obvious?" said Jen, packing the last of the chairs away.

"Maybe a little, yeah," said Faith. "Look, I wouldn't stress about it too much. There isn't really any wrong answer, more of an expectation, you know?"

"An expectation? To do what, always come up with the right answer? I'm trying my best, Faith. But I still feel I'm falling short of whatever it is she expects. I mean, what if she decides I don't measure up? What will she do then—not allow me any of her blood? You know what that means—I'll die. You've seen what the virus can do. I don't want that to be me."

"Don't think like that," said Faith. "It only leads to doubting yourself. You'll end up looking weak. If there's one thing she hates, it's weakness."

"I'm sorry. I'll try not to from now on."

"No," said Faith, placing her hands on Jen's shoulders. "Here, trying isn't good enough. Here you must fully commit. Go all out, and I promise you that everything will fall into place. You'll see."

She hoped she sounded convincing.

"Thanks, Faith, at least I know I can always count on you."

"Don't sweat it. Now let's finish up and get ready for fight training."

Faith returned to the remaining book on its stand. She closed it, picked it up, and turned to face Jen with a smile.

"Who knows, maybe I'll get a chance to kick Meredith's ass!"

"Who knows? Maybe you will," chuckled Jen.

Both knew Meredith was the most proficient fighter by far amongst all the girls. Any thought of kicking her ass was wishful thinking.

4

Each afternoon's fight class observed a set routine—a brief warm-up followed by a seemingly endless repetition of punching and kicking techniques. Then, much like Kata, the girls would practice set sequences of blocks, turns, strikes, and kicks. Anastasiya's fighting technique incorporated a mix of the different oriental fighting styles she had mastered over the years. Attaining these skills had not been achieved by chance. She had learned from the best. Her survival depended on it. For the same reason, she demanded a high level of competence from each of her acolytes. Relying on the strength and agility afforded by the virus was not enough. Each day, hour after intense hour, every technique was practiced until the girls' muscle memory allowed instant and effortless response to any attack.

The last hour of each four-hour session was devoted to actual fighting. The girls were paired off against each other and encouraged to employ the skills they had learnt. The fighting was brutal with no quarter given. After all, the virus infecting each one meant broken bones and cuts healed quickly. The enhancement of muscle and tendon forming part of each girl's transformation also meant that even those previously less athletically gifted found themselves more than a match for any human foe. Fighting each other, however, was a different matter. Some of the girls were naturally more attuned to fighting. Faith was not one of them. This meant she usually got beaten. Today felt like one of those occasions.

"Come on, girl, you gonna have to do better than that!" taunted Judith.

She evaded Faith's snap kick easily before delivering a vicious counter punch.

Faith fell back onto the floor. She twisted to the side to avoid Judith's heal-strike and grunted with pain as her broken rib bones ground against each other. Conceding defeat at this point was allowed, but that meant being the other girl's servant for the next week. The mundane tasks of cleaning and laundry felt the same whether human or vampire.

Faith was not about to give in easily. She rolled to her left, narrowly avoiding another strike and jumped to her feet. The girls circled each other once more, each looking for an opening. Faith followed Judith's movements but maintained distance, attempting to slow the fight. She was buying time for the virus to mend her damaged ribs.

"Stop backing away, girl. You know I'm gonna whip you good!" growled Judith.

She moved quickly then, feinting with a left jab then shifting her weight to deliver a right-hand strike. Ordinarily the blow would have landed, but this time it missed as Faith side-stepped. Judith followed through with a spinning back-kick, but Faith blocked it easily and countered with a right-hand strike to her attacker's neck. Judith stumbled back with a choke.

Faith blinked, equally as surprised as her opponent. Somehow, she'd sensed Judith's attack before it had been delivered but had no clue how she'd done it.

Her opponent circled warily now, looking for another opening. Faith danced back and forth on her toes, a new confidence surging through her. She felt something else too—a kind of sentient awareness that radiated from her being like an aura. Faith now saw in her mind's eye Judith's next attack even though her opponent was yet to strike.

Judith attacked a fraction of a second later, and Faith evaded the blow, following through with a quick right-left combination to the midriff of her off-balance opponent. Judith grunted in pain but spun about quickly, fists raised to counter any follow-up. But Faith was still trying to understand her newfound power and hung back content, for the moment, to see the uncertainty in her opponent's eyes.

"You got lucky. Let's see how good you are on the attack," snapped Judith.

"Luck? I don't think so. Maybe you're getting slow. You ever consider that?"

The truth was Faith didn't really know whether she'd been lucky and was reluctant to test herself, lest Judith be proved right.

Encouraged by Faith's hesitation, Judith struck again, this time with a high roundhouse kick to the head. But Faith countered easily, deflecting the kick with a flick of her arm before delivering a vicious counter punch to Judith's solar plexus. The girl doubled over with a gasp, yet Faith failed to follow through again, preferring instead to move back to admire her handiwork. At that moment she sensed rather than saw the lance Anastasiya flung at her and found herself moving instinctively to counter the attack.

Her block sent the shaft spinning harmlessly away, but she was already moving to counter Judith's attempt to capitalize on the distraction. Block, spin, and elbow strike to her opponent's ribs followed with lightning speed. Judith let out a cry of pain and stumbled back, nursing her broken ribs. It was then that Faith realized everyone in the room had stopped to watch their fight.

"How did you do that?" asked Mia, another of the girls, with undisguised envy.

"Do what?" answered Faith, feigning innocence.

"She means—how did you see that spear?" said Meredith, stepping forward.

"I don't know," said Faith. "Maybe I didn't. Maybe it was a lucky block."

"I don't believe you. Besides, you know we don't believe in luck," pressed Meredith.

She wanted an answer. They all wanted an answer. Faith wanted one too, but not right there. She needed time to figure it out for herself, away from the scrutiny of the others.

"What can I say? Maybe the stars aligned this one time," she said.

"Or maybe you're full of—"

"The intent of the spear was not to test reflexes," interrupted Anastasiya sharply. "The spear was a reprimand."

She turned to Faith.

"Why do you think I threw that spear at you?"

"I failed to press the advantage," said Faith.

She sensed this was what her mistress wanted the others to hear, but the real question lurked in Anastasiya's eyes. An explanation would be demanded at some later time.

"Correct, you failed to press your advantage," said Anastasiya, looking around at the other girls. "Never allow your enemy a moment to recover. Be relentless and press your attack until he lies dead at your feet. Nothing less will suffice."

She looked intently at each of the girls in turn. Was this to see if they understood or was it to ensure they no longer cared about Faith's sudden display of martial prowess. There was a noticeable ease of tension in the room.

"Class is over for today. You may return to your rooms," she said.

◊ ◊ ◊

It was late. Faith sat at the open window and looked out over the mansion grounds. She liked the way the moon's cold light distorted the everyday shapes of tree, hedge, and shrub. It lent these otherwise mundane objects an air of mystique and freed her mind to imagine whatever she wished.

"Faith?"

"Yes?"

Faith had hoped Jen would've taken the "I don't feel like talking" hint but also understood her roommate's burning curiosity. What everyone witnessed earlier had been extraordinary, she supposed, even allowing for the fact each of them was already superhuman.

"You mind if I ask you something?"

"Look," said Faith without turning around, "I know what you're going to ask, and the answer is I don't know. One minute, Judith was beating me the way she always does, and the next I was all over her. Every attack she threw at me I countered and then some. That's all there is to it."

"Oh, I thought maybe…"

"Maybe what?" snapped Faith, turning to face Jen. "You thought that maybe I'd planned it all along? That I'd let her beat me all this time to see the look on her face when she finally got her ass whipped?"

Jen hesitated. Faith was her only friend. She would need to weigh her words carefully or risk upsetting her.

"No, it's not like that. I mean, maybe I am thinking you were waiting for a chance to make her look stupid, but that's not really you, and that makes me wonder what the hell did happen today?"

Faith folded her arms across her chest. "What are you trying to say?"

"Well, isn't the virus supposed to change us all the same way?"

"You really believe that?" said Faith arching her brow.

"It's what Meredith told me when I first woke after, you know, the change," said Jen. "She said I'd be better than I ever was before—stronger, faster, prettier, and all that. Like a god, she said."

Faith stood up and went to sit on the bed alongside her friend. She took Jen's hands in hers. "All gods aren't equal, Jen. Besides, we're not gods. We're humans with an advanced viral infection."

"You really think that?"

Jen looked a little disappointed. Up to that point, she'd always felt special—one of the chosen—and had assumed Faith felt the same.

Faith let go of Jen's hands. "I didn't mean to shit on your dream, girl. Look, all of us have gone through some pretty heavy shit in our past lives. That's what got us here in the first place. That's why Anastasiya chose us, besides the fact our bodies could handle the change. But it's still a lot to get your head around. This is my way of dealing with the whole thing. Doesn't mean I hate what I am. Like you, I'm working through it, but in my way. Maybe the thing today was a one-off, my body reacting to the virus or something."

Faith searched her friend's expression. Had she alienated Jen? She hoped not.

"I don't know, Faith," said Jen. "That was pretty full-on today. But you know what, I think you're right."

"Right about what?"

"About our bodies reacting differently. It kinda makes sense in a way. I mean, your eyes haven't changed color either."

"Then you've noticed," said Faith with a faint smile.

"Sure, all the girls have."

"Oh? What've they been saying?"

Faith wanted to believe she didn't really care what the others thought, but part of her did.

"Only that your eyes haven't changed and then wondering why that is. You know, things like that."

Jen's tone hinted at something more.

"And how do you feel about it?"

Was she challenging Jen or merely asking? Faith wasn't sure herself.

"Honestly, I haven't thought much about it. Sure, I noticed right off, but I figured things were moving slower with you. Anyway, I've had my mind on other things. Like making sure I don't piss off the countess."

"I thought we'd talked about this. Stop overthinking everything and you'll be fine," said Faith, placing a reassuring hand on Jen's shoulder.

"I want to believe that, Faith, and don't want to fuck it up. That's what I always seem to do. When things start going good then somehow, I fuck it up. Like when I was in school. Things were going bad at home again. One of my teachers, Mr Jones, was someone I could talk to. Pretty soon, things between us got serious, and for a while it was great. I mean, it all felt so right. He listened to me and was caring. Then my mom found my diary. She was furious. Called me a slut. It hadn't ever seemed to bother her when her boyfriends all hit on me."

Her voice trailed off. The pair sat in silence for a while.

"Mark lost his teaching job. I had to move schools. Then Mom met JT, and he didn't take no for an answer. He, you know... I got outta there soon after that. I thought maybe I could start over some place new. But it's never that easy, is it? Anyway, I guess you can figure the rest."

"We've all been there, Jen. It doesn't help to think on it all the time. Keep looking ahead. Isn't that what Anastasiya tells us?"

"I suppose you're right. Look, can you keep this between us? I don't want the countess to think I'm ungrateful or anything, and I'm not, really. But when you think about it, she's right. She has granted us a better life. I sorta lost my way before I came here. Getting through each day was a struggle. Now I've finally got something to look forward to."

"Look forward to?"

Faith wondered if Jen meant feeding on men, but she realized it had to be something else.

"Sure, haven't you ever thought about it?" asked Jen, surprised.

"Thought about what, Jen? You're gonna have to be more specific."

"Well, being how we are. It means we're gonna live a long time. The countess has lived for hundreds of years..."

"You don't know that, Jen," interrupted Faith. "She could be fifty years old or a thousand years old. She's never said."

"But the way she talks, the stuff she knows. She's gotta be at least a few hundred years old. Imagine what she's seen, Faith. Imagine who she's met," said Jen, becoming more animated. "Haven't you wished you could go back in time and meet a famous person? Or thought about seeing a historic event firsthand?"

"We don't have the power to go back in time, Jen," observed Faith dryly.

Jen laughed. "I know that. But you're missing the point. Think about it!" she said, settling back on the bed.

She stared up at the ceiling and explored the possibilities.

"The world will keep changing, and we'll be there to experience it. We'll see fashion evolve not over seasons but over centuries. We'll get to hear new types of music, maybe on instruments they haven't invented yet. We'll see movie effects no one's even thought of. We'll get to see people travel to other planets. Mars, Saturn. Holy shit, there's so much it could make your head explode thinking about it all."

Faith smiled at her friend's optimism but remained unconvinced. She doubted Anastasiya would allow any of them to live fifty years, never mind a few hundred. The countess controlled every aspect of their lives here. The longer any of them lived, the more they would want to test that control. It was only natural. Besides, how much would they get to experience living as they did, in the shadows?

She let Jen talk on, her voice becoming a comfortable drone that allowed her mind to drift away, unfettered from this place and time.

5

Three days passed. To Faith, it felt like forever. She needed time alone to figure out what was happening to her. But between Anastasiya's lessons, fight practice, and Jen always hovering close, it had been impossible. She understood her friend wanting to be with her. They had been excluded from the group. Meredith had seen to that. No doubt their mistress was aware of this toxic dynamic but appeared ambivalent to it all. Perhaps she was intrigued to see how it would play out. A game within a game.

Faith snuck out of the room the moment the opportunity presented itself. She stood alone in the mansion's gardens. The kiss of the moon bathed the manicured lawns, trees, and shrubs in a silvery light, and she noticed too how her skin appeared to glow. She raised her hands against the night sky and moved them languidly back and forth, her fingers tracing lines between the stars. A faint luminescence seemed to trail in their wake.

Was this her imagination? It was difficult to tell. She knew something within her had changed—something that had caused her to become different from the others. A being more evolved. She closed her eyes and breathed out slowly. Her body relaxed as she did. She could feel her consciousness expand, searching out every life essence, no matter how small. A great horned owl perched in a tree, two hundred feet to her left, pale-yellow eyes glaring balefully. There, thirty feet to her right, the beating hearts of two mice moving furtively in the shrubbery. In the flower beds twenty feet behind her, a wolf spider pounced upon its prey. She could sense them all and yet more still.

Much like her heightened awareness, her newfound combat skills appeared to be further manifestation of the change within her. She smiled. The ability to anticipate her attacker's every move and pick the perfect counter had given her the edge in fighting. But she was not foolish enough to flaunt her skills, sensing that what set her apart also made her a target.

Since her fight with Judith, she'd "lost" as many practice fights as she'd won and even allowed her arch-rival, Meredith, to beat her. Did Anastasiya suspect the change in her? Faith did not know but realized the countess would feel threatened if she did. And if threatened, would it be enough to drive her to kill? Knowing how ruthless Anastasiya could be, she had no reason to believe otherwise. All the woman needed do was refuse her access to her life-giving blood. She had seen how the virus picked its victims clean. Without the blood, how long before it devoured her? She shuddered involuntarily.

But what if her new self no longer needed Anastasiya's blood? What if she was now Anastasiya's equal? Was that even possible? The only way to know was to refuse the blood at the weekly communion. That would mean challenging Anastasiya, which could only lead to death. But for whom? She realized then she did not care to find out. At least, not yet.

"You can come out from there now, Jen," she said without turning.

Jennifer stepped out from her hiding spot. "You're not supposed to be out here, you know," she hissed.

Faith shrugged. "I know. But some rules beg to be broken, don't you think?"

Jen giggled. "Go tell that to the countess."

"Tempting, but no thanks."

The pair stood silently in the evening quiet, each lost in thought. All about them, the universe moved, but they were still.

Jen sighed wistfully. "The girls should be back soon."

"Yeah, back with their prey. Back to fuck and feed."

"You make it sound disgusting."

"I'm not trying to. I'm stating it as a fact. You know, on a biological level. We'll be no different when our turn comes next week. It's a part of what we've become now. We are the hunters," said Faith.

"And you don't think there's something more to it than that?"

"Like what?"

Jen clasped her hands together. She raised them to her lips and considered her friend for a moment, weighing her words. She dropped her hands with a shrug.

"I don't know for sure, but there's a feeling I get, you know, in the days leading up to us going out. It's like a craving, but then it isn't. And then choosing my lover, tempting him back here, seducing him, feeling him inside me before I take his life essence. That feeling, it's like a madness that builds inside you and keeps on building. Like a pressure cooker. Then when I taste his blood, I feel that rush and then the serene calm that flows through me. It's... Why, it's almost spiritual, you know?"

Faith knew Jen was attempting to rationalize the whole idea of their being. Perhaps even find a meaning through doing that. Of course, she understood what Jen was attempting to say, because she too had felt much the same way in the beginning. She reflected then that they really were no different from the humans they fed upon. All sought a meaning to their lives. All wanted the comfort provided in believing that somehow one's own existence transcended the Darwinian idea of cellular organisms struggling against each other to survive. Ultimately one could either embrace the stark reality of nature or seek comfort in believing in some deeper meaning to it all.

Faith smiled briefly. "You know what? I think you're right. Their sacrifice allows us to live. So maybe on some level this whole thing is very spiritual. I mean, the way I feel everything is pretty much the same way as you, right?"

"I guess you're right."

"And I wasn't trying to trivialize it before. I was having a dig at you," said Faith, playfully punching her friend's arm.

Jen laughed. "Hey! That's not fair."

They heard the groan of the mansion's front gate opening on its old iron hinges and then the low rumble of the approaching limousine.

"The girls are back. I think maybe we'd better get inside."

"I won't argue with that!"

They laughed and sprinted back towards the waiting house.

6

The school was a haven, a self-contained world created by Anastasiya. Each of her acolytes knew the fear that came from being powerless. They had experienced it firsthand in the horror of their previous lives. She had released them from that fear. She had given them back control of their lives, or at least the illusion of it.

Here, time flowed seamlessly from night to day and back again, from one season to the next. The names of days and months held no meaning. Their mutated physiology meant their monthly periods had ceased too—another cycle discarded with their human past. But there was something they could not escape—the hunger. It gnawed at them constantly, growing and growing until finally sated in an orgy of blood.

Anastasiya sat in her private room and watched the screens arrayed before her, a world within a world. This one vantage point allowed her to see everything captured by the surveillance cameras located in the mansion's grounds as well as those hidden in her acolytes' rooms.

Her eyes moved restlessly between screens before focusing upon two. One monitor showed the interior of Faith and Jennifer's room, the other that of Meredith and Judith. It was another hunt night, which meant sending out a pair of girls to lure a man back so that a selected group might feed. Ordinarily, the pair chosen would be roommates. It made sense—the girls sharing the same room were more attuned to the emotional nuances of the other. This allowed them to better anticipate each other's actions when netting their prey.

But tonight she had chosen differently. Tonight, Meredith and Faith, two girls who openly disliked each other, would be paired. She smiled. There was, as always, an ulterior motive to her decision. In this case, it was to ensure the continuing enmity between the two girls. Maintaining control over her acolytes required more than the threat of withholding her life-giving blood. It also required a certain amount of competitiveness and conflict.

This meant preventing strong friendship bonds from forming between any of the girls. To this end, Jennifer and Judith would be confined to the mansion while their roommates went on the hunt. Two would be left to brood upon why they had been excluded, and two would contemplate the meaning of them being paired. It was perfect.

Anastasiya watched the girls as they prepared themselves for the hunt. Though each chose their own preferred look, the intention remained the same—to entice a suitor, a moth to their flame. What of the moths—those young men lured to their deaths, their lives snuffed out? And all so that the needs of the chosen should be satisfied. As she had done many times before, she wondered at the possibilities each life represented. Lives of promise reduced to a singular reason for existence—to be a source of food.

But was it not the right of a god to decide a mortal's purpose? Whether to satisfy their hunger or their pleasure? Yet pleasure could be found in more than the momentary thrill of the carnal. It could be found in art—human creativity at its finest, at times profound and at times, ridiculous. Art was timeless.

Her mind shifted to another time and another life—as Anna Schaller, a high-class prostitute living in the Vienna of 1886. She remembered the young artist she had spared. The spark of artistic genius she recognized and easily could have snuffed out. Even now, many years later, she could feel his heart beating as their bodies entwined in hedonistic coitus. In that moment, he fell beneath her spell. Had she wanted, he would have offered his life to her. But she stayed her hand, preferring the infinite enjoyment she knew his art—an individualistic style he had yet to create—would provide her.

She had not been disappointed, though it meant travelling back to Europe from time to time to attend his exhibitions. There had been others, of course. The Vienna of that time had teemed with the unconventional—artists and musicians eager to embrace the new philosophies that challenged the old order of things. She smiled at the memory. Was it long ago, or was it yesterday? At times it was hard to tell. Time was of little consequence to her.

Anastasiya focused on the screens again. The girls were almost ready. She pushed the button on the intercom.

"Lotho, bring the car to the front. The ladies will be with you shortly."

She watched the big man's image moving across an array of monitors, alternately disappearing then reappearing as each camera captured his progress towards the garage.

Moments later, the sleek black limo pulled up at the front of the mansion. He got out, walked round to the passenger door, and opened it. Meredith and Faith emerged from the mansion and got in. Lotho closed the passenger door and proceeded back around to the driver's side. He got in, clipped in his seatbelt, then put the car in gear.

After watching the car pull away from the house, Anastasiya got up from her chair. The night was young, and her memories of Vienna had filled her with a desire to hear some Mahler.

7

Stanley Silverfeld was a collector. Some men collected cars, some men baseball cards, and others comic books. Stanley preferred collecting women. More precisely, he enjoyed collecting his sexual encounters with them. Since that first fumbling grope with Mary-Ann Parker behind the school bleachers, he'd been hooked. Brunettes with small, pert breasts. Blonde, tanned surfer-chicks. Generously proportioned redheads. Dusky beauties with dark, beguiling eyes. Asian girls, Swedish, German, Hispanic—Stan had enjoyed them all. Six hundred and twenty to date. Each fucksploitation had been neatly filed away in his head. Each accessible in picture perfect high definition whenever the mood took him—like in those interminable weekly sales meetings.

At thirty, Stan could have been more than the slick salesman he was. He was good-looking. He was charming. And he had a mean, cutthroat business sense. This should have made the prospect of early career advancement a certainty. But he'd deferred, more than once. He preferred the transient lifestyle afforded by the constant travelling his job demanded. Besides, how else could he have met this many different women? Stan may have bedded a lot of women, but that didn't mean he didn't respect them. Quite the contrary. He loved women. That was the problem. He loved them too much. He loved the smell of them. He loved the way they moved. It was an addiction that no one woman could save him from. Each sexual adventure served only to kindle his hunger for the next and the next.

Which brought him to this night. A stopover in another town, trawling another nightclub, looking for that special woman. Not that he had anything specific in mind. He never went out with a clear picture in his head. He preferred the pleasure of not knowing. He preferred the pleasure of watching. Waiting until he saw something about a woman that he liked, be it the vulnerability in her eyes, the sensuous way she swung her hips, or her smile. In a way, he felt much like a tiger stalking its prey. He felt omnipotent.

Stan had positioned himself at one of the small tables near the busy dance floor. He was dressed in a combination of casual pants, coat, and open-necked shirt taken straight from the pages of the latest issue of GQ. The look, together with his tanned trim physique and chiseled features, was meant to ooze studied cool. In the past, he'd had little trouble netting the girl of his choice with this approach, but lately things had been a little slow. He'd even had to settle for women he'd ordinarily never look at twice.

His eyes roved over the girls gyrating hypnotically to the techno beat. There was plenty to choose from tonight. Unless he struck out again. He brushed the negative thought aside quickly, promising himself he'd leave with nothing less than a prime piece of ass.

He took another sip of his drink and watched the girls dancing. The music was loud and not the sort of thing he liked listening to. The people dancing seemed to be enjoying it though, their bodies jerking rhythmically, like puppets moved by an unseen hand. It was then the realization struck him. He was getting old. He looked at the sea of faces and tried to gauge the average age. Nineteen or twenty perhaps? The thought afforded Stan a rare moment of introspection. What did he look like to them? Did they think of him as a thirty-year old has-been, bedding younger women in some desperate attempt to cling to the last vestige of his youth? Was he a joke? Or was he something more pathetic? The more he attempted not to think about this, the more the thought nagged. It was like having a throbbing mouth ulcer you couldn't stop running your tongue over. He looked at them now and tried not to hate their youth.

"You mind if I join you?"

Stan turned to answer. A young woman sat down in the chair opposite him. She was strikingly attractive and, in his opinion, dressed to kill. Her blonde hair hung in long ringlets that ended above a pair of firm breasts seductively exposed by the dress's plunging neckline. His eyes hovered a second over the twin globes, erect nipples pressed against the thin fabric of the dress. Her skin was pale—almost translucent. His gaze moved up to her face. She had pinched, model-like features and full red lips. It was her eyes that most caught his attention. He felt himself drawn into their ice-blue depths. A drowning man unable to resist.

She flashed a seductive smile. "I'm Meredith."

"Stan."

"Hi, Stan."

"What if I did mind?"

He might've had a more charming line, but she'd caught him at a vulnerable moment, and he was unwilling to let go of his newly discovered angst.

"Mind?" she said, leaning forward so she didn't have to shout over the music. "Oh, I don't think you mind. Besides, you looked kinda lonely sitting here."

"Lonely? How'd you know that? Maybe I'm waiting for someone."

"Sure, you have. You've been waiting for me."

"That depends on whether the wait turns out to be worth it or not." He smiled, the old instincts kicking back in.

She winked. "Oh, it'll be worth it. Would you like me to buy you a drink, or do you want to go somewhere quieter?"

"Let's go somewhere quieter," she said.

"Somewhere quieter it is then."

Stan pushed back his chair. The girl followed suit and allowed Stan to guide her through the crowded nightclub towards the exit. The cool night air greeted them as they stepped outside the club entrance. He turned left towards where he'd parked the rental car.

"No, this way," said the girl, pointing in the opposite direction. "We'll use mine."

She took his hand and started leading him down the street, the music receding to a dull background throb the further they got from the club.

"Are you sure?"

Stan would've preferred to use his car, but only because he felt uneasy about leaving it in the street overnight.

"Of course, why wouldn't I be?"

The tone of her voice and the dark look that flashed across her face caused him to hesitate. The last thing he needed was trouble.

"See over there," said the young woman pointing to a sleek black limo parked a short way along the now quiet street.

A large man in a chauffeur cap and suit got out and proceeded to open the passenger door.

"Yours?" asked Stan, failing to hide his surprise.

"Who else?" she laughed and pulled him onward.

A few more steps, and they stood at the limo's passenger door. Meredith got in and slid gracefully across the backseat. She patted the place beside her and smiled. The invitation was clear. Stan glanced up at the imposing chauffeur. The man appeared to ignore him and looked straight ahead. Stan looked back at the lights of the nightclub down the street. Should he back out?

"Are you coming with us or not?" demanded the girl petulantly from inside the limo.

Us?

Stan bent forward to peer into the car. A second girl sat on the back seat opposite.

She smiled invitingly. "Hi, I'm Faith," she said.

"Uh, hi. The name's Stan," he said, suddenly feeling a little out of his depth. Two knockout girls on the prowl, and they chose him?

He looked back at the chauffeur, apparently indifferent to his presence. He shrugged to himself and slid into the limo beside Meredith. The chauffeur closed the passenger door, walked round to the driver's side, and got in. The limo pulled away from the curb before slowly accelerating up the quiet street. Stan watched the nightclub glide silently by. He turned to his fellow passengers and smiled.

"So, are you ladies from around here?"

"You could say that," said Faith. "And you?"

"Nope. Denver. I'm here on business. Aerospace."

It was a lie of course. But it sounded far more impressive than "mechanical bearings salesman."

"Really? That must be exciting," said Meredith, placing a restless hand on his leg.

"It can be, I suppose. But I prefer not to talk about my work. What about you two? What do you do?"

"We're both at college. I'm majoring in philosophy, and Faith, would you believe, is in religious studies."

"You're kidding, right?"

She giggled. "Could be, but I'll leave it to you to guess."

She straddled him with a sinuous grace. Stan could feel the heat of her sex against his crotch. Hungrily, he slid his hands up her thighs, but she stopped him.

"Slow down, cowboy. We've got plenty of time. You sit back and enjoy the ride. We'll be home soon."

Meredith leant forward and placed a long leisurely kiss on his lips. He responded, his tongue urgently seeking hers, and soon the pair were locked in simulated coitus, their mutual pleasure rising with the passing minutes.

Faith watched the pair dispassionately. Ordinarily, she'd have felt her own mounting desire—a mix of blood hunger and sexual need that only the taking of life could satisfy. But she also felt pity. This man would die tonight, his life extinguished to satisfy their need. No matter how productive this person had been with his life, or how good or bad, he had still, in some way, contributed to human society. He would be missed. But not she and her kind. Death was their only contribution. They lived a life in the shadows, indifferent spectators to the world passing them by. Was there an alternative to this existence? She watched as Meredith dry-humped the man and could think of nothing. The limo sped onward in the dark, a black vessel sailing the river Styx to deliver a man called Stanley Silverfeld to his end.

◊ ◊ ◊

By the time they reached the mansion, Stan's lust had dulled any misgivings he might otherwise have had. He submitted willingly to the blindfold and allowed himself to be led down a disorientating number of corridors into a room. He heard light classical music. The perfumed fragrance of musk hung heavy in the air. But Stan smelt a hint of something else. Something with a distinctly feral quality. The blindfold was removed. He blinked. Meredith stood naked next to a large four-poster bed. She was everything he'd imagined. To his left, the second girl, Faith, walked towards an ornate chair in the corner. She stood facing away from him, unhooked her dress, and allowed it to fall from her body with a shrug. She wore nothing beneath. His gaze moved hungrily down her toned back to her firm rear, and he felt a familiar stirring in his groin.

"Well? Are you going to stand there all night?"

"I was enjoying the moment," he said with a self-satisfied grin.

Stan was back in the game, and he was in control. He started slowly unbuttoning his shirt, but Meredith grew impatient and walked over to him with a sinuous grace.

"Here, let me help you with that," she said, ripping his designer shirt open.

Stan responded and kissed her fiercely, one hand squeezing her derrière while the other moved to her breast. She returned the kiss hungrily, her hands moving down to undo his belt buckle. In moments, his pants were open, her hand encircling his engorged penis. She pulled him back towards the bed by his rigid member, Stan shrugging off his ripped shirt along the way. Meredith suddenly spun about and pushed Stan back onto the bed.

"Now let's get the rest of these clothes off you," she purred as she slithered on top of him.

She pulled his pants and shorts down in one movement. Although he preferred taking the lead, allowing the woman to take the initiative was nothing new to Stan. He found it usually led to more adventurous sex, and based on the evening thus far, he was in for one wild ride. He looked back over to the corner. The second girl was staring at him with an odd expression.

"Hey, baby, why don't you come over here?" he said, motioning to Faith.

Faith did not move, watching instead as Meredith proceeded to straddle the supine man, raising her hips to guide his penis into her sheath. She moaned a low animal-like growl and shuddered. Stan reached for her full breasts, rubbing the erect nipples between the thumb and forefinger of each hand.

"Well, sister? Care to join us?" Meredith winked at Faith.

She turned back to her prey and started to move her hips, rhythmically stroking the penis trapped within her.

Faith watched Meredith fucking the man. The couple's frantic coitus had released a heady pheromone brew that now aroused her sexual desire. The ambivalent feeling of before had passed. She moved lithely towards the couple and stopped at the foot of the bed. Stan, sensing her presence, turned to look at her. He extended an inviting hand as Meredith continued to ride him, her hips thrusting back and forth in mounting pleasure. She looked across at Faith with a self-satisfied grin. Their eyes locked, each attempting to read the other. Faith smiled then suddenly lunged forward, sinking her fangs into Stan's extended forearm. He cried out with a look of horror at the vampire latched firmly to his arm.

Meredith had little choice but to join, wrenching Stan's head back to sink her fangs deep into the struggling man's exposed jugular. The smell of blood suffused the air—life's vital essence spilled. It was the signal for Jennifer and Judith to join the feeding. They entered quickly from the adjoining room and joined their acolyte sisters to gorge upon the helpless man—Dionysius's maenads slithering over their blood offering. It was soon over.

"What the hell, Meredith?" shouted Judith.

She was voicing the surprise both she and Jen felt at how unusually quick things had proceeded. Meredith didn't answer her friend, looking past her at Faith.

"You bitch! You fucking bitch!" she screamed and lunged across the corpse at her antagonist.

Her prescient edge allowed Faith to anticipate the attack. She rotated her hips as Meredith hit her, using the energy to send her attacker tumbling to the floor in an undignified heap. Faith leapt upon her before she could recover and in the ensuing grapple trapped Meredith in a neck choke. The girl struggled desperately to escape, but Faith held on, grimly increasing the pressure on Meredith's carotid artery until she passed out. It turned out a vampire was no different than a human in at least one respect—neither could function without blood flow to the brain.

Faith released her grip and pushed Meredith's unconscious body off her. She stood up as an angry hiss alerted her to the next attack. Judith had recovered from her initial surprise and now wanted revenge. She jumped from the bed and hurled herself at Faith but dropped to her knees in pain as her opponent blocked and countered with a bone-crushing punch to the ribs. Judith recovered quickly and fired off a front snap kick as she rose, but Faith evaded easily, spun about, and delivered a sharp elbow to her opponent's solar plexus.

Judith dropped to the floor with a grunt, and Faith backed away, aware of movement on the floor to her right. Meredith was coming around. Faith allowed them to recover, confident she had the measure of them. The girls squared off against each other, Judith and Meredith circling their opponent as they attempted to find an opening.

"Enough!" cracked Anastasiya's voice like a whip, freezing the girls in mid step. They all turned and looked apprehensively at their mistress.

"You." She pointed at Jennifer. "Why are these girls fighting?"

"I... I don't know, ma'am."

"Meredith," said Anastasiya, turning to the most senior of her acolytes, "perhaps you can answer?"

"It was nothing, ma'am, a small misunderstanding," said Meredith, looking down at the floor.

"Nothing but a small misunderstanding? And this is how you attempt to resolve it?" she growled. "I am disappointed in you all. Have you learned nothing from my teachings? Is this how you repay my gift to you? You fight amongst yourselves like humans. Perhaps you tire of being one of the chosen. Perhaps you would prefer to cast your lot with the rest of humanity, yes?"

"No, ma'am. I shouldn't have allowed my emotions to control me. It won't happen again. I promise," said Meredith. She shot an angry glance at Faith.

"Good, see that it doesn't," said Anastasiya. She turned to Faith. "Well?"

"I apologize, ma'am."

"Then it is settled. Now, take your things and go to your rooms."

The girls picked up their discarded clothes and proceeded to file from the room. Anastasiya stopped Faith at the door.

"I will talk to you tomorrow morning, an hour before class."

The girl nodded mutely before following the others.

Anastasiya stood in silent contemplation. Perhaps she'd allowed the hatred between Meredith and Faith to fester too long. Competition between the girls was one thing, but not if it threatened the group. Had Faith become a threat? Perhaps it was time to remove her from the equation. A decision would have to be made. She walked over to the bed and looked at the corpse. The change had started. She walked into the small adjoining room where Judith and Jennifer had waited and spoke into an intercom on the wall.

"Lotho, you are required in the Red Room."

By morning, nothing would remain of a man named Stanley Silverfeld.

◊ ◊ ◊

"What the fuck, Faith? What were you thinking?" hissed Jennifer when they were back in their room.

Faith shrugged. "I don't know. A brain snap, I guess," she said, closing the door behind them.

"A brain snap? Is that what you're gonna tell her tomorrow?"

"Stop stressing, mom. I'll be fine."

"Fine? I'm glad you're taking this so well, girl. Because if you were me, you'd be totally freaked out."

"But I'm not, so chill already."

"Chill? Jesus, Faith, I still can't figure why you did that. And to Meredith of all people. She's the last person I'd want to cross. So, why?"

"Like I said already, I don't know why. I wanted to wipe that smug look off that bitch's face, I guess."

"Is that what you're going to say tomorrow?"

"No, obviously."

"Then what? I need to know. I mean, what if she calls me in to verify your story? What then, Faith? You know she already has it in for me."

"Don't worry, Jen. You weren't there anyway. It's my word against Meredith's."

"But the fight. You and her and Judith and..."

"What you saw was Meredith attacking me."

"I know, but before that."

"Before that was maybe me getting a little too excited. I'll say I got lost in the moment and couldn't stop myself from feeding before Meredith was finished."

"Is that it? You really couldn't stop yourself?"

"That's what I'm going to say."

"Okay. Don't do it again, okay? I don't think I can handle any more stress like this."

"I won't let it happen again, okay? Does that make you feel better?"

In the cold glare of hindsight, Faith had begun to regret her actions. The truth was she wasn't sure why she'd done it. Had it been merely to piss off Meredith? Or had there been another reason she'd wanted to finish him off quickly? Had it been a form of penance? Or had she begun to hate what she was? She could not tell.

Faith walked over to the window and looked out into the night. She felt lost. Jennifer was saying something to her, but she no longer cared to listen. So much for flying under the radar.

8

An hour before class the next morning, Faith opened the door to the library. Anastasiya sat in an ornate chair, reading. She did not bother to look up. Faith closed the door behind her. Classical music played in the background, its leisurely tempo setting a relaxed mood. She recognized it as "Air" from Bach's *Orchestral Suite No 3*. A year ago, in her other life, it would have sounded no different to any other classical piece. A benefit of Anastasiya's teachings? That depended upon one's perspective. She could appreciate its beauty, but it still didn't resonate with her in the way modern music did. Punk, rock, electronic, soul, she enjoyed it all. She was, after all, a product of her time.

Anastasiya continued to read while Faith stood waiting. It felt like an eternity.

Anastasiya looked up from her book. "Come, sit," she said pointing to the chair opposite her.

Faith walked over to the chair and sat down. She looked at Anastasiya and tried to gauge her mistress's mood.

"What was the cause of the fight between you and the others?"

Faith hesitated. Should she be candid? The impenetrable ice-blue eyes staring back at her offered no hint.

"I had a disagreement with Meredith."

"What was this disagreement?"

"I chose to feed before she had finished enjoying herself."

"Why?"

"Honestly, I'm not sure, ma'am," said Faith.

"Perhaps you still blame Meredith for the death of your lover, John? Although it was you who took his life, was it not?"

"He gave up his life to save me," said Faith, griping the arms of the chair. "Meredith was the one who infected me. He knew the only way I could live was to feed on him. He wanted me to live. I only did it because he wanted me to live."

"But he did not save you. He only stayed your hunger. It was Meredith who saved you. It was she who gave you the blood gift. And it was I who allowed you the choice. Do you not recall? The both of you, in that room?" she said, pointing in the general direction of the so-called Red Room. "I could have killed you both. But I allowed you the choice, and you chose, did you not?"

"But maybe the choice wasn't really mine. Wille zum Leben. The will to live. You taught us that. The biological drive within all of us to survive."

Anastasiya smiled. "Yes. The will to live. Though the will is not strong in some. Some prefer death. Perhaps you have grown to regret taking the gift. Perhaps that is why you antagonize your sisters. Is that not so?"

Faith realized answering in the affirmative might invite death. The truth was, she wasn't sure what she should regret anymore. She could no longer tell right from wrong. Right and wrong—what did that even mean? Killing was meant to be wrong. It was evil. But killing gave them life. Any other choice could only end in dying an agonizing death. What choice was that? She looked into the cold eyes that regarded her and knew there was only one answer.

"No, ma'am."

"So I ask you once more, why did you do it?"

"I think maybe I was challenging her. Maybe that was it."

"Have I not said you are all sisters?"

Faith nodded.

"So why then would you want to challenge your sister?"

"Meredith likes to say we are gods amongst human cattle."

"That is what I have taught you," corrected Anastasiya.

"Last night...watching Meredith with that man. Suddenly I didn't feel like a god. I felt like a cold-blooded killer. And maybe I felt sorry for him, so I put an end to his suffering."

"Empathy is a luxury we cannot afford, Faith."

"But isn't it natural for people to feel that way? We were like them once. Human, I mean."

"No, that is where you are wrong. You, like me, were never like them to start with. Only humans die at the virus's touch. We did not die. We evolved. How if not because we were different to begin with? We were always more than them. We are beyond human. We are gods."

"If we are gods, then why do we hide in the shadows?"

Faith instantly regretted her question, but it was too late. The words hung in the air like a challenge. The two women eyed each other as the seconds ticked by.

"Do you not think I have thought about this?" said Anastasiya. "A thousand years ago, we would have been worshipped by them. They would have erected temples in our honor and sacrificed slaves to please us. They suffer one short life, but we enjoy a life near eternal. A thousand years from now, who is to say we will not be worshipped once more?"

"So we wait for a better time," said Faith, unconvinced.

"Yes. The cycle of life, the ebb and flow of it. Birth, death, and rebirth. It is the fate of all humans. Things will change, as they always do. Only we will remain untouched. Enjoy your time. For each day that passes is one never to be regained."

Enjoy your time. Was this a veiled threat? Was she living on borrowed time? Or was Anastasiya simply attempting to reassure her that she would feel better about herself in time.

"I understand, ma'am."

"Good. Then it is settled. You may return to your room."

"Thank you, ma'am," said Faith, standing up.

Anastasiya watched the girl leave the room. Her eyes narrowed. She realized nothing had been resolved. For the present, the girl posed no real danger. She would wait, she decided, to see which path the girl chose.

9

Dave Black walked along the foot of the perimeter wall that enclosed the luxury mansion's grounds. The comfortable way he cradled his M4 assault rifle marked him as ex-military. He stopped, slung the rifle over his shoulder, and retrieved a pack of cigarettes from his inner jacket pocket. His hard-jawed features were illuminated for a brief second as he lit up then dissolved back into the dark. He sucked the acrid smoke deep into his lungs then looked up at the night sky as he exhaled slowly. Funny, he thought, the stars looked no different whether in Baghdad or Sacramento.

"You got to that faulty camera yet?" crackled Trent's voice in his earpiece.

"I'm on it," muttered Dave quietly into the mouthpiece of his headset.

The man was an untrained idiot, he decided. He took another drag from his cigarette. Trent was team leader for his four-man security detail and took his job very seriously. Their current assignment was a wealthy businessman named Jeremy Faber. The details were sketchy, but as Dave understood it, Faber and his partners were under investigation for money laundering and fraud. There'd been a falling out between Faber and the others, probably because they suspected Faber of doing a deal with the Feds.

Whatever the facts, Faber had retreated to his walled mansion in the Sierra Nevada foothills and hired protection. The fact was Dave didn't really care. The pay was good, and there was less risk involved. No roadside IEDs or trigger-happy fanatics to worry about here. All he had to contend with, it seemed, was some tight-ass prick insisting that no one smoke on his property.

No smoking, my ass, he thought irritably.

Dave stopped. The light located near the faulty camera was out. Coincidence? His instinct told him otherwise. He unslung the assault rifle, raised it to his shoulder, and peered through the night-scope. The camera's cable had been cut! He opened his mouth to speak but instead let out a surprised gasp of pain as the blade of Goran's fighting knife pierced his ribs and heart. Goran held the big man firmly then allowed his body to slowly crumple to the footpath. He pulled the knife out of the corpse. Then he wiped the blood from the blade on the dead man's jacket before sliding it back into the sheath strapped to his chest. One obstacle removed. He unslung his silenced HK MP5 submachine gun.

Goran had been given the property's blueprints so was familiar with the position of each camera and infra-red sensor. This allowed him to move quickly but stealthily along the footpath towards the house, negotiating each device in turn without slowing his pace. He knew it only a matter of time before the dead guard's disappearance raised suspicions, and he needed to be in position by then.

Faber's house was a sleek rectangular affair in the modernist style with large plate-glass windows forming part of each outer wall. The windows allowed clear views into the well-lit interior. Goran smiled to himself. Whoever was running security was either an amateur or had been ordered not to encroach on their client's lifestyle. He sidled up to a door at the rear of the building's lower level, avoiding the security camera as he did.

This was the door someone sent to find the unresponsive guard—now dead—would use. He did not wait long. The door swung inward, and an armed man appeared. Goran stepped out from the shadows and fired, hitting the surprised man with two headshots. The dead man fell back into the hallway, his weapon clattering loudly on the marbled floor.

Goran stepped over the corpse with his submachine gun raised and moved quickly towards the second door to his right. This was where the security monitors were located and where at least one more of the security detail would be. By now, the man inside would know he was there, either because he'd seen him on the hall camera monitor or from the distinct noise of the MP5's silencer. He crouched low, pulled the pin from a stun grenade, and lobbed it into the open doorway. It hit the floor with a dull thud and rolled further into the room.

A man swore, there was the sound of panicked movement, and then the grenade detonated with a deafening thump. Goran followed up quickly, spraying the smoke-filled interior with quick bursts of automatic fire as he entered. His wounded adversary slumped against the far wall, firing desperately at Goran as he did. The shots ricocheted wildly off the wall behind Goran, who unflinchingly fired a final burst into the guard. The man groaned and left a bloody smear on the wall as he collapsed.

Goran looked up at the images flickering from the undamaged security monitors and watched the remaining guard usher Faber and his wife into the master bedroom. The police or possibly more security would be on the way by now, so speed was essential. He moved quickly through the house towards the curved stairway that led to the upper level. Goran took the stairs two at a time, stopped briefly at the top to get his bearings then moved carefully down the hall towards the master bedroom with his submachine gun ready. He placed a small Semtex charge on the door lock ensuring as he did to remain to the side and out of the line of any gunfire from the room beyond.

With the charge set, he moved out of blast range by stepping back into an adjacent room and detonated the explosive. The lock disintegrated with a sharp crack, and the door swung open. Goran rolled another stun grenade into the bedroom without leaving his cover. There was a loud thump as the grenade detonated, and then he followed up swiftly, firing quick bursts from the MP5 as he moved into the bedroom. The nervous guard fired blindly through the bedroom's ensuite bathroom door, but Goran had rolled instinctively to the side and out of the line of fire. He returned fire, emptying a full clip into the ensuite's hollow-core door. The ammo clip was ejected, the next inserted, and the weapon re-cocked in one fluid motion before Goran moved forward, firing from the shoulder as he did.

He kicked open the bullet-ridden bathroom door, lobbed in a stun grenade, and stepped quickly to the side. The small confines of the room amplified both the sound and effect of the grenade's detonation. Goran moved into the smoke-filled room and fired a burst into the prone guard then turned to the disorientated man and woman cowering in the corner.

"Wait, please," stammered Faber, raising his hands, "I have money. I will pay you. I will—"

Goran fired twice, the hollow metallic thud of each silenced round ringing loudly off the tiled walls. The dead businessman slumped back against the wall. Goran finished with a headshot before turning his attention to the man's wife. He noticed then that she'd been wounded and was struggling to staunch the blood flowing from her stomach. She looked up at him with an expression of hopeless resignation but made no sound. He fired twice.

◊ ◊ ◊

Police officers viewing the security footage later would comment on how calm the killer appeared, strolling nonchalantly out through the front door and into the waiting night. The fact the killer wore a full-face respirator throughout the attack made identification impossible.

Goran had felt no emotion during or after the hit. After all, he bore no personal animosity towards the people he'd murdered. Killing had been a way of life for so long that he knew little else, and the work paid well. But now that the contract was completed, he could get on with the real reason he'd come to America—to get revenge on his brother's killer. This time, it would be personal.

10

Charlie Ainsworth, proprietor of the Gateway Motor Inn, sat at his dusty reception desk paging through a copy of *Big Butts*. It wasn't his favorite porn magazine—*Lusty Latex Sluts* was top of his monthly reading list—but it passed the time. Ever since they'd rerouted the interstate, he'd been reduced to scratching a meagre living off the few truckers, travelling salesmen, or occasional lost tourist. Each monotonous day dragged by much like the one before until he no longer cared what week it was, reckoning time by his monthly porn subscriptions instead.

The cheap office chair protested loudly as he shifted his corpulent frame to release a loud fart. He yawned, turned another page, and flicked absently at the annoying fly that landed on his arm. A car pulled into the empty motel car park. Charlie looked up from his magazine. A man of medium height dressed in a dark suit climbed out of the car. He looked like a salesman, Charlie decided and watched as the man strolled towards the motel reception. What struck him was the way the man moved. It reminded him of a panther.

The small bell above the front door jingled weakly as the man entered. He closed the door behind him and ignored Charlie as he studied the room. Apparently satisfied, he turned and approached the front desk.

"Good morning. Can I help you?" said Charlie.

"Yes, I want to hire room," replied the man.

"Sure, we have rooms available for rent. Do you want any room in particular?"

"You have room away from road?"

It was not a request.

"Sure," said Charlie, studying the man over his glasses. "We have a few around the back, if that's what you want."

"Yes, give me one of them."

"Certainly. If you would like to confirm your credit card details and fill out this form," said Charlie, handing over a yellowing piece of paper. "Will that be for one night only?"

"Maybe few weeks," replied the man, retrieving a wallet from his coat inside pocket.

"A few weeks?" repeated Charlie, raising his eyebrows.

The man slid his credit card across the desk.

"A few weeks it is then. Okay then, Mr umm..." He read the name on the credit card. "Okay, Mr, er, Smith."

He looked at the stranger with the sharp angular features and foreign accent and smiled thinly.

A short time later, Goran opened the door to one of the motel's rooms. He closed the door behind him then proceeded to move through the room and its adjoining small bathroom, studying each in turn. Once satisfied, he returned to the car, retrieved a single suitcase, and went back to the room. He placed the suitcase on the bed, opened it, and removed a small battery-operated screwdriver, an MP5 submachine gun, three full magazines, and two fragmentation grenades. He used the screwdriver to unfasten the cover to the room's air-conditioning vent and proceeded to slide the items into the opening. Then he refastened the cover in place.

Goran usually avoided an obvious hiding spot such as this but reasoned the overweight motel manager wouldn't venture more than a cursory snoop through his luggage. Besides, the hidden weapons were a last resort. He preferred the Glock 9mm in his shoulder-holster or the fighting knife strapped to his right ankle. He slipped the screwdriver into his pocket and walked back out to the car. A moment later, he returned to the room with a large brown envelope.

Goran sat down at the small desk provided and retrieved some documents from the envelope. He spread the paperwork on the desk in front of him. The documents detailed the police investigation into the apparent gang-related murders of his brother and associates that had occurred a year before. He picked up the police report and started reading. About half-way in, he stopped, frowned, and reread part of the paragraph. It concerned two of the bodies that were discovered in an advanced state of desiccation. Both had been decapitated. One of the bodies had been identified as that of his brother, Dragan Millovic.

Goran thought for a moment. The condition of the bodies reminded him of a story from his childhood. He and Dragan would sit before the fire in their grandmother's kitchen listening to the old woman's stories. Each night, she would skillfully weave the stuff of legend and folk tale into the fabric of her story, leaving the boys wondering whether they were fact or mere fantasy. He was reminded of one specific story. It was a favorite of hers, one she had told them many times.

It concerned a young woman who appeared late one winter's night in their village—alone, lost, and afraid, her ragged shawl clutched tightly about her. Predrag, the village elder, took her into his home, since he and his wife had no children of their own. The young woman was extremely beautiful, and it was not long before she began attracting the attention of the young men in the village. This provoked the jealousy of all the young women. The fact the girl made no attempt to befriend any of the other women only added to their envy.

When two of the village's young men mysteriously disappeared, rumors accusing the mysterious beauty began circulating. Naturally, Predrag and his wife defended their adopted daughter. The girl though, remained coolly aloof from the whole affair, apparently unmoved by the accusatory glares and whispers greeting her wherever she went. Yet despite everything, the young men, seemingly bewitched by her allure, continued competing for her attention.

Then, early one morning, one of those young men stumbled into the village, no longer a man but a shuffling creature. Stojan, the man's best friend, called out but instead of answering the thing had only growled and ground its teeth, eyes staring lifelessly. So Stojan ran up to his stricken friend only to be attacked by the creature. The villagers watched, transfixed in horror, as the undead creature proceeded to tear at the flesh of the dying man. Then one of the older men stepped forward and shot the creature, which did not die but turned instead on the terrified old man. The sight of this unholy thing tearing at the flesh of another of their number galvanized the rest of the villagers to attack it with anything at hand.

But it refused to die and continued towards its attackers, who began retreating beyond its searching grasp. The macabre dance moved through the village until at last one of the men decapitated the thing with his scythe. The true horror soon became apparent when the villagers turned to find both Stojan and the old man now shuffling towards them, no longer dead yet neither alive. Another bout of attack and retreat ensued until the villagers also managed to decapitate both these creatures. The villagers watched as the corpses began deteriorating until all that remained were their dried-out husks. Their mummified remains disintegrated at the slightest touch.

His grandmother would pause at this point in the story and lean in close to the boys. "Who else do you think had disappeared from the village that morning?" she would enquire, her eyes sparkling fiendishly.

"The strange girl!" the boys would reply in chorus.

"Yes! The strange girl! Then we knew she was the one who had taken the young men, and then old Predrag understood too the horrible truth. He had invited the girl into our village. Except she was not a girl. She was vampir. So then Predrag went back to his home, and not wanting more horror to come to the village, he and his wife took their own lives. From then on, the villagers vowed never to speak the young girl's name lest she return. But on cold winter's nights, we would often lie in our beds and listen to the wind howl outside and wonder. We would wonder when she would return to take the rest of us."

Their mother always admonished the old woman for scaring the boys and reminded them the story was nothing more than a fairy tale. But now Goran was no longer sure.

He leant forward and continued reading through the documentation, his eyes skimming over the sentences searching for key words.

Mutilated remains, multiple fractures and broken bones, massive internal hemorrhaging, throats torn out, injuries similar to wild-animal attacks, a large quantity of shell casings discovered, but only from the dead men's weapons.

He sat back in the chair. As fantastic as it seemed, all the clues seemed to point to one conclusion. His brother and the other men had been killed by something like the girl from his grandmother's story. He shook his head. Was such a thing—a vampir—even possible? And what was the connection to his brother? He realized there was not much to go on. No suspects had been named in the report. No other known associates. That left the site of the murders—the house. Perhaps that was the key. He scanned through the remaining pages and found what he was looking for. The property belonged to a Father Samuel O'Connor.

Apparently, the detective on the case had attempted to interview the priest but found the man had been registered as missing and had not, to date, been found. With no evidence connecting the missing priest to the dead men, and no clue as to their killers, the case had been shelved.

Goran decided then he would visit the church where the priest had served. Perhaps that was where he would find the information he needed.

11

Detective Jack Holland sat at his desk staring intently at his PC monitor. In his youth, he'd been slim but now had the comfortable paunch, receding hairline, and lined face displayed by most middle-aged men. He looked at his watch. It was 9 p.m. He cursed. It would be past ten by the time he made it home. Cue the same old routine—dinner in the oven, Janine asleep in bed, and he in the dogbox another week. What else was new?

At least this time he had good reason, and besides, he owed it to Don Stone. The man's death had been ruled accidental, but Jack had always suspected there was more to it. Water hemlock in a salad? There was just no way. His friend had been strictly meat and potatoes. The word "vegetable" wasn't in his vocabulary. But with no leads and a mounting caseload, the department had taken the easy route. The case of a disgraced ex-cop screwing up his ingredients and poisoning himself had been put to bed with the minimum of fuss.

Jack had decided to continue his own unofficial investigation. His workload had made this difficult, and almost a year later he'd been no closer to the truth. Until today.

He adjusted his headphones and increased the volume.

"Look, man, I told the detective everything I know."

The voice belonged to Brad Jefferson, a known hacker with a drug habit. He'd been pulled over earlier in the day for running a red light. A search of his car had uncovered enough amphetamines to raise the charge to possession with intent to sell. Brad was facing hard time. Back at the precinct he'd offered the interviewing detective information on Don Stone in exchange for leniency. The brother detective knew of Jack's interest in the dead PI and had invited him to sit in. Brad's unkept hair, oversized tracksuit and designer sneakers were the type of obnoxious that irritated Jack. He watched himself on the recorded video.

"You say you did, but now I'd like to hear what you said to Detective Miller for myself."

Brad shifted his lean frame in the chair. "What do I get out of it?"

"That really depends on what you've got for me."

"Does that mean I aint gonna do time?"

"That's really up to you now, isn't it?"

"What do you mean?"

"Exactly what I said."

"How do I know you won't stiff me?"

"You're gonna have to trust me on that."

Brad crossed his arms and leaned back. "Trust you? A cop? I want something more. Something in writing. Something about no jail time."

Jack leaned forward menacingly. "Let's get something straight, shit bag. You're not the one in the driver's seat here. I am. You give me something worthwhile, and I talk to Detective Miller, and who knows? But say you give me nothing, we both know where that's gonna get you."

This type of approach could get a case thrown out of court for police intimidation. But Jack didn't care about building a case, he wanted information.

Brad gripped the armrests nervously. "Look, I don't wanna be screwed over. That's all I'm sayin."

"You don't want to be screwed? Interesting you say that. Don't you say, Detective Miller? Screwing and prison. Prison and screwing. The two go hand in hand, don't you think? It's almost like they're made for each other. Now, what's it gonna be, Brad? You gonna start talking, or do I get Detective Miller here to throw the book at you?"

"Okay, man. I'll tell you everything I know. Don was working some case. It had something to do with a woman named Anastasiya Strajinski. I think that was her name. I mean, he didn't give me the details, but he asked me to look into her background."

Jack paused the video and reached into his pocket for his cigarettes then remembered the office no smoking policy. He swore under his breath. At least they hadn't extended the policy to the department's vehicles, yet. He opened his desk top drawer and took a stick of gum from the pack he kept there. He closed the drawer, opened the aluminum paper wrapper and shoved the gum unceremoniously into his mouth. He squeezed the wrapper into a tight ball and tossed it into the wastepaper basket before resuming the video.

"She's the head mistress of this finishing school. The Whitby Foundation Academy for Girls, or some such. Anyway, there wasn't much to go on. No social security number, no license, no personal bank account. What I did find went back to this trust fund managed by some old law firm out of New York. When I told Don, he got more interested and wanted me to find out who'd set the fund up, who really owned the school property, and things like that. But by the time I got the info, he was dead."

Jack leant forward to rest his elbows on the table and eyed Brad speculatively. "What did you find out?"

"The trust fund had been set up by a man named Richard Granger in the nineteen twenties. He was from old money but didn't go into the family business. Looks like he saw himself as an adventurer. He joined up in nineteen seventeen to fight in France and was sent home after being wounded at the Argonne a year later. He had some sort of mental episode back home and disappeared. Then he resurfaced a few years later when his parents died."

"Let me guess. His parents didn't die of old age."

Brad shook his head and moved his chair closer like a fellow conspirator. "No, they were murdered. It caused a sensation at the time. Something about the way their bodies looked. And they'd been decapitated. The cops never do find the killer, and Richard wasn't a suspect. Had an alibi for the night in question. After the funeral, he up and sells off the business and leaves New York for good. A few years later, he gets the law firm to set up the trust fund. The fund's sole beneficiary is an Anna Stibor. A while after that, he dies in a fire in a Chicago brothel."

"And this Strajinski broad?"

"She comes into the picture around '65 when Stibor names her as sole beneficiary."

"Well, this is all very interesting, but I still don't see motive."

"Don't you see? Both these women pop up from nowhere. No record of them before, then suddenly they're the only beneficiaries of some serious money. Also, they've got the same initials – A.S. I'm thinking they're the same person."

Jack pushed his chair back from the table and turned to his associate. "Hell, Detective Miller, if you'd told me I was gonna listen to fairy tales I might have passed. Saved myself the trip over here."

"I'm telling you, man. They're the same person! It all makes sense. Someone must've hired Don to investigate her. She finds out, and the next thing he winds up dead."

Jack shook his head. "You know what I think? I think the thought of prison has got your imagination working overtime. That's what I think."

"No! Please, I'm not making any of this up. Why don't you check it out? Look through his case files. Maybe go to that school and question her. You'll see I'm right."

"The case is closed, Brad. It has been for almost a year. Death by misadventure. You want me to reopen it with this bullshit? To risk my career? Frankly, I don't know whether to be insulted or amused."

"Look, this isn't bullshit. Believe me!" said Brad wringing his hands.

"I think I'm done here, Detective Miller. I'll leave you to sort out the details relating to this man's drug charges."

Jack stood up to leave.

Brad's voice rose an octave betraying his panic. "What about the broad he was banging?"

"What about her?"

"Tammy Sloane. She's married to some real estate tycoon. Maybe he found out they were fucking and had Don killed."

"I think maybe you'd best stop talking, boy. Don Stone was a good man. There's no need for you to use his death trying to get outta the shit you're in!"

"Come on, man. Please! There's gotta be something I can say."

Jack stopped the recording at this point and leaned back in his chair. He'd hoped for more from the perp when Miller had first called him that morning. That said, he still had two potential leads—the two women. The only way he'd know for sure whether any of the information was worthwhile was to investigate. He'd have to see how the two women reacted to questioning.

He nodded to himself.

He'd have to pay the two ladies a visit. The question was—which would be first?

"Hey, Jack, are you coming or what?" called Dan Miller from across the open-plan office.

"What?" said Jack, annoyed at having his thoughts interrupted.

"I said, are you coming? You owe me a drink, remember?"

"Yeah, sure. Why not?"

He looked down at the two names he'd written on his notepad. Anastasiya Strajinski. Tammy Sloane. Head mistress or two-timing wife? Jack thought a moment and smiled. He knew exactly the type of women Don liked.

"Well, Ms Sloane, let's see what you have to say about Don," he said to himself.

He got up from his desk. First, he'd have a couple of beers with the boys and then head home. With a little luck, Janine would be asleep by then. He shook his head and thought about the fucked-up year he was having. First, his good friend died, and then he'd been dragged through a messy divorce. His kids wouldn't speak to him, and now the broad he was living with was pissed at him too. How was it that life always knew when to kick you when you were down?

◊ ◊ ◊

As Jack sat down to his first beer, a man three time zones away was involved in an investigation that shared a common link—Anastasiya Strajinski. Dr Michael Webb sat at his desk in a small office located in one of the CDC's large laboratories. He had the soft physique of someone unused to physical labor but was extremely intelligent. A cosseted childhood had led to a lack of social skills, which had made high school unbearable. His relationships with people in university and beyond had fared no better. Webb's superiors in the CDC tolerated his eccentric personality only because he had the ability to get results. But their patience had worn thin over his quixotic quest for what he claimed was an alien virus.

Almost a year to the day, the LA police had been presented with a bizarre crime scene at a small holding located outside the city. The peculiar condition of two of the seven bodies discovered had intrigued the county coroner, and he'd spent weeks attempting to understand the reason. Eventually realizing he was unlikely to discover the answer, he'd released the bodies for burial but had, as an afterthought, sent tissue samples to the CDC in Atlanta. The samples had eventually landed on Webb's desk, presenting him with a riddle he was still no closer to solving.

Webb looked nervously over the top of his PC monitor to the deserted laboratory beyond then back down at the screen. He input the police case file number and waited. Hacking into the LAPD database to retrieve the details he needed was risky, but the shadow organization funding his private research had started demanding results. Losing their financial support was one thing, but the thought of the unpleasant ways his foreign backers might show their displeasure was what really motivated him.

The file opened, and he started to scan the report to ensure it was the one he needed. Seven dead bodies. Five horribly mutilated. The remaining two in an advanced state of desiccation. These two had also been decapitated, he noted. His eyebrows furrowed quizzically.

"How did it go?"

Webb gave an involuntary start and looked up from his PC. It was Dr Malik, one of the other scientists.

"Christ, Glenn, what are you still doing here?" asked Webb, quickly minimizing the page on his screen.

"I didn't mean to startle you, Michael," said Malik, grinning amiably. "I wondered how the meeting with Jenson went."

Webb scowled. "How do you think it went?"

"Not good, obviously," he said and sat down.

At almost seven feet tall, Malik looked ridiculous perched on the unstable office stool—his long legs splayed awkwardly to steady himself. Webb had purposely requisitioned the chair and placed it inside and to the left of the doorway of his little kingdom.

"Obviously," said Webb, eyeing him suspiciously. "An alien virus hiding in bacteria is pure science fiction. If you ever go over my head to the board again with this fantasy, I'll have you fired. Jenson's words, not mine."

"Look, for what it's worth, the way the bacteria consumed the inside of each host cell—I've never seen anything like that before. What did you call it?"

"Strip-mining on a microbial scale."

Malik nodded. "Yes, that's right. Strip-mining. It certainly is unusual. Bacteria tend to adapt to feed on specific cells. It's in their interest to keep their host alive for as long as it takes to transfer to a new host that is."

"Don't try to teach me my job, Glenn. Or need I remind you that it was my unique staining protocol that allowed identification of this strange bacteria in the first place?"

"That wasn't my intention, Michael, but to say the only way an organism infected with the bacteria could survive is to be modified itself, and to then claim the mutation is achieved via some kind of alien virus... Well, you must admit that might be stretching credulity."

Webb's face reddened. It was annoying that someone he considered his intellectual inferior should think to question him.

"Given the apparent virulence of the bacteria, how else do you propose the infected organism transfers its cargo to a new host before dying?" he said. "From what I've seen, this organism would have to balance the bacteria's high energy requirements with its own, and to the best of my knowledge, no such organism exists."

Malik chuckled. "From what you've seen? We weren't given any living microbes. And we've never located any infected host either."

"We haven't identified an infected host yet. It's out there, Glenn. An animal that has been modified to allow this type of commensal relationship. An animal unlike anything we've seen."

"That's what you say."

"Yes, I do say. And until someone comes up with something better, I'm going to stick to my theory."

"Okay, Michael, but if you want my advice, perhaps you should keep the whole 'alien virus hiding in a bacterium' theory to yourself from now on."

"Is that an order? I didn't realize you were my boss."

"I don't mean it like that. I don't think going on some wild goose chase is productive. It isn't what the CDC does 'to protect America from health, safety, and security threats.' Isn't that our mission? Besides, you don't want to mess with Jenson. He will follow through on his threat, mark my words."

"I'll take that under advisement," snapped Webb. "Now, if you'll excuse me, I have work to finish."

Malik shrugged. "Suit yourself," he said and stood up.

Webb waited for Malik to leave the laboratory before bringing up the police report on screen again. He continued reading. Besides the crime scene's address and the identity of three of the victims, there was not much more in the file. He knew he'd have to enlist the help of an expert. The question was, who?

With that thought, he copied the file to one of his personal flash drives. A short while later, Webb exited the CDC building, the flash-drive with its information secured in his top shirt pocket. Perhaps a small part of him regretted the treason of serving a hostile foreign power, but mostly he felt justified in his decision. His own bosses had refused to support him. Theirs was a clear lack of vision. How else then could he further his research? Besides, the promised financial payoff was beyond anything he could ever have imagined.

12

n their appearances, Clark and Wilson looked the way most people expected FBI special agents to look. They had neat, conservative haircuts, wore sports jackets of a similar style, and had completed their respective clothing ensembles with gaudy ties and pressed grey trousers. The pair sat squeezed into a booth in a downtown LA fast-food joint and studied the pale, white-haired man opposite them with an impassive interest.

"As you can see, gentleman, I'm new to this sort of thing," said Webb with a tentative shrug. "But honestly I feel I've run out of options."

"So let me get this straight," began Special Agent Wilson, leaning forward to look intently at Webb. "Sometime earlier this year, you were given human tissue samples to study. Your examination led you to conclude that some type of alien virus was the cause of death."

"Bacteriophage," corrected Webb.

"What?"

"The bacteria are what initially infects the human host. The virus hiding inside the DNA of each bacterium is a bacteriophage. In this case, it is the bacteria that appears to be extremely virulent. It is my theory that this virus either helps accelerate the infection or delays it by modifying the host. I'm not sure really. It's all conjecture at this point. I need hard evidence."

Webb was nervous. He'd contacted the two men in front of him via a deep web site specializing in guns-for-hire type work. Murder, kidnapping, extortion. All services were available at a price. But these men looked more like cops, and he wondered whether he'd been set up.

Wilson frowned. "You hacked into a police database?"

"I might have."

"You hacked into a police database. And then you get the case file that you hope might help track down the source of this thing."

Webb nodded.

"So why hire us?" said Clark. "Why not do the detective work yourself?"

"I'm a microbiologist. I specialize in studying infectious diseases, not crime scenes."

"I don't know, Dr Webb. This seems to be a lot of effort to prove your manager wrong," said Wilson.

"Our services don't come cheap, Webb. Your line of work must pay well for you to want to hire us," cut in Clark with a tone that said he best not waste their time.

"Look, I don't think you both realize what this could mean. If my theory proves correct, imagine the implications. It would be like discovering life on another planet. I could publish my findings. There will be awards. Who knows, perhaps even a Nobel prize. I'll be famous," said Webb glibly.

The fact was he didn't believe it was alien. Some sort of mutation possibly, but not alien. The reasoning he'd offered the two men and why he'd also used his real name was to appear naïve. That way if he were to get caught, he could ascribe his actions to over-enthusiasm for his work. The reality was he recognized the potential to develop a biological weapon. A weapon that, sold to the highest bidder, could prove a far more lucrative prospect.

"I would've thought your bosses would jump at the chance of a discovery like that," pressed Wilson, eyeing the doctor distrustfully.

"My bosses are morons!"

"Isn't that always the case? It still doesn't seem a good reason to choose this way. Don't you have any peers? You know, scientists in other organizations who would support your theory? Why not approach them?"

"And have them share in the reward? What kind of imbecile do you take me for?"

"Ah, I see," said Wilson turning to his colleague. "What we have here is a man of scientific principle. Don't you boys have to take the hypocritical oath or something?"

"It's Hippocratic oath, and no, because I'm not that sort of doctor."

"A doctor without a sense of humor. Now that I didn't expect," said Wilson, deadpan.

"Are we going to do business or not?"

"Okay, say we do take your case," said Clark. "What do you expect us to find?"

Webb retrieved a USB from his coat pocket and placed it on the table.

"When you read the case file," he said, pushing the USB towards the men, "you will find there's not much to go on. The police seem to think its gang related. The dead men were all criminals of one sort or another. I don't have the know-how to investigate those types of people. But I do think either one of them or someone connected to one of them was or is the source of this infection."

"I assume you have a deadline?"

"Two weeks?"

It was a hopeful request rather than a demand.

"Two weeks?" said Clark with a raise of his eyebrows. "That's not a lot of time, but we'll see what we can do."

"I need you to do something else for me."

"Go on," said Wilson.

"I need to visit the crime scene—the house where these murders occurred. It could be a possible source of the infection, and I might be able to retrieve some samples or other clues. At the very least, I'd like to be sure nothing has been missed. But since it is the scene of a possible gang-related crime, I would prefer if I were accompanied."

Wilson smiled. "You mean, you want backup?"

"Yes, something like that. I don't know who or what I might run into up there."

"We can take you there. But first there is the matter of the down payment. The money must be deposited into the account specified by the close of business today," said Clark smoothly.

"I'll send you proof of payment," said Webb, looking at his watch. "I'm staying at the Marriot. I'm supposed to be attending a conference there, and I've got a paper to present in less than an hour, so if you two gentlemen will excuse me."

Webb got up to leave.

"Close of business today or no deal," said Wilson.

Dr Webb nodded briefly then made his way quickly towards the restaurant's exit. He did not look back.

"Slimy little cocksucker," observed Wilson as he watched Webb leave.

"Of that I have no doubt, Nate," said Clark and pocketed the USB. "Be that as it may, it's paying work that fits nicely into the case the bureau's got us on right now."

"Think he's legit?"

"As legit as any of the creeps we've done work for in the past. Legal or otherwise."

"He didn't give us a lot of time, expecting us to come up with something the LAPD missed in their investigation into this bullshit. And we still have to maintain reasonable progress on our real case or raise suspicions we're not doing our job."

"There were over nine thousand murders in the greater LA area last year, Nate. You really think the cops managed to put more than a half-assed effort into a gangland mass-killing? They got more important things to worry about."

"There still doesn't appear to be a lot to go on."

Clark grinned. "You really are a glass-half-empty kind of guy, aren't you?"

"I prefer to see myself as a realist, Allan. It'll be hard pleasing the little prick no matter what we come up with," said Wilson, taking a sip of his coffee.

"Why don't we see for ourselves before we make that call? Besides, I think he might be onto something."

"What do you mean?"

"The property where the killings took place. I think a good place to start is to find out who owns the place, don't you?"

"You think the cops didn't check that out themselves?"

"Could be. But let's assume they didn't. Anyway, so long as we get paid I really don't care how this pans out."

The pair settled into a relaxed silence. They sipped their coffee and idly watched the people rush by.

"Ever think about the Lambert case?" said Wilson.

"From time to time. Why do you ask?"

"No reason."

"There's always a reason with you, Nate. What? Is dealing with a little prick like Webb that annoying?"

"It's not that. Sometimes I wonder about the girl. You know, if we'd followed up on that lead like we were supposed to. Could she have survived?"

"I can't answer that, and neither can you. The fact is when they found her, it was too late. Maybe it was always going to be too late. All I know is they had to blame someone, and we've been paying for it ever since."

"You think after ten years McNeil would let up. But we still get assigned the shit no one else will touch."

"What can I say? She was the only daughter of a billionaire. Anyone else and things might've turned out different."

"But they didn't, and here we are."

"Don't grow a conscience on me now, Nate. The side hustle we've had going has paid well up till now. There's no reason to change that."

"I'm not saying we should."

"Alright then," said Clark.

The men returned to their silent contemplation, watching the people whilst sipping their coffee every now and then.

Clark chuckled. "Jesus, I've never seen so many fat fucks in one place."

"We are in a fast-food joint," said Wilson. "What did you expect, sexy twenty-somethings chatting up muscular young dudes?"

"Is it too much to ask? I don't understand why the hell people let themselves get that way. Don't they ever look at themselves in the mirror and wonder? Are they happy like that? They sure don't look happy. Most of them, anyways."

"Not everyone feels the need to work out every day. Not all of us watch every calorie we put in our mouths. Maybe they're not unhappy with the way they look. Maybe it's the dead-end job they're forced to work every day. You ever think of that?"

"It's an observation, Nate."

"An observation? You mean like the one about the GFC being a communist Chinese plot to destroy the West's economy? Or your other pet theory about project Blue Book and UFOs being a fact?"

"Area 51 is real."

"I didn't say it wasn't. But the whole alien spaceship and dead bodies thing is pure science fiction."

"I've read the reports."

"What, the ones on those crackpot websites you like to visit? Tell me, have you ever had a visitation? Were they little green men?"

"Fuck you."

"Was it the ten inch or the twenty-inch anal probe they used?"

"Fuck. You."

"It would explain a lot."

"Fuck you and fuck you some more."

"That's quite a retort you've developed. Good to know you've put that college degree to good use."

"Look, are we gonna sit here the rest of the day talking shit, or are we gonna get to work?"

"I was waiting on you, Allan," said Wilson with a sly grin.

13

Tammy Sloane reclined on a lounger by the poolside, a red micro bikini scantly covering her tanned, well-toned body. The sunlight glinted off the cool water's surface as it neared its midday zenith. The heat and the steady trickling gurgle from the pool's tiered water feature combined to lull Tammy into a dreamy, sensual languor.

She roused herself and reached over to pick up a tall glass of chilled spring water. Tammy took a sip and placed the glass down next to the unread copy of whatever it was the ladies' book club had on its recommended reading list for that month. She glanced at the book again and immediately felt annoyed. She'd attempted to read it, but the lengthy descriptive passages and exotic wording had left her feeling stupid. And that made her hate the stuck-up bitches from the book club even more. What did they know about real life anyway?

She smiled to herself. Most of their husbands were having affairs, in every case with younger women. That was because they didn't know how to keep their men in line. Not like her. She knew exactly how to keep George interested. Only that morning she'd allowed him to fuck her, mostly because having rejected his advances of late she'd judged it time to service his need. Maintaining the perfect balance between frustrated desire and contented fulfillment was a skill she prided herself in. It was a skill she had discovered more by circumstance than by design, and unsuspecting men the hone she'd since sharpened her skills upon. Tammy was a consummate manipulator of men.

Playing the role of trophy wife always carried the danger of being displaced by the next young hopeful. But she was not the type to relax her hold and never lost focus. It required, she believed, a certain art but also meant devoting part of each day to maintaining herself. A light breakfast each morning was followed by a strenuous workout at the local gym before moving on to whatever other activity she'd planned—whether tennis with girlfriends at the local country club, shopping, her scheduled beauty treatment, or a discreet liaison with her current secret lover. This morning, tennis had been cancelled, so she'd decided instead to spend a few hours lazing by the pool.

The large patio door slid open, and Maria, the Hispanic housemaid, emerged followed by a man. Tammy frowned. How many times had she told the girl to check with her first before letting anyone in? She studied the man as the pair approached. Tall, reasonably slim, receding hairline, weathered face. Probably in his late forties. The shabby clothing ensemble of faded sports-jacket, functional tie, crumpled long pants, and scuffed shoes pointed to a man preoccupied with his work. A cop, she decided.

"Excuse, Senora Tammy, this man he says he is policia, a policeman," said Maria, introducing the stranger.

"Good morning, ma'am. I'm Detective Holland," said Jack, noting idly that the woman made no attempt to cover her half-naked body.

"Good morning, Detective. You must be here to see my husband," replied Tammy, regarding him impassively from behind her large sunglasses.

"No, actually I'm here to ask you a few questions."

"Oh? What about, Officer?"

"It's detective."

"I'm sorry, Detective."

"Donald Stone," said Jack noting the sudden tenseness in Tammy's posture.

"Donald Stone?"

"Yes, Don Stone. You knew him, didn't you?"

"Don?"

There was a pause.

"Maria, don't you have cleaning to do?" said Tammy, glaring at the curious housemaid hovering nearby.

"Si, Senora Tammy." Maria retreated reluctantly towards the house.

Tammy sat up and reached for her robe.

"I'm sorry, Detective. You were saying?"

"I asked whether you knew Mr Stone," replied Jack, mildly amused that she'd suddenly discovered her modesty.

"Oh yes, Mr Stone. Yes, I knew Don," said Tammy, slipping her arms into the robe and pulling the tie about her waste.

"What was your relationship with Mr Stone?"

"Just a friend, a casual acquaintance really."

"And you would say your relationship with Don wasn't serious in any way?"

"Serious?" said Tammy, appearing puzzled by his question. "I don't know what you mean."

"We have information that your relations with Don Stone were more than him being just a friend."

"Information? From whom?" snapped Tammy indignantly.

"That has to remain confidential at this stage of our investigation, Ms Sloane."

"Investigation? The newspapers said his death was accidental."

"Then you knew he was dead?"

"Yes, I read about it in the papers."

"Did reading about his death upset you?"

"Yes, I suppose. I did know him after all. But I still don't know what this has to do with me."

"As I said, we've received new information. I'll ask you again, Ms Sloane. Was your relationship with Don Stone of a more personal nature?"

Tammy appeared to hesitate for a moment.

"I do love my husband, Detective," she said finally, her voice hinting regret. "And I wouldn't want to do anything to hurt him. But I don't get to see him very much. He's very busy, you know. It was about eighteen months ago. I met Don at the gym. Anyway, I don't know how it happened really. He was so charming, and I suppose I was lonely. One thing led to another, and I had a brief relationship with him. It only lasted a month or so. I hated myself for it. I told Don I couldn't see him anymore. He seemed to understand. Anyway, we went our separate ways. I felt it best if I didn't run into him again, so I started going to another gym."

She picked up the glass of spring water, took a sip, and placed it down again.

"A few months later, I read about what happened to Don in the papers. Of course, I was upset. I mean, it seemed so pointless. You know, dying because he put the wrong thing in a salad."

"Yes, regrettable," said Jack, eyeing her suspiciously.

"I've told you everything now, Detective Holland. I don't know how this is going to help you with whatever it is you're investigating," said Tammy, searching the detective's expression for a clue.

"Do you know Brad Jefferson?"

"No, why?" she replied.

"Another part of our investigation, Ms Sloane. Part of filling in the blanks, so to speak," said Jack.

"Filling in the blanks? Why, did he have something to do with Don's death?"

"That depends on what our investigation uncovers."

"You still haven't told me how me admitting to an affair with Don helps you, Detective Holland."

"Every bit of information helps in some way or other, Ms Sloane.

I'm following up on information received. It's standard police procedure. Now, if you'll excuse me, I have other business to attend to." Jack and turned to leave.

"Detective," said Tammy, standing up from the lounger.

He stopped and turned to face her. She moved closer, her eyes searching his.

"The affair. Please say my husband won't hear of it. It would kill him to know. He doesn't deserve any of this. It was my mistake. He shouldn't have to pay for..." She looked down.

"Don't worry, Ms Sloane, details of the investigation will stay confidential. Of course, that could change if say, something else was to come to light. Something pertinent to your involvement with Mr Stone."

Tammy smiled weakly. "Of course," she said. "Well then, goodbye, Detective."

"Goodbye, Ms Sloane, and thank you for your candor."

◊ ◊ ◊

Maria escorted Jack to the front door.

"Cuántos años ha trabajado para la señora Sloane?" asked Jack.

"Desde hace tres años," replied Maria carefully.

"Three years? You enjoy working for her?"

Maria shrugged and opened the door.

"I thought as much. You have a good day now."

He walked back to his car, opened the door, and slid behind the wheel. He pushed the key into the ignition when something occurred to him.

"The wrong thing in the salad."

Ms Sloane had said that. He sat back, sure the newspaper report had never mentioned anything about a salad. Accidental poisoning from water hemlock, yes, but no mention of salad. He'd have to check to be certain. What if it turned out he was correct? Did that mean Tammy Sloane murdered Don? And if she did, how could he prove it?

Then there was the Strajinski woman. Why had Don wanted a background check on her? What had she done to cause him to be suspicious? There was no denying the information on her didn't add up. Could there be a link between Sloane and Strajinski? It was another line of enquiry he knew he'd have to pursue. The only thing he was sure of was that his friend had been murdered. Proving it would take time, but he was a patient man. He turned the ignition, put the car in drive, and pulled away from the curbside.

14

G oran started his day with his usual five-mile run. Then he took a shower, dressed, and went to a roadside diner for breakfast. He ordered four eggs, sunny side up, two slices of whole wheat toast, and an espresso. While he waited for his meal, he scrolled through his cell phone searching for local costume-for-hire stores. The nearest was twelve miles away. He scanned the store's webpage and found what he was looking for.

Two hours later, he pulled up opposite Saint Augustine's Catholic Church, backed into a parking spot, and turned the ignition off. He sat in the car and studied the large sandstone building and its leafy suburban surrounds. Adjusting the starched dog-collar that dug uncomfortably into his neck, he scowled as he recalled the shop assistant's smirk.

"A priest's costume?" he'd said with a sly wink. "We don't get too many requests for that one. Popular with De Sade fans though, if you know what I mean."

Goran had killed men for less but had chosen to ignore the insinuation. There would always be another time. He flicked down the sun visor and looked at himself in the mirror. His disguise appeared convincing enough, he decided. With that thought, he exited the car and strolled across the street towards the waiting church.

Father Okoro sat in his small office working on the weekly parish newsletter. It had been about a year since he'd taken the position, yet he still felt the need to prove himself to his new flock. The spacious homes and manicured lawns of the upper middle class were a far cry from the low-income Detroit parish he'd served before. A discreet knock at the door interrupted him.

"Yes?"

The door opened, and Mary Green, his secretary, peered in.

"I'm sorry to disturb you, Father," she said, smiling politely, "But there's a Father Dubcek to see you."

"Please send him in."

Mary opened the door to allow a fit-looking man of medium height to enter the room. He was dressed in a black suit and clerical collar, yet Okoro felt uneasy.

"Father Okoro? My name is Father Dubcek," the man said, extending his hand in greeting.

Father Okoro stood up and walked round his desk to shake the stranger's hand.

"Good day, Father Dubcek. What is it I can do for you?" he enquired, his accent betraying his West African origins.

"I am old friend of Father Samuel O'Connor, but I have not seen him for many years and wanted to visit him today," said the man. "But your secretary says Father O'Connor is not at this church anymore."

"I'm afraid that is correct. Father O'Connor has been gone about a year now. I am the new pastor."

"Ah, I see. I was hoping to see him. It has been a long time since we see each other. There is much I want to say. Can you tell me where he is now?"

Okoro shrugged. "That I am afraid I cannot say," he said, noting the stranger's flash of annoyance. "This is not because I do not want to tell you but because I do not know. You see, Father O'Connor has been missing all this time. The police came here, there was an investigation, but still there are no answers. It is all very unfortunate."

"I am very sorry to hear of this. We are good friends, you know. There is much I wanted to talk about."

"This you have said," said Okoro, eyeing the man suspiciously.

"Do you know if Father Samuel has family? Maybe I can visit them and..."

"He had no family."

"That is not good."

"Yes, unfortunate. I'm afraid I will have to cut our talk short, Father Dubcek. It is almost time for me to leave. I minister to some of the patients at the oncology ward at Saint Josephs."

"I am sorry to disturb you. Thank you for the time," said the man, shaking Okoro's hand before turning to leave.

"Father Dubcek."

The man stopped at the door and turned to face Okoro. "Yes?"

"I must apologize for my rudeness for not asking before. Which is your parish?"

"Parish?"

"Yes, your parish. In case I hear anything about Father O'Connor. Then I can contact you."

"Ah, I see. It is not here in United States. My church is in small village in the mountains in Serbia. Travel, communication—all is very difficult. It is no matter. Maybe when I am in United States again, I will come visit."

"You are here on holiday then?"

"Yes, I am on holiday. Maybe we will meet again another time."

Okoro watched the stranger leave his office in silence. A priest on holiday would have dressed informally. But this was not what convinced him of the man's deceit. It was what he'd seen in the man's eyes. Once, years ago, as a boy in Africa, rebel soldiers raided his village. He'd seen the same look in those men's eyes. Men of violence and murder. Men he hoped never to meet again.

◊ ◊ ◊

Mary Green sat at her front desk and watched as the priest passed by. When she'd reflected upon it later, Mary couldn't quite tell why she'd called out to Father Dubcek. Or why she'd handed the man Father O'Connor's personal Bible. Perhaps she'd felt sorry for the priest who'd come all this way to visit his friend. Or perhaps the impulse had been to do with something more pragmatic—the chance to close a chapter in the parish's history and finally accept the new order of things.

◊ ◊ ◊

Goran stopped at the foot of the sandstone stairs outside the church. He was about to toss O'Connor's Bible into the nearby shrubbery when he thought better of it. It would only confirm the suspicions he realized Father Okoro had concerning him. Goran flicked through the book, and found some prayer cards tucked between the pages. He pulled out one. "Act of Contrition," it read. He turned it over and started to read.

Oh my God, I am heartily sorry for having offended you.

He stopped reading and placed it back between the pages. He flicked through more pages and pulled out another.

"The Blessed Sacrament."

He turned it over. More empty words. He found another.

"Prayer for the Dead."

Then another and another. One caught his eye—it showed a knight on horseback with a halo about his head. The knight was plunging a lance into a dragon's head.

"Saint George—Patron Saint of soldiers."

He turned it over and read the words scribble across the back of the card.

"Anastasiya Strajinski – Whitby Foundation Finishing Academy."

A potential lead? He was about to replace the card but slipped it into his wallet instead. He would follow it up, he decided. After all, who could fathom the fickle nature of chance? As he walked back to his car, he failed to notice two men watching him from a parked car further down the street. Goran got into his vehicle, dropped O'Connor's Bible onto the passenger seat, and started the car. He pulled out into the traffic and headed towards the motel unaware he was being followed.

"You sure it's him?" said Clark.

"Positive," said Wilson, his eyes fixed on Goran's car. "If you'd read the file like I did, last night you'd know Dragan Millovic was one of the dead found at the old house O'Connor owned. I did some background checking on Dragan last night and came up with a mugshot of his brother, Goran. He's wanted by Interpol. War crimes. According to the intel, he contracts himself out as a hit man these days."

"You think he's here looking for his brother's killers?"

"That's the only explanation I can think of. He's probably got the same intel we have. No doubt he's here looking for information on the priest. I say we keep following the asshole and see where he's going. Besides, this place isn't going anywhere. We can always come back if we need to."

"Synchronicity."

"What?"

"Synchronicity, you know, when seemingly unrelated things all line up."

"I know what it means but I don't think its relevant in this case."

"Meaning what?"

"Meaning in this case everything is related. Dragan killed in that house, the house owned by a priest since presumed missing, Goran turning up here, the priest's last known location."

"Yeah, but him walking out the church when we were about to go in. Think about it. That doesn't happen every day. That's like winning the lottery."

"If you check the odds on winning the lottery, you'll find this easier to believe. Besides, we don't know where this asshole might be leading us."

"Maybe, but I reckon its better than anything we could get back at the church."

"At least we agree on that."

Wilson accelerated smoothly and moved across into the adjacent lane, his eyes never straying from his target.

◊ ◊ ◊

The agents had followed Goran back to the Gateway Motel, Wilson choosing to continue past rather than turn in at the place itself. At this point, Clark had argued that they pose as salesmen enquiring about accommodation so that they could discover which room Millovic was staying in. But Wilson did not want to alert the hit man and had instead stopped a discreet distance from the motel. An uncomfortable hour passed as they watched the place. The car was hot and stuffy, even with the windows rolled down.

"I'd kill for a beer about now," muttered Clark.

"Me too. Fuck, you'd think after twenty years we'd be used to this bullshit. Or at least found a better way to make a living."

"But here we are."

"Suppose it could be worse."

"How so?"

"We could be stuck in some mindless nine-to-five desk job, getting shot at in some dirty Afghan village, shoveling shit in a pig farm, or..."

"Okay, I get the picture. We should be happy sitting here while our nuts slowly dissolve in a puddle of sweat."

Wilson offered a wry smile. "Something like that. Anyway, it'll be dark in a few hours. I say he'll be on the move by then."

"If you're so sure about that, why don't we go get takeaway and coffee and come back later?"

"I didn't say I was. It's a hunch. The way he was paging through that book back at the church, looked to me like he was onto something there."

"And if he was, then why not go there straightaway?"

"Maybe he didn't have enough information and needed to do some research first. Maybe he wanted to change out of that priest outfit. Maybe he wanted to take a shower."

"That's a lot of maybes."

"Look, whatever the case, the odds are running in our favor right now, and I say we keep playing 'til our luck changes."

"Okay, you've made your point. I still think we'd miss nothing getting takeaway," grumbled Clark. The vinyl leather upholstery squealed in protest as he shifted uncomfortably in his seat.

Wilson shot a sideways glance at his partner and grinned. He felt a subversive pleasure in seeing Clark's own discomfort even though he was no better off.

15

It was Faith and Jennifer's turn to go out on the hunt night. But Anastasiya had changed her mind. Mia and Lily were going instead. Meredith and Judith would join them at the bloodletting. Faith was not surprised. She understood Anastasiya's motives. But the fact they had been excluded and would go hungry for another week stoked Jen's paranoia.

Faith had offered to help her improve her weapon skills, if only to provide them both with the distraction. They passed the other girls' rooms on their way to the dojo and heard the music and animated conversation. It was like a regular girls' night out. The music was Meredith's choice. Anastasiya would allow her access to the streaming app once a month to update their selection. As much as she despised Meredith, her music taste wasn't too bad.

Faith turned the dojo lights on as they entered. She walked over to the weapon's rack.

"Katana, naginata or yari?" she said.

"Naginata, I guess," replied Jen.

"You guess?"

"Anastasiya would say I suck pretty much at all of them, but I think I'm not too bad with the naginata."

"All the more reason to try one of the others, don't you think?"

"I know you're right and all, but can we stick to something I am reasonably good at tonight?"

"Okay."

Faith lifted two of the polearms from the rack. She tossed one to Jen, who caught it with one hand and then whirled it expertly about her body.

"We'll practice blocks and strikes then maybe a few kata before we get on to the sparring," said Faith.

They walked onto the mat and adopted hasso-no-kamae, the ready stance with the naginata angled across the body, its sharpened steel blade pointed upward.

"Remember, no tension in the shoulders and hands. The body immediately follows the weapon."

"The body immediately follows the weapon," repeated Jen.

She followed Faith through a set series of blocks, their naginatas slicing through the air as they moved to parry imaginary attacks. Uchi otoshi—the naginata sweeping down to deflect an incoming blow, suriage—an upward parry, harae, nagashi uke, kaeshi uchi, each block performed rapidly in succession, their bodies perfectly balanced as they moved. Then they moved on to the strikes, men—a powerful downward cut aimed at the opponent's head, do—a strike to the body, gyaku do—a reverse strike to the body, suni, tsuki, kote, migi kesa, and so on, their movements a study of power and precision as they transitioned fluidly between each deadly strike.

Faith moved to a combination of block and strike. On and on they went, moving with inhuman speed, their enhanced bodies betraying no sign of fatigue.

◊ ◊ ◊

Anastasiya watched Mia and Lilly get into the limo from the monitors in her room. Meredith and Judith were still in their room. They would move to the small room adjoining the killing room an hour or two from now. She turned to a third monitor that showed Faith and Jennifer training in the dojo. She smiled. The girls had taken their disappointment well. It was nothing less than what she expected of them.

◊ ◊ ◊

The big limo purred down the winding driveway towards the waiting front gate, gravel crunching beneath its wheels. The gates swung open as though moved by an unseen hand as the vehicle approached. Lotho slowed the car a fraction at the entrance, turned into the street, and pulled away as the gates swung closed once more. The limo passed a black sedan approaching in the opposite direction. Lotho looked instinctively into the rearview mirror and watched the red taillights of the sedan recede into the distance. It did not stop. Satisfied, he turned his attention back to the road ahead and depressed the gas pedal. The big V8 motor growled appreciatively as the car accelerated towards the waiting city.

◊ ◊ ◊

Goran drove another hundred yards before executing a U-turn in the street. He stopped a discreet distance away from the mansion's front gate and turned off the ignition. Two cars drove by. He watched both disappear. He waited. Five minutes later, he exited his vehicle. He proceeded at a leisurely pace up the street, slowing as he passed the imposing iron gates.

"The Whitby Foundation Finishing Academy for Girls," read the sign.

Goran noted the remote camera monitoring the entrance and kept walking. When sure he was beyond the camera's visual arc, he stopped. He looked down the quiet street in each direction and, satisfied he was alone, turned to face the high stone wall. He slipped a set of night vision goggles over his head and then scaled the wall. The rough stonework provided easy purchase. Stopping at the top of the wall, he peered into the dark shadows of the mansion's grounds. He flipped the night vision goggles down, flicked a switch, and was rewarded with a ghostly green vision of the world beyond. He adjusted focus until he could make out each tree, hedge, and flower bed and scanned the grounds slowly from left to right.

Scattered in an apparent random fashion were small points of light reflecting off various surfaces. He smiled. The reflected dots of light indicated the presence of infrared sensor beams. He flipped up the goggles, pulled a thermal vision scope from his pocket, and raised it to his eye. Small heat signatures became visible in some of the trees. Security cameras. He had seen enough. Slipping the scope into his pocket, he climbed back down to the street, pulled off the night vision goggles, and walked briskly to his car.

He sat in his car and stared at the school's imposing iron gates. Why did a school require so much security? He could think of no reasonable explanation. Unless whoever was running the place had something to hide. Something like hiding a nest of vampires? Or was it something more mundane? A paranoid head mistress perhaps? Or a smooth-talking security system salesman? There was no way to know without gaining more information.

This presented its own problem—a way to reconnoiter the grounds without alerting anyone. And he knew the man to help provide a solution. He pulled out his cell phone, punched in a number, and waited.

"Tony's Electronics, Tony speaking." said a voice.

"It's Mr Smith," said Goran, "Tomorrow morning, six thirty, the usual place."

"I'll be waiting," said Tony, ending the call.

Goran started the car and headed back towards the motel.

A short while later, a car further down the same street rumbled to life. Its headlights flickered on as it pulled away from the curb following in the direction Goran had gone. The car slowed outside the entrance to the school.

"The Whitby Foundation Finishing Academy for Girls," read Agent Clark. "What the fuck do you think he wants with a bunch of schoolgirls?"

"Not sure, but it must be related somehow," replied Wilson.

"I hope you're right, Nate. I hope this is more than some creepy sex-fiend thing. The last thing we need is to go off on some wild goose chase."

"Have a little faith."

"Okay, fine, I'll run a check on the place in the morning and see what comes up. Now, let's get something to eat already for Christ's sake!"

"Now? Don't you think we should follow Millovic back to the motel?"

"Fuck you!"

"Whoa, slow down, big fella. I'm not that much of an easy lay you know. You gotta at least buy me a drink first."

"Fuck you, and fuck your sense of humor!"

"Too easy. You make it too easy, Allan," laughed Wilson.

The agents' car accelerated slowly away from the school, its large wrought iron gates standing like an ancient sentient being jealously protecting the terrible truth within.

◊ ◊ ◊

Having finished the sequence of katas, Faith and Jen moved on to sparring. They took up stances and then began to circle each other, their weapons held firmly at the ready as they looked for an opening. Jen moved first, darting forward to deliver an overhead strike. Faith parried easily and countered with a wicked cut to the body, slowing her speed enough to allow Jen to block her attack. They moved apart and commenced circling again.

"Pretty good, but I think you can do better," said Faith.

"You think?"

Jen moved in quickly, stooping low to sweep her naginata's blade like a scythe aimed at Faith's legs. Faith skipped backwards and delivered a downwards block, easily deflecting her opponent's blade. The girls continued moving around each other. Strike, parry, counter. Strike, parry, counter. On they went. Faith slowed her block a fraction on Jen's next attack, allowing the blade to nick her exposed midriff.

"Oh! I'm so sorry, Faith. I didn't mean to," exclaimed Jen.

Faith laughed. "You know you can't hurt me, right? You did good."

"I'm sorry, Faith," said Jen, stepping back and dropping her hands to her side, with the naginata held loosely.

"What do you mean?"

"I mean, I'm sorry. I thought I could to this tonight but I... Well, there's too much in my head right now."

"I know, Jen, but you've got to focus on something else. You let too many negative thoughts in your mind, and they crowd out the good stuff, you know?"

"I know, but Anastasiya has a way of getting in my head. When I think I'm measuring up, she goes and does something like this. I mean, what is she really saying by taking away our hunt night—that she has the power to starve us or that I'm one step away from death?"

"It's not you, Jen. It's me," said Faith. "I fucked up the other night, and she's punishing me. You're my roomie, so I guess she figured it was easier to punish the both of us."

"But why? You apologized to her. You said she seemed happy with what you said, so why do it now so long after?"

"That's the way she works. She's reminding me. She's saying, 'I got you figured and don't you forget it, bitch!'"

"You think so?"

"Pretty much. So don't sweat it, okay? I've got your back. You and me are like real sisters."

"Thanks, Faith, you always know what to say."

"You wanna go back to the room?"

"Yeah, okay."

The girls walked to the side of the mat then turned and bowed.

"Here, give me your weapon."

Jen handed the naginata to Faith, who racked the weapons.

"Maybe we can sneak out into the gardens later," suggested Jen.

"I'd like that," said Faith.

16

The horizon flushed pink in the early dawn, and then the color began to bleed into the sky, turning a deep orange that faded to a warm yellow as the light slowly drew back the curtain of the night. It kissed the tops of the undulating hills surrounding the I5 highway and then moved inexorably down the slopes, driving the darkness back into the deepest folds and ridges. Birds began to sing as they stirred from their roosts, and a gentle breeze ruffled the chaparral, wild lavender and sage that covered the hillsides. A red-tailed hawk surfed the air current high above, its keen eyes scanning the earth for an early morning snack.

A little after six-fifteen, a plain white van turned into a secluded area located an hour's drive off the highway. This was Tony the man he'd spoken to the night before. He watched as the van pulled up alongside his vehicle. Tony turned off the engine, looked across at him, and gave a curt nod in greeting. They then got out of their vehicles.

To the casual observer, the pair could not have been more different, the short, scruffy bearded individual the antithesis of the athletic, well-dressed killer. Tony pulled back the side door as Goran approached to reveal a cornucopia of electronic gadgetry.

"Well, whaddya need?" he asked with an impish grin.

"Surveillance equipment. The place I watch, there is plenty of security on the property. Infrared, security cameras, perhaps more. It is difficult to get close to house without detection."

"Why don't you use a high-powered telephoto lens?"

"No. The house is back from property wall. Too many trees, too many bushes."

"Why don't you use a drone then?"

"I have thought about it, but drone is too noisy, battery life too short."

Tony smiled smugly. "Maybe back in the day when you flew the old kind, but not anymore."

He turned to retrieve something from one of the containers.

"Let me introduce you to this little baby," he said, revealing a small quadcopter drone with a magician's flourish.

"Is drone," said Goran, unimpressed.

"No, this is not just any drone. This here is one of my own designs."

"So?"

Tony raised his eyebrows in mock surprise. "Let me explain a few things here. First off, it's very, very quiet. See the props?"

He pointed to one of drone's propellers.

"My own design. This shape doesn't generate as much noise. Also, I've set the motors out of sync. It controls the harmonics better. Basically, a greater frequency spread means less noise. Second, battery life. Not a problem when you go solar. Check this out."

He pointed to the drone's semi-translucent shell.

"These are small solar panels. Now, I know what you're thinking. The panels are too small to generate power quick enough for the motors in flight, right?"

Goran nodded.

"Ordinarily, you'd be right. Except this isn't what they're meant for. See, the idea here is to fly this baby to a good vantage point and set it down out of sight. Then you sit back and record the live-stream high-def video direct to your tablet without ever having to worry about battery life."

"Never?" challenged Goran, unconvinced.

"Okay, it's got some limitations," conceded Tony with a shrug. "Obviously, no sun, no juice. Also, you'll want to keep an eye on the LiPo battery charge. If it gets too low, you won't have enough power to fly if you need to get it out of Dodge in a hurry. But you won't need to worry about that. I've set up the system with an in-built minimum charge warning."

"Range?" enquired Goran.

"About fifteen hundred feet, give or take. The system's WiFi-based, so it depends on local conditions."

"How much?"

"For you, eight thousand," said Tony, reaching back into the container, "and I'll even throw in a tablet to connect to the controller and a case to store everything in."

"First let me test," said Goran.

"No problem, it's all set up to go. Here, let me show you."

Tony placed the drone on the ground a short distance away then walked back to Goran. He turned on the controller and tablet.

"It'll take a minute to go through the start-up sequence," he explained.

Goran watched as the drone rose silently into the air before hovering in place about ten feet above the ground.

"See?" Tony tapped the screen. "You've got all your readings here—remaining charge, altitude, distance, speed, and so on. Controls are easy. Push the right stick forward, and she moves forward, left stick forward to increase altitude, stick down to decrease altitude, to yaw right you..."

"I know how to fly drone," interrupted Goran, holding out his hand for the controller.

"Okay then."

Goran quickly familiarized himself with the controls before

expertly putting the small drone through its paces. He watched the drone weave and roll through the air as it responded to his touch and had the beginnings of an idea.

"You make bigger drones?"

"Of course," answered Tony.

"Your drones can carry a few kilograms?"

"I can go up to twenty pounds or so. Of course, the bigger the drone, the bigger the payload. But the drawback is the bigger the drone, the more noise, the easier to spot."

"Can you program drones to fly to plan?" enquired Goran, maintaining his focus on the controller's screen.

"Whaddya mean, program? You mean program the drone to fly a set route? Yeah, I can do that."

"Not one drone. Many drones. You can program to fly in formation to set route?"

Tony thought for a few seconds. "Others have done it, so I don't see why I wouldn't be able to. I'll need some time, but tell me what you need."

"Later," grunted Goran. "First, I use this one. Maybe no need for others."

He maneuvered the small drone to hover in front of them before setting it down.

"Okay then," said Tony, rubbing his hands. "Let's get down to business. I believe we agreed on eight thousand?"

"Seven thousand."

Tony sighed inwardly. He'd expected as much and had adjusted his price to suit. Still, he found the whole business of negotiating irksome. Didn't anyone appreciate great craftsmanship anymore?

"Okay then, seven thousand five hundred, and we'll call it a deal," he said finally.

17

Detective Holland pushed the button on the intercom once more, but this time he kept his finger in place.

"That ain't gonna help. Either nobody's home or they're not interested in talking to us," said Ed Jablonski, Jack's partner. He shoved the last of his tuna on rye into his mouth and compressed the wrapping into a tight ball in his large fist.

"See that security camera?" Jack pointed to the camera perched above the gate. "It keeps moving. That means somebody's home, and I'm gonna make sure that somebody speaks to us, even if it means we sit in this car all day."

Jablonski wiped the crumbs from his lap. "Tell you what, why don't I stick the red light on the roof, and you switch on the siren, and we see if someone answers then?"

"I think you might be onto something there, Ed."

He knew his partner was joking. The pair had worked together for ten years and were used to each other's quirks. As his ex-wife had remarked on more than one occasion, he knew his partner better than anyone else.

"Run this by me again. We're here to question the principal of this finishing school about Don Stone because you got a tipoff he was investigating her?"

"About covers it," said Jack, his finger still firmly pressed on the intercom's button.

"You know the case on Stone's closed, don't you?"

"Yep, that I do. What about it?"

Jablonski counted the points off on his stubby sausage-like fingers, "One, we're doing this at the city's expense. Two, we've got a full caseload as it is. And three, the captain will have our asses if he finds out."

"Well, maybe if Cole and Dickson hadn't done such a half-assed job investigating Don's death, we wouldn't be sitting here right now."

"Okay, I'm not a fan of those clowns either, and I know Don was a close friend and all, but I've read over the case file, and I see nothing to suggest foul play."

"As you said, Ed, I knew the man, and I'm telling you that something about this case doesn't add up. And I aim to find out what that something is. Are you with me or not, partner?"

"Sure, I'm with you," said Ed, holding up his hands in mock surrender. "But don't lose focus on the other stuff, that's all."

"Duly noted, partner." Jack took his finger off the intercom button.

"Can I help you?" enquired a stilted voice over the intercom.

"Yes, this is Detective Holland from the Los Angeles Police Department. I'd like to speak to Ms Anastasiya Strajinski."

"Ms Strajinski is very busy at present. May I ask what this is about?"

"We think Ms Strajinski might be able to provide some important information relating to a homicide we're currently investigating. Of course, if she's too busy now, she can always come down to the station later. We can interview her then."

The seconds ticked by, and Jack began wondering whether his empty threat had worked. He was rewarded as the large wrought iron gate's opening mechanism engaged with a metallic groan.

"Looks like we gonna have that conversation with Ms Strajinski after all," said Jack, winking at his partner.

He steered the big sedan slowly past the gates and down the winding gravel driveway towards the waiting mansion.

◊ ◊ ◊

Meredith led them from the mansion's large foyer into the equally imposing library.

"Please wait here."

She turned and opened the door to leave.

"A bit old fashioned, isn't it?" said Jack.

She frowned. "Excuse me?"

"Your uniform. I didn't think schools went in for that type of thing anymore. Does it annoy you? Having to wear the uniform, I mean."

"The uniform is the symbol of this school. Like police or firemen wear uniforms to show who they are, we wear this to show who we are."

She closed the door behind her without waiting for a reply.

"The girl needs to lighten up," noted Jablonski idly.

He walked over to a large painting that dominated the wall opposite.

"In a place like this?" snorted Jack as he looked around. He walked over to the tall bookshelves loaded with row upon row of books. The place reeked of antiquity.

"If I didn't know better, I'd say this was an original," said Jablonski, peering closely at the painting.

"Why do you say that?" asked Jack over his shoulder as his eyes drifted casually over the mostly foreign language titles.

"This painting is called *Philosophy*. It was painted by Gustav Klimt, and it was destroyed by the Nazis in '44."

"That so?"

"Some black and white photos were taken of it back in the day. So apart from one art critic's account, there's no way of knowing what it actually looked like in color," said Jablonski, stepping back to admire it better. "I'll tell you something. This is the way I always imagined it though. In fact, maybe even better. The color, the texture, brush strokes. Every detail. Incredible."

"Hold on," said Jack, turning to look at his partner with amusement. "Am I missing something here? Since when was Ed Jablonski an art lover?"

Jablonski shrugged unapologetically. "It can't all be beer and football, you know. A man's gotta have some hobbies. Mine is art."

He stepped up to the painting again and bent forwards to study the brushwork closely.

"It has to be a copy. There's no other way."

"Perhaps it is as you say. But then is not a painting a copy of the artist's vision?" remarked a voice coldly behind them.

The surprised men turned around to find a statuesque woman standing at the door. She walked up to the painting, ignoring the men as she did, and touched its surface lightly with an elegantly slender hand.

"If this is true, if a painting is only a copy of the artist's vision, then the original is destroyed the moment the artist leaves his final brush stroke upon the canvas. In the end, all the world is left with are copies."

Anastasiya traced the brush strokes with her fingertips. She smiled faintly. The men watched her. The scent of her perfume filled the air. It was sweet yet wild and strangely erotic. She turned to face them, her eyes enigmatic pale blue, her face a picture of studied disdain.

"Ms Strajinski? I'm Detective Holland and this is Detective Jablonski."

"Why do you wish to speak with me, Detective Holland?"

"We would like to ask you a few questions."

"Concerning what?"

Jack produced a photo of Don Stone from his coat pocket. "Do you know this man?" he asked, holding up the photo.

"No. Why do you ask, Detective?"

"We're currently investigating a homicide, Ms Strajinski. Does the name Donald Stone mean anything to you?"

"No, I'm afraid not. Is he the man in the photo?"

"Mr Stone was a private investigator. Do you have any idea why Mr Stone was investigating you, Ms Strajinski?" enquired Jack, sliding the photo back into his coat pocket.

"No, I do not. Perhaps you should ask Mr Stone that question."

"Unfortunately, Mr Stone is dead."

Anastasiya clasped her hands comfortably in front of her and regarded him with what appeared to be polite indifference. A clock ticked steadily on the far wall.

"You really have no idea why someone would want to have you investigated?"

"This is an exclusive finishing school for young women, Detective. Our students come from very wealthy families. Their parents would expect only the best when seeing to their education. It would not surprise me if perhaps the family of a prospective student decided to undertake a background check on the person, in this case me, who would be responsible for their daughter's welfare."

"Being investigated doesn't bother you?" Jablonski looked surprised.

"I consider it a small price to pay for their continued patronage," said Anastasiya, turning to the short balding man. "Besides, I have nothing to hide."

"Are many girls enrolled here?" asked Jack.

"A select number of students are admitted each year. We teach foreign languages, social etiquette, and art appreciation to better prepare them for entry into wealthy society."

"You actually have to turn girls away?" said Jablonski.

"On occasion, yes. Why do you ask, Detective? Do you wish to enroll your daughter here? Or a favorite niece perhaps? The cost can prove prohibitive for some."

"No thanks, I thought this kind of place wasn't that popular anymore."

"Schools such as this have experienced a recent resurgence in popularity," said Anastasiya, flashing him an icy smile. She turned back to Jack. "Do you have any further questions, Detective?"

"No, not at present," he said and handed her his card. "These are my contact details, in case you remember something."

"Thank you, Detective," she said, taking the card. "Though I'm not sure what it is you would like me to recall."

"Every bit of information helps with our investigation, Ms Strajinski."

"Of course. And now if you will excuse me, I have a class waiting. I will have Meredith show you out."

The door opened, and the uniformed girl from before appeared. "Good day, Detectives."

"Thank you for your time, Ms Strajinski. Goodbye," said Jack.

The two men followed Meredith out of the room.

The door closed, and Anastasiya turned back to the painting. She reached out and let her fingers run lightly over the brush strokes again.

◊ ◊ ◊

The two detectives walked over to their vehicle.

"That's one stuck-up broad," noted Jablonski sourly as he opened the car door.

"Let me guess. Next you're gonna say she needs a good screw," said Jack, climbing into the driver's side.

"Maybe," said Ed, dropping heavily into the passenger seat. "But that wouldn't be PC, would it? Guess I'll have to settle for hoping she gets run over by a bus or something. You know she's hiding something, don't you?"

"Probably. But there's no way to tell for sure. And I don't have enough to go on anyway." Jack turned the ignition.

"And so what now?" asked Jablonski.

"Right now, nothing. Besides, I'm working on another lead. Only this one looks a lot more promising."

"Another lead?" Ed sounded surprised. "You gonna tell me what this promising lead is or keep me waiting in suspense?"

"Not yet, Ed. Let me do some digging first. I'll let you know if I turn up anything worthwhile."

"You'll let me know? I thought we were partners."

"And we are. But you said so yourself earlier that this isn't an official investigation. Anything we do now is gonna have to be off the books. That means putting in plenty of our own time, and I know the short leash Cathy keeps you on. Besides, it could turn out to be nothing."

"Make sure you keep me in the loop, Jack. I know how obsessed you can get with these things."

"Sure, I will. You're my partner, aren't you?"

Ed eyed Jack suspiciously. "And don't you forget it."

◊ ◊ ◊

Anastasiya stood in front of the array of security monitors and watched the car approach the front gate. She knew all trace of her dealings with Donald Stone had been erased, yet somehow there was still a link to him. How was this possible? More importantly, what did the police know? She watched the detectives' car leave as the wrought iron gates closed behind them.

She sighed. Less than one hundred years ago, she'd have eliminated the two men the moment they'd showed up at her door. It was no longer as simple as that. Cell phones, GPS-tracking, video surveillance in every suburb, all of these increased the risk of identifying their last-known location. It was a risk not worth taking. Besides, she reasoned to herself, if they'd had any evidence, they'd have confronted her with it. She thought of Don Stone and shook her head.

He had taken it upon himself to investigate her. What had he hoped to discover? It would have profited him little of course, since she had always intended to deal with him the moment his usefulness had expired. In the end, he'd been murdered by someone else. Who and why? These were still mysteries. But she was sure of one thing. The person had been a woman. She'd smelled the bitch's perfume on Don's clothes when she'd discovered his body. Humans and their petty games!

The thought at once annoyed and amused her.

She would hunt tonight, she decided. She would hunt, and in the killing she would release all her frustration.

18

The drone hovered high in the morning sky. Its digital eye scanned the mansion's grounds below, faithfully relaying every detail to its master. It drifted slowly overhead before dropping altitude to hover at roof-line level about four-hundred feet from the mansion. Guided by the unseen hand, the drone proceeded to follow a wide circle about the building, training its camera on the windows as it did. On its third lap, the drone stopped and resumed hovering, its camera focusing on a row of windows.

Goran tapped the tablet's display, and the drone's camera zoomed in to focus on a tall, attractive blonde woman. She was speaking. He nudged the controls gently, and the drone edged closer, its camera panning along the row of windows to reveal a group of seated females. They looked to be in their late teens or early twenties. It looked like a teacher instructing her class—it was a school after all. He found it strange that these were the only students he had seen, or the only teacher for that matter.

He focused the camera back on the attractive blonde. This must be Anastasiya Strajinski, he reasoned. He took a few photos of her to provide his police source.

The drone continued to hover as Goran watched the screen. On the face of it, nothing appeared out of the ordinary. It looked like a teacher instructing her students. Not quite what one would expect from a nest of vampires. But then, what exactly would one expect in the first place—night creatures hiding in their coffins, or partially clad nubile women draped sensuously over antique divans? He could think of a host of movie clichés, each as ridiculous as the next. Why not hide in plain sight? It was as obvious as it was simple. But he needed to be sure.

The drone's low-battery warning flashed on the tablet's screen. It was time to find a roosting spot, preferably one that gave a good view of the classroom. He maneuvered the drone towards the roof of the conservatory that extended perpendicularly from the main house. He'd noticed a gryphon-shaped roof finial on the conservatory roof apex earlier and aimed to land the drone there. Soon the drone was hovering above the back and extended wings of the gryphon. Goran depressed the control's left stick slightly, and the drone dropped gently onto the weathered cast-iron surface. It'd taken skill to land the drone, but he knew it would require a little luck to ensure it remained undetected. Besides the possibility of it being blown off by high winds, the drone's perch was over two hundred feet from the mansion's windows—easy enough to spot for anyone observant enough.

But he didn't have the luxury of time for a more elaborate approach, and even if it were found, there'd be no way for them to know what he planned. It was a risk worth taking. The camera rotated on its small gimbal mount to focus on the target row of windows. He watched the tablet screen. Was this a regular class? He noted the time. A few more hours of surveillance then he'd leave. He would return tomorrow morning, albeit to a different position to resume his watch. A few days would confirm whether there was any routine to their schedule. By then, he felt sure his suspicion would prove either correct or not.

"He's still just sitting there," noted Agent Clark as he watched Goran through a pair of binoculars.

The agents had tailed the assassin to a quiet leafy suburb located a block from the school earlier that morning. They'd parked some distance away and had been observing his every action since.

"He's got that drone flying recon over the school," said Agent Wilson, not bothering to look up from his iPad.

"I reckon you're correct. But why? There has to be some kind of connection."

"Oh, there's a connection alright," said Wilson, tapping the screen to access another website. "That school's a front for something. I'll put money on it."

"For all your searching, you haven't come up with dick. Which is strange, I'll give you that. Every school and campus out there pimp their wares online these days. Then there's FaceFuck and all those other social media sites. You name it, most are on it. But not this one." He peered through the binoculars again.

"You'd think some of the students would post about it at least, but nothing. The only thing I can come up with about the place is a lousy one-pager with a contact number and name. No board of trustees, no parent's association, no nothing. They're keeping a low profile for a reason, and I'm betting that reason connects them to Millovic."

"And the principal, Strajinski? Have you got anything on her yet?" asked Clark, placing his binoculars on the dash.

"Nope, which is odd in itself."

"Why do you say that?"

"There's no driver's license, no social security number, and no passport. At least, none in her name that I can find."

"If she works, she'll pay tax, so she'll have a tax ID number."

"You don't think I thought of that?"

"And?"

"Nothing. I have found something on who runs the finances though. The school appears to be part of a trust fund managed by a law firm, Whitcomb, Newton & Moore," said Wilson, scrolling through the webpage on his iPad. "Established eighteen sixty-seven. Appears to specialize in corporate and property law. Strictly old-money clients. Operates out of NYC. That's about it. We want anything more, we'll have to approach the firm formally."

"We obviously can't do that, not without raising a whole lot of questions. I guess that leaves watching Millovic and hoping he's on to something."

"We'll give it an hour or so then head off to the office," suggested Wilson. "McNeil's gonna start asking questions if we don't start progressing on the other case. Besides, there's the GPS tracker we've put on his vehicle early this morning. We shouldn't have much trouble keeping tabs on him."

"And Webb?"

"What about him?"

"Do we keep him in the loop or what?"

At that moment, the sound of Pink Floyd's "Money" filled the car's interior. It was the ring tone from Agent Wilson's cell phone, the one he reserved for his special business. He pulled the phone from his coat pocket and looked at the number. He smiled.

"Speak of the devil," he said.

"Webb?"

"Yep."

"What you gonna tell him?"

"Only what I think he needs to know," said Wilson, letting the song play on a few more seconds before answering.

19

Morning had become afternoon, and with it the watchers had departed. Inside the mansion Anastasiya continued to instruct her acolytes, the morning's philosophical study now replaced with martial arts instruction. The first two hours consisted of practicing the set fighting moves and sequences over and over to enhance each student's muscle memory.

Anastasiya signaled the girls to pair up for fight training. This was a break from the usual set routine, but the girls did not question her—it was an opportunity to release the pent-up frustration each of them felt from being forced to stay indoors so much of the time. Their mistress was no fool, realizing her hold over them did not guarantee obedience. She relied upon the hunt and fight training and even on occasion assigning mundane tasks to distract her acolytes.

Anastasiya walked the mat watching intently as the girls fought each other—strike, block, counterstrike. Faith paired with Jennifer, the newest acolyte. She watched the pair a moment. Strike, block, counterstrike. Her eyes narrowed. It was as though each girl was merely going through the motions. There was no energy, no intensity, no ferocity.

"Everyone, stop now!"

The fighting ceased after some hesitation. Her acolytes turned to her, wondering why she had stopped everyone so abruptly.

"I see a lack of conviction in your fighting. I have told you many times, fighting is not a game to us. It is a matter of our survival. Nothing less."

Her acolytes looked around at each other. Who did Anastasiya mean? Was it all of them or someone in particular? They looked expectantly at their mistress.

"Meredith, stand over here," snapped Anastasiya, pointing to the center of the mat.

"You," she said, pointing at Faith, "Join her."

Both girls stepped obediently to the place indicated.

"The rest of you will step off the mat."

The acolytes moved back obediently, and Anastasiya turned to the two girls.

"Now you will fight. There will be no quarter asked and none given. You will fight for your survival. You will fight for the survival of your sisters. You will fight until I say otherwise. Do not disappoint me!"

Meredith assumed a fighting stance, with Faith reacting in like fashion. The pair circled each other, ready to exploit an opening in the other's defense. Meredith was first to strike, feinting with her left before immediately following with a right jab to her opponent's head.

Faith used her right hand to both block and then counter the blow, her fist smashing the bridge of Meredith's nose. She danced back from her stunned opponent, content to watch Meredith's expression of pain and anger. Meredith recovered quickly and, fueled by her anger, moved swiftly into the attack again. She feinted with her left again but this time followed with a high-front snap kick that would have decapitated a human opponent. Faith avoided the strike with ease, and Meredith suddenly found herself desperately blocking an overwhelming combination of punches before succumbing to a roundhouse kick that sent her tumbling off the mat. There was a collective gasp from the other girls.

None of them had ever come close to beating Meredith. Faith stood quietly and watched her opponent jump to her feet and move resolutely back onto the mat.

Meredith felt humiliated yet somehow managed to gain control of her rage. Giving in to her anger would make her less effective, she realized, but it took some effort. She looked back at the others. Their expressions were mixed. Was she in danger of losing her place as their leader?

Her gaze moved to her mistress. Anastasiya's impassive expression betrayed nothing. She looked back at Faith. Their eyes locked, and Meredith saw the contemptuous amusement lurking there. Faith smiled then closed her eyes and dropped her hands to her side. She stood still, as though serenely unaware of Meredith's existence. The anger surged within Meredith, and she launched herself at the waiting figure. She struck with a high, spinning roundhouse kick, but Faith evaded it easily and delivered a bone-cracking counterpunch to Meredith's ribs. Faith resumed her relaxed stance and closed her eyes. Meredith attacked again.

Strike, block, counterpunch. Strike, block, counterpunch. The one-sided fight continued, Meredith's attacks slowly losing their power with the virus struggling to repair the damage inflicted by Faith's increasingly vicious blows. Strike, block, counter strike. On and on until finally Meredith's battered body refused to obey her will. It was over.

Faith looked down at her vanquished opponent. She knew she should pity her, but she did not. Nor did she feel satisfaction. She felt no emotion, and that unsettled her. Meredith's body would heal quickly, but not so the damage done to her status amongst the others. Faith looked at them. What did their expressions reveal? Hate. Fear. Envy. Each was there in some measure. She looked at Anastasiya and understood. This had not been a lesson about survival. This had been a lesson aimed at her. Only recently she had argued she had no choice but to accept Anastasiya's blood. That wanting to live was a natural part of nature and nothing more. Yet beating Meredith the way she had, was that simply the will to live? Anastasiya had taught them the philosophy of Nietzsche. He had written each living thing would strive to become dominant because all life was simply a will to power. Was this what Anastasiya wanted her to acknowledge? That she had accepted Anastasiya's blood not because of a need to survive but because she'd instinctively wanted the power it promised.

"The lesson is ended," said Anastasiya, looking at Faith. "Some of you, take care of your sister, Meredith."

Anastasiya left the training room, making a point to ignore Faith as she did.

No one moved at first, then Judith and Mia stepped forward and helped the battered Meredith to her feet. Supported by the pair, she glared balefully at Faith as they shuffled past. The other girls filed silently from the room until only Jennifer remained.

"Is everything okay?" she asked.

"I don't know. You tell me," said Faith, searching her friend's expression.

"I don't know if I can, Faith. I mean, I'd like to say it is, but after what happened..."

"Why? Are you worried I would do the same to you?"

Faith wasn't threatening Jen but was annoyed at her friend for stating the obvious. Why ask when they both knew the opposite to be true?

"Of course, I'm not. How could you think that?" objected Jen. "But I've never seen you like that before. You took Meredith apart. It looked so calculated. Nobody could take their eyes off you. But as the fight went on, I started wondering what everyone was thinking. Then I looked back at the countess."

"And?"

Faith felt she already knew the answer.

"She couldn't keep her eyes off you, like the others. But there was something in her expression that got to me. It looked, I don't know, it looked like fear. I know it sounds stupid. I mean, I haven't been around as long as you or any of the others, so what the hell do I know? But that's what I started thinking. Then she caught me looking at her, and it was surreal. She knew that I knew, and I knew that she... Fuck it, you get the idea, right?"

Faith nodded.

"What if I'm right? What if it was fear? That means she sees you as a threat and that means she'll want to get rid of you, don't you think?" said Jen, taking Faith's hands in hers. "All she has to do is refuse to give her blood to you. And then you'll die. We've all seen what the virus does. I don't want that to happen to you."

"Stop worrying, Jen. That won't happen," said Faith with little conviction.

"How can you be so sure?"

"Call it a hunch," said Faith, attempting a reassuring smile. "If I don't step out of line, she'll be content to let me be. Leastways, for now. I mean, if I'm no threat, then why go to the trouble, right?"

"And what about a month from now or a year from now when she decides otherwise? What are you going to do then?"

"Let me worry about that Jen, okay? I said I'd handle it, and I will, trust me."

"I do trust you, Faith, but..."

"Look, I know you're worried for me, and I really appreciate it. You're my friend. My only friend. But right now, I need some time alone. Give me an hour or so to clear my head, and I'll see you back at the room, okay?"

"All right, if that's what you really want," said Jen reluctantly.

"For a little while, I promise."

Jen nodded then turned and walked to the door. She looked back, attempted a reassuring smile, and then let Faith be alone.

◊ ◊ ◊

They did not speak when Faith returned to their room. Each furtive glance, each nervous movement, betrayed the questions her friend was desperate to ask but did not. They sat on their beds pretending to read while the void between them grew.

Later, she slipped out of the room into the night and the solitude it promised. She walked through the mansion's gardens, a wraith drifting aimlessly in the silent darkness. She looked up at the infinite black of the universe. If only she could float away, up, up amongst the stars. Away from all this. Perhaps if she wished hard enough it would be. If only.

She looked around. Jen had not followed her like she usually did. Why? Did she understand her need to be alone, or was it something else? The more she turned it over in her mind, the more doubts surfaced.

She's afraid of me. She saw what I did to Meredith, and she's afraid. She saw my anger. Is she worried I'll do the same to her someday?

But how could she think that? She cast her mind back to a time before the change, back to the Faith of then. Had she been any different as a person? Had she been any less determined? Any less strong willed? Hadn't she always remained true to herself? But if that were true, what about Manny? His cruel face appeared, uninvited, in her mind.

"You came to me willingly. You didn't stop me. I took what I wanted, and you didn't stop me. You deserved those beatings. You could've walked away, but you didn't. You were weak," he'd said.

She shook her head. What choice did she have? The will to live. She had not fought back. She'd endured and had survived. Did that mean she'd compromised herself? In surviving, had she cheated the person she believed she was? Did that person even exist? Perhaps she was nothing more than a human chameleon—constantly changing to suit her needs. Pragmatic. Soulless. Calculating. How else could she explain what she did—drinking the blood of innocent humans. Was she only responding to the biological drive to survive—the will to live, or was there something more sinister to her motive? A god amongst human cattle. The will to power. The opportunity to take power and never fear people like Manny ever again. Perhaps Anastasiya was right. She'd accepted the blood for the power it'd promised. But at what cost? What part of the idealistic young girl now remained? Had she ever been that girl? Perhaps the real Faith—the thing she was now—had always existed, hiding in the shadows of her psyche, waiting to emerge.

Jesus Christ! Who the fuck are we all really anyway? Do any of us know for sure?

Faith stopped and looked around. She'd strayed close to the boundary wall. She turned and looked towards the mansion then back at the high stone wall. She could leave right now, she realized. She could climb over the wall and run off into the night. Climb the wall to find the person she'd once been. How long would she have before the virus started to eat at her? A week? Maybe two? She knew without Anastasiya's blood she would die. But at least it'd be her choice. She'd have that.

She looked up at the wall and then turned away to head back to the mansion. She wouldn't run. Not because she was afraid of dying but because running felt like quitting. No matter how bad things got in the past, she'd never given up on herself. She would stay and figure out some positive use for her power. At the very least, she'd be able to protect Jen. She took a deep breath. Maybe then she'd finally find a way to accept the darkness within herself.

20

G oran sat patiently in his car. Two hours had passed since he'd followed the sleek black limo from the school to one of the trendier nightclub districts. He'd watched two girls exit the vehicle and enter a club. Dressed in strapless, short cocktail dresses and flashy stiletto-heeled shoes, they appeared to be nothing other than two girls having a night out on the town. The limo had driven a few hundred yards further and turned into a quiet side street. Goran did not follow the girls into the club—a grizzled forty-year-old would stand out amongst the crush of bright young things.

There was also the off chance he might lose them in the busy club. And there was no reason they wouldn't leave the way they'd entered.

The minutes crept by. People came and went. Goran waited. Another half hour and then he saw the two girls exiting the club, a smiling young man between them. They talked and laughed as they walked. He watched as the girls guided the man down the side street.

Goran started his car and pulled away from the curb. He slowed the vehicle and watched the girls and young man climb into the limo as he passed, then he accelerated smoothly to turn down the next side street along. He glanced at the street map on the car's electronic navigation system and saw that both streets joined the same arterial road. He slowed down before the intersection and waited for the limo to pass. He turned into the busy road and proceeded to tail the black limo at a discreet distance.

He soon realized the limo was headed back to the school. As he followed, he considered the possible reasons the girls would take a man back to their school. He kept coming back to the same conclusion—the man was vampire food. He shook his head as though that might dispel the idea. It seemed too fantastic. A fairy tale come to life. The stuff of legend. A horror walking the earth. Perhaps his desire to avenge his brother's murder had swayed him to believe his grandmother's tale. It offered him redemption for having failed his brother. He could be at once his avenger and a demon slayer.

There was only one way to know for sure. He would have to watch the school and wait for the man to leave. But if he failed to reappear, did that prove the school hid vampires? Not necessarily. The truth was that Goran hoped it did. The idea of eradicating a nest of vampires was altogether too enticing. The limo sped through the night with Goran following at a discreet distance. He looked in his rearview mirror. The headlights of the now familiar sedan followed a few cars behind. His source had confirmed they weren't government agents.

The authorities didn't even know he was in the country. That narrowed it down a little. He'd considered confronting them but decided against it. Eliminating them might cause further complications. For the moment, it was convenient to allow the charade to continue.

He would watch the school, and they would watch him. A grim farce with death as its punchline. He was certain they had no connection to the place nor had they any way of knowing what he planned. When the time came, they would not be able to stop him. Still, it was a distraction he'd have preferred to do without.

The traffic thinned as they left the city. The limo turned off the interstate. The two cars followed. They came to an intersection and the limo turned right. Goran followed suit. There were no other cars on the road. He would have to drop back further or risk detection. He looked in his rearview mirror. The sedan was gone. He smiled. Whoever was following had figured where the limo was headed. They had probably decided the risk of being spotted outweighed any benefit of tailing him. He knew he would see them back at the school. Either later tonight or tomorrow. He'd have preferred doing the same, but he could not.

He needed to see the young man delivered to the school. Then he would wait. No matter how long it took. He would wait to see his suspicions confirmed.

21

Detective Holland took a sip of his morning coffee and watched the gym across the street. The large plate-glass windows fronting the establishment allowed an unobstructed view of the people exercising inside. He had always wondered why most of these establishments allowed this potentially intrusive view. Was it a kind of exploitation—a way to get free advertising off the sweat of their paying customers? Or were they simply pandering to the exhibitionist within each of us?

One of the gym's patrons held his attention—Tammy Sloane. He'd followed her to the gym that morning. After thirty minutes watching her push herself through a grueling exercise routine, he'd decided to risk grabbing a coffee and doughnut from the fast-food joint around the corner.

When he'd returned Tammy had moved onto the Stairmaster. Jack took another sip of coffee and shook his head. If nothing else, he admired her workout ethic. He reached over and switched off the radio. Perhaps it was his age, but these days stations didn't seem to be playing the music he enjoyed. He yawned and took another sip of coffee. He stretched his legs as best he could in the cramped confines of the car. Placing the styrene cup into a cup holder, he reached into his shirt pocket and pulled out a pack of cigarettes. He lit up, took a long draw, and slowly exhaled.

Ed Jablonski had accused him of becoming obsessive about a case more than once. What he was doing now—taking a week off from work to tail a woman he barely knew—probably fell into that category. But he and Don Stone had started off in the academy together. They'd been partners for almost fifteen years. Don had been his best friend. He had been best man at his wedding. Godfather to his children. The man would have done the same for him. Deep down in his gut, he knew Tammy had something to do with Don's death. The real problem, as he saw it, was proving she did. The lack of physical evidence made it almost impossible. As he watched her climb the Stairmaster, he began thinking about how else he might get justice for his friend.

Tammy finished her workout and headed to the changing room. She emerged from the gym a half hour later dressed in a stylish, short summer dress and high heels. She slipped on a pair of Bvlgari sunglasses and strutted over to her sports car. Her hips swayed with a restless sexual energy. Jack smiled. He could see why Don had been attracted to her. A few moments later, she pulled out of the gym's parking lot with Jack following a few car lengths behind.

◊ ◊ ◊

Another hour went by before Tammy turned into the parking lot of a motel. Jack pulled into a parking spot across the street and watched as she exited her car and walked into the motel's reception. She emerged a short while later, took the stairs to the first floor, and walked along the external corridor to a room located near the end. She unlocked the door and entered.

Jack waited. A quarter of an hour later, he was rewarded when a metallic-green Dodge Challenger pulled into the motel parking lot. An athletic young man exited the vehicle and headed straight for the stairway. Jack watched as he took the stairs two at a time. He turned to his left at the top of the stairs and walked along the same corridor Tammy had before. He stopped outside the door she had entered. He knocked, the door opened, and he slipped inside. Jack waited fifteen minutes before getting out of his car.

He strolled across the street, took down the Challenger's registration, then headed for the motel reception. No one was at the desk, so he rang the counter bell.

"Be with you in a minute," called a man's voice from the small adjoining office.

A few minutes later, a short, balding man dressed in crumpled shirt and pants emerged. He wiped the last flakes of Danish from his thick moustache before speaking.

"How can I help you?"

"Are you the manager?"

"Yes, I run this establishment."

"Detective Holland, LAPD Homicide," said Jack, casually flashing his badge.

"Homicide? We haven't had any murders here, Detective," said the manager, regarding Jack warily over the top of his bifocals.

"You have a guest register?"

"Yes, as required by law. We do everything by the books here."

"I'd like to take a look at it."

"I don't know if I can allow that, Detective. I mean, I think I need to see a warrant first."

"I could do that. Then again I might choose to cite you on some fire code violations I've noticed," said Jack, leaning over the counter. "The choice is yours."

"Suppose that's fair," said the manager, turning the PC screen round to face Jack. "Are you looking for anyone in particular, Detective?"

"Show me the people who checked in today."

The manager tapped on the keyboard and a short list of names appeared. Jack scanned the list. There was no Tammy Sloane.

"There was a woman who checked in earlier."

"A woman?"

"Yes, she came in here about thirty minutes ago. Blonde, five-seven, tanned, easy on the eyes."

"Ah, yes, I think I know who you mean. That would be Ms Starr."

"She come here often?"

The manager hesitated. Jack could see what he was thinking—was he really a cop, or was he a jealous husband or a possessive ex-boyfriend? Was he going to pull out a shotgun, break into the room, and gun down the cheating woman and her lover? He watched the play of emotions on the man's face.

"A couple of times a week, yes," said the manager finally.

Jack thought he detected more than a hint of self-righteous satisfaction.

"A couple of times a week. Any days in particular?"

"Mostly Tuesdays and Thursdays. Why do you want to know, Detective? Is she in some kind of trouble?"

"That depends on what you term trouble."

"Well, I'm not sure really."

"Are you a law-abiding citizen, Mr..." Jack looked down at the man's name tag. "Robert?"

"I like to think so, yes."

"What if I said Ms Starr was a prostitute?"

"Is she? She certainly didn't strike me as one. But if it turned out she was, why then I suppose I'd have to call the police, of course. You know prostitution is illegal in this state."

"That I do. Of course, if we found she had been plying her trade from this establishment, then things might get a little messy."

"Messy? Look, Detective, I assure you I would never allow anything like that here."

"Sure, you say that now."

Robert turned the PC screen back away from Jack as though in doing so everything would return to normal. He licked his lips nervously.

"Please, Detective, I don't know what else I can tell you."

"I might have a proposition for you."

"A proposition?"

Jack pushed his hands into his pants pockets and looked around the reception area as though assessing the place. "Would you say you run a respectable establishment here?"

"Yes, I would. I mean, I do."

"So you wouldn't want anything to come out that might damage its reputation, would you?"

"No."

"I'm glad to hear it. That means you'd want to help me any way you could. Is that right?"

Robert's hand strayed to the pen used by guests that lay on the counter. He straightened it. "What are you asking me to do, Detective?"

"I haven't asked you to do anything yet."

"I'm sorry, but I thought..."

"Ms Starr, does she rent the same room every time?"

"Not every time, but most times, yes."

"But you could arrange that she does, right?"

Robert adjusted the pen again. "I suppose I could."

"That's good to hear, Robert. When she gets here, is it always around this time?"

"Mostly, yes."

"Mostly?"

"Maybe once or twice she hasn't but mostly she's on time."

"Good. Say that morning, a few hours before, you were to leave the keys to the room in an envelope here." Jack tapped the corner of the counter.

"Yes, but why would I..."

"I'll be bringing some camera equipment with me."

"Oh, I see. But what you're proposing, isn't that breaking the law?"

"You'd want Ms Starr to be caught if she were breaking the law, wouldn't you?"

"Yes, I suppose."

"Okay, Bob, you don't mind if I call you Bob, do you?"

Robert offered a thin smile. "No."

"Bob, you don't know me, but I like to think I'm a fair man. Most of the time anyways. If we work together on this, I get what I want, and you get what you want. We both walk away happy. But if say, something was to go wrong, that could make things awkward. At least for you more than for me. Do we understand each other?"

"Yeah, we understand each other."

"That's good. I like that. I'll be in around eight Thursday morning. Make sure the keys are on the counter."

Jack was about to open the door when he stopped. "Oh, and Bob?"

"Yes?"

"Not a word about this to anyone. Is that clear?"

"Yessir, clear."

◊ ◊ ◊

It was an hour before midday. Goran watched Anastasiya dismiss her class, their every movement transmitted from his rooftop drone to the tablet device he held. The young man from the previous evening was yet to emerge from the school. Goran was convinced he never would, and each hour that passed merely strengthened his conviction.

A flick of Goran's thumb and forefinger on the tablet screen focused the drone's camera on Anastasiya's face. He studied her a moment. Beautiful? Undeniably. Elegant. Controlled. Aloof. Cruel. The more he watched her, the more certain he was of something darker lurking beneath those poised features. She turned suddenly and looked directly at the camera. Goran's fingers hovered over the screen. Had she seen something? He held his breath. Time stood still.

Her ice-blue eyes burned into his soul. Then, as suddenly, she was gone. He pulled back on the camera's zoom and watched as she left the room. Goran let out his breath. Had she spotted the drone? Only time would tell, he decided. He jotted down the time of the class. It was the same as the day before.

He picked up his cell from the passenger seat and punched the keys rapidly. He waited for Tony to answer.

"It's me. I want six drones. All must carry twenty pounds minimum. All must be linked to each other to fly in formation to set target coordinates," he instructed. "Can you supply?"

He listened carefully before replying. "You say X8 configuration. Is okay. How long?"

He scowled. "A month? No, you have two weeks."

He waited for the protestations to abate. "And the price?"

He raised an eyebrow at the reply. "Less fifteen percent and we have deal."

He smiled. "Good, is deal. Delivery in two weeks, the usual place." He hung up.

Goran switched the drone to record mode then turned off the tablet. The young man was dead. He was sure of that now. How many more, he wondered, had suffered the same fate? Countless no doubt, but only one mattered to him—Dragan.

It was decided. He would destroy this nest of vampires to revenge his brother. The Strajinski woman had murdered his brother, and she would die. The drones would provide him with the means to carry out his revenge. There were still some other items he'd require, however. Goran began to systematically go through a list in his head. Obtaining these would take time, but that would provide him the opportunity to continue his surveillance and plan his attack. And if in that time he found he was mistaken about the school? He immediately brushed the thought aside. In his mind, there was no doubt.

He started his car and pulled away from the curb.

22

Jennifer stood at the window and looked down at the well-tended gardens. Everything appeared to shimmer with a sparkling intensity that hurt her eyes. She couldn't remember ever being sensitive to the light. She placed her hands against the glass and felt the sun's warmth permeating through the transparent barrier. It was oddly comforting.

She shifted her gaze from her hands to her lean, muscled arms. Her skin was like porcelain, unblemished by the freckles she once had. She knew she should feel this was a better version of herself. Perhaps, in time, she would. A new self for a new world.

Lotho appeared and strode over the manicured lawn towards a row of rose bushes. He produced a set of secateurs and began cutting and collecting the flowering stems. Jen watched, intrigued by the hulking brute's delicate handling of the flowers. He turned and looked up at the window where she stood, as though aware she was watching.

She stepped back from the window. Something about Anastasiya's manservant filled her with unease, although quite why she couldn't figure. She turned around. Faith was sitting on her bed, her back against the wall with a book cradled in her lap.

"You know what? I don't miss it," said Jen.

"Don't miss what?" responded Faith without looking up from her book.

"The daylight. Being out in the sun like I used to, being by the pool and all that."

"Uh-huh."

"Hey!" laughed Jen, reaching over and snatching the book away. "I'm talking here."

"I heard you," said Faith, looking at Jen patiently. "You don't miss sunning yourself by the pool. Now can I please have my book back?"

"Fine, I was trying to have a conversation," said Jen, turning the book over to read the cover. "*The Society of the Spectacle*. What's it about?"

"Mass consumerism. How we've allowed ourselves to be defined by what we own rather than who we are. How we can only find value through the image we project."

"You mean like through social media?"

"Something like that. I mean, I think Debord wrote the book in the 1950s, so he wouldn't have known about the internet back then. But maybe I'm reading more into this than he meant."

"Sounds boring," replied Jen, handing the book back to Faith.

"It's not an easy read. Pretty depressing really."

"So why read it?"

"I don't know. Maybe I thought it'd help me figure out some meaning to it all, I guess."

Jen sat down next to her. "Meaning to it all?"

"To life?" said Faith.

"Life? You really think one book can do that?"

"I guess not, but we all gotta start someplace."

"So do you miss it?"

"Miss what, life?"

"No, silly! You know what I mean. Going out in the daylight."

"Sunlight can't kill you, Jen. You can go out there if you really want."

"Sure, I can. But then I end up feeling sick in the stomach with a splitting headache. No thanks. That's not much of a choice."

"But it's still a choice, and it's yours to make. Anyway, don't you prefer the way you are now? After all, you said your life was pretty fucked up before."

"You know I do, Faith. I mean, when I think back now, how bad things got, it scares me, and part of me gets really angry. And it's not like I'm complaining or anything. I'm just thinking out loud."

"And it's okay. We all have those moments when we think back to the way things used to be. Theres nothing wrong with that, really."

"And?" pressed Jen.

"And what?"

"I know you want to say something else. I've been your roomie for long enough to know. Why don't you tell me already?"

"Look, you know you can say anything to me. You know I've got your back. But I'd be more careful in front of some of the others, that's all I'm saying."

"You mean, Meredith?"

"Yes," said Faith. "But right now, I think any of the girls would use the chance to show you up in front of Anastasiya."

"Thanks for laying that on me, bestie. As if I'm not paranoid enough about stepping out of line."

"Don't take it that way, Jen. Anyway, you'll find in time the old part of you mattering less and less until finally this life is the only one you will want to know. Trust me."

"In time. Well, I've got plenty of that I guess."

"You said it," chuckled Faith, opening her book up again. "Can I go back to reading now, bestie?"

"Sure," said Jen with a faint smile.

She looked at Faith and suddenly felt afraid for her friend. Was this an irrational feeling or a premonition that something bad was going to happen? She had no way of knowing and decided it was best to say nothing. Besides, her friend looked happier than she had in weeks.

Jen stood up and walked back over to the window. The big man had gone, she noted idly and then looked up at the sky.

She sighed wistfully. "It seems to be a deeper blue today, don't you think?"

◊ ◊ ◊

While Jennifer day-dreamed, another embraced her rage. Meredith showed no sign of the physical trauma suffered in her fight with Faith, but her emotions threatened to consume her all the same. She had been beaten by someone she'd always considered inferior. Worse, she'd been beaten by someone the other girls also viewed as inferior. They might not have said as much, but she'd seen the looks on their faces. She was in danger of losing her position as their leader.

As first chosen, Meredith enjoyed the fawning admiration of the other acolytes. Now the thought of losing that cherished place gnawed at her fragile sense of self-worth, and the festering rage of old came bubbling to the surface again. It was a rage born from the abuse first suffered in the wretched confines of her trailer home. A rage continually fueled by every vindictive taunt, every snide comment and every social indignity endured at the hands of girls who society had placed above her. She wanted to scream out loud. Scream at the unfairness of it all.

Despite Meredith being an outcast of society, a reject tossed on the scrap heap of humanity, Anastasiya had selected her as one of her favored. And she'd done everything to validate that choice. She had proved herself the most adept at luring their prey. She had proved herself the best fighter. She had never questioned her mistress, not even once. It was she who, till now, the other acolytes had looked up to. Now she wondered how many of them were laughing behind her back. The thought of it threatened to overwhelm her.

She clenched her fists and took a deep breath. Then she breathed out slowly as she took up a fighting stance in front of the makiwara striking post. She would find a way, she decided. She would find a way of getting even with Faith. No matter the cost, she would find a way. She breathed in and focused. Then she fired off a lightning-fast right-hand punch. The post snapped back with a satisfying twang. She pulled her arm back and struck the post again, a little faster and harder this time. Ka-twang! Pull back, snap the punch. Ka-twang! And again. Ka-twang! Ka-twang! The punches followed harder and faster until finally the post sheared clean off its base.

Meredith looked around the silent training room. She giggled. Then she began to laugh wildly. Its sound rang in the empty dojo, brittle, manic and tinged with bitterness.

23

Over a week had gone by since Jack first followed Tammy Sloane to the motel. He shifted uncomfortably in his car seat and looked down at his watch. Then he looked across the street to where the lone green Dodge Challenger stood in the motel parking area.

"Come on, fuck her already and be done! I haven't got all day," he growled.

He reached into his top pocket and pulled out a pack of cigarettes. He tapped the back of the pack, and a cigarette slid part way out. Taking the cigarette between thumb and forefinger, he pulled it out and placed it between his lips. He returned the pack to his top pocket with his left hand whilst extracting his lighter from the side pocket of his coat with his right. Then he lit the cigarette, took a long drag, and exhaled slowly. He dropped the lighter back into his pocket and glanced across at the large brown envelope on the passenger seat. He smiled. He could afford to wait.

One hour and another cigarette later, he was rewarded as the motel room door opened. Tammy's lover emerged, closed the door behind him, and strolled casually over to his car. Jack watched the green Challenger pull out of the motel parking lot and merge with the busy midday traffic. He waited a minute, got out of his car, and jogged across the road, narrowly avoiding the oncoming traffic. He walked up to the motel room door and produced the master key Bob had given him earlier from his pocket. Inserting the key, he turned it and pushed open the door in one movement. He stepped inside and closed the door behind him.

Tammy was still in bed. Gasping in surprise, she pulled the bed sheets over her bare breasts. She was about to scream for help when she recognized Jack.

"What do you think you're doing? Get out!"

Jack locked the door and walked over to the foot of the bed.

"Oh, I think you and I both know exactly what I'm doing here."

"Look, Officer Holland, I don't know what you're playing at but..."

"It's detective," interrupted Jack. "And I've got a little business proposition for you. But first I think we need to get a little more comfortable."

He reached down and yanked the bed sheet off the bed. Tammy gave an indignant squeal as Jack was treated to a view of her naked body. She reached back to grab a pillow.

"You, motherfucker," she snarled, pulling her meagre covering close. "What the hell do you want?"

"What I want is justice."

"Justice? I don't know what you mean. Justice for what?"

"For the murder of Donald Stone."

"Don? Murder? It was an accident. The papers said so."

"The papers got it wrong. It was you," said Jack, jabbing his finger menacingly at her.

"No, I loved him," she sobbed.

"Bullshit. You were fucking him, like you're fucking Steve."

"Who?"

"Don't play the dumb broad with me," he said, pulling a small notebook from his jacket and flicking it open. "Steve Taylor. Drives a green Dodge Challenger. Employed as a personal trainer at Shape & Trim Fitness Centre. Currently residing at..."

"Okay," snapped Tammy, her expression hardening. "I know Steve. That still doesn't prove anything."

"Maybe, maybe not. But here's my theory. Don wasn't your first. He was probably only one fun fuck of many you've had over the years. One day something changes. Maybe you get bored and decide to move on. But you find Don's fallen for you and doesn't want to let go. He threatens to spill the beans to Mr Sloane. You can't stand the thought of losing everything, so you decide to kill Don."

"I would never do that!"

"It's a solid theory except for one thing. I knew Don. He wasn't the type to go falling for any woman. Especially a two-bit whore like you."

"You son of a bitch," snarled Tammy, her eyes blazing defiantly.

"Here's what I think really went down. Don got tired of you. Probably the thought of sticking his dick in that diseased twat of yours one more time made him sick to his stomach. He tells you it's over, and you get mad. Being tossed aside like some broken-down car sends you over the edge. You decide to get even, so you invite yourself round for one last meal. You even offer to cook for him. A cozy dinner for two. Easy to slip the water hemlock into the salad. What excuse did you give him for not eating, I wonder?"

"You're mad," snorted Tammy, shaking her head. "There's no way you can prove any of this."

"Who said anything about proving it?" said Jack, reaching into the large brown envelope he had with him. He pulled out a set of color photos and tossed them on the bed. "Here, some happy snaps for your family album. I especially like the one of you on all fours with Taylor's dick up your ass. Real class. You think Mr Sloane would agree?"

Tammy snatched up the pornographic images scattered across the sheets, her nakedness temporarily forgotten. Clutching the photos close, she pulled the pillow up to cover herself again.

"What do you want, Detective Holland?" she said, her eyes filled with hatred.

"Like I said before, I want justice. Justice for Don. I want you to pay for what you did."

"You want me to pay? You mean money, don't you? You want to blackmail me."

"Who said I was blackmailing you?"

"Then why take the photos?"

"Maybe I wanted to see you squirm."

"And then?"

"I haven't decided yet," said Jack, pulling back his coat to reveal a Glock pistol in its holster.

Tammy gasped, her eyes widening in terror. "Oh Jesus! You can't mean it! Please, why don't you believe me? I didn't kill, Don."

Jack took a threatening step toward the bed, his hand on his pistol. "You keep saying that, but I still don't believe you."

"Stop! I'll give you anything you want. Please don't kill me!" cried Tammy dropping the photos as she raised the pillow in front of her like a shield.

Jack removed his hand from his pistol with a mocking laugh. "If I'd wanted to kill you, you'd be dead already."

Tammy pulled the pillow close looking bewildered. "Then what? What do you want from me?"

"You know Don had a daughter?"

"Yes, of course I do."

"What's her name?"

"I... I don't recall," said Tammy adjusting the pillow nervously.

"Her name's Stacey. You ever wondered about her?"

She frowned. "Wondered? What about?"

"What would happen to her if Don ever died?"

"She has her mother to take care of her," said Tammy.

Jack shot her a condescending look. "Anne barely makes enough to cover the rent. She relied on the alimony Don was paying."

"Why are you telling me this?"

"I'm starting a college fund for Stacey, and you're going to be the sole contributor."

Tammy's eyes narrowed. "So that's it. After all the theatrics, all you want is money. I thought blackmail was against the law, Detective?"

"This isn't blackmail."

"Oh? Then what would you call it?" she demanded.

"It's an insurance policy."

"An insurance policy? What do you mean?"

"You pay a small premium of, say, fifty thousand dollars, and your husband never sees the photos."

"Fifty thousand!" she exclaimed gripping the pillow tightly "I can't get my hands on that kind of money without George knowing."

"A smart girl like you can figure out a way. I'm giving you a week to come up with the cash."

"I'll need more time. Please, you've got to give me more time!"

"A week and not a day more," said Jack. "And if you can't squeeze the money out of George, you could always hit the strip. With a knockout body like yours, you should be a real hit with the johns."

"You fucking asshole!" she yelled hurling the pillow at him.

"I'd be careful with that mouth, Ms Sloane," said Jack bending to pick up the pillow. "You hurt my feelings and then, well, who knows? You might become an overnight internet sensation. That's the great thing about digital cameras—there's always a copy."

He tossed the pillow onto the bed, and she snatched it up to cover herself again.

"Get out!" she screamed.

"Here's a number to reach me," said Jack, flicking a slip of paper on the bed. "I'll give you the details for the drop when you contact me. Don't be late. You have a great day, Ms Sloane."

He turned and let himself out as Tammy hurled a stream of invective at him.

Jack strolled back to his car and got in. He looked at himself in the side mirror and wondered if he was doing the right thing. He consoled himself with the thought that Stacey had been all Don had ever really cared about. In the end, he'd have wanted his death to count for something. At least that was what Jack told himself.

Had he chosen to analyze his feelings a little more closely, he might have conceded that deep down he wanted revenge. Not only for his friend, but for himself. The acrimonious divorce he'd endured had left him feeling embittered. Maybe this was his way of striking back. Not only against his wife but against Tammy and women like her. But he preferred not to think on it. Believing anything other than that he was doing this for Don would've taken the shine off the whole affair, and right now he felt good about himself.

◊ ◊ ◊

Agent Clark sat at his desk and stared vacantly at the PC monitor. His daydream was interrupted by a phone ringing nearby. He refocused on the flickering screen image—a scan of a handwritten ship's manifest. He scrolled down the seemingly endless list, his eyes scanning each barely legible line. That the shipping company had been unable to provide digital records was annoying enough, but the fact their supervisor had refused to assign a junior to help with the work made him angrier still. He looked up from the screen to the glass cubicle located in the far corner of the office. The balding head of the supervisor was visible above the large twin monitors perched on his desk. He scowled. The man was probably asleep.

He looked at his watch. It was almost lunch time, and Agent Wilson had still not returned. This only added to his annoyance. They'd agreed he would take on the monotonous task of checking the shipping manifests to allow Wilson the time to run a check on their client. That had been three hours ago. Either Webb's life was more complex than first thought or his partner was avoiding having to work on the manifests.

He sat back in his chair and rubbed his temples attempting to avert the migraine he felt coming on.

"Found that needle yet?"

"Huh?" Clark looked up to find Agent Wilson standing at his desk.

"Come on, Allan—needle. Get it?"

"Yeah, I get it, Nate. I don't find it funny, especially when I'm the only fucker neck deep in the haystack."

"Well, I had that thing to do."

"And?"

"It's almost lunch. Why don't we get a cup of coffee?"

Clark winked and stood up.

"Coffee? Yeah, sure. So long as you're buying, I'm in."

He grabbed the coat from the back of his chair and pulled it on. The pair strolled from the office towards the waiting elevators.

They ignored the Starbucks situated across from the office and instead headed down-town. Salvatore's Coffee was a good fifteen-minute walk, but there was less chance of being overheard by snooping work colleagues. Besides, old Salvatore took a special pride in roasting, grinding, and blending his own coffee, which was more than could be said for the bland blend of mediocrity on offer at most other establishments.

"Well, what did you manage to find out?" asked Clark once they'd sat down with their coffees.

Wilson pulled out his notebook and began reading out the dot points he'd made earlier.

"Dr Michael Webb, born 10th November 1975, Athens, Georgia. His parents were George and Martha Webb. Guessing from Martha's age she had him pretty late in life. Graduated..."

"I should've figured he was a Scorpio," interrupted Clark before taking a sip of his coffee.

Wilson looked perplexed. "And?"

"Well, it fits. He's self-absorbed, moody, sneaky. All typical Scorpio."

"You really believe in all that shit?"

"Trust me. Four of my ex-girlfriends were Geminis. Real lookers. All high maintenance. A real pain in the ass. These days, I go out on a date, the first thing I find out is what day they were born. Anytime between May 22nd and June 21st, and I say I need to go to the rest room. Then I leave the back way."

"You're all class, Allan. You must be a real hit with the ladies."

"I haven't had any complaints yet."

"I find that hard to believe, but stranger things and all of that. Can I continue?"

"Sure, go ahead," said Clark before taking another sip of his coffee.

"Graduated summa cum laude in bioscience at Vanderbilt University before going on to get a PHD in microbiology. Got a job at the CDC in Atlanta soon after, probably to be closer to his folks. His personnel records show that up until a few years ago he was a real little worker bee. Scored well on his work performance reviews, published a few papers, even won an award or two."

"And what happened?"

"Looks like there was some sort of sexual harassment case. A young intern. Anyway, looks like the top dogs there didn't want to lose one of their stars, so she was transferred, and the whole thing quietly went away. It affected him though. His work quality became erratic. Ended up having some run-ins with superiors. Word is he's difficult to work with."

Wilson closed his notebook.

"It still doesn't explain his connection to the school or Ms Strajinski," said Clark.

"Who says there is one?"

"There's gotta be. Strajinski, the Millovic brothers, the priest, and Webb. There must be a link. Maybe we need to start thinking outside the box."

Wilson sat back in his chair and sighed. He knew the way Clark's mind worked.

"Okay, Allan, so what's your theory?"

"See, the whole alien-virus thing is bullshit. You wanna know what I think?"

"Enlighten me."

"I think Webb's really into the manufacture of narcotics. Probably crystal meth. The school's a front, more than likely set up by someone in the Russian mafia. Strajinski's their pawn. Probably some high-class whore they smuggled in from the old country. That's why we have so little on her."

"Are you saying the school's a whorehouse? Either business is slow or they don't know how to entertain, because we haven't seen any visitors."

"Correction, we haven't seen any visitors those times we've been there. And what about the limo we've seen leave the place? The girls are being taken to meet their johns."

"To what? Fuck them in a nightclub?"

"Why do you have to be so contrary? How many times have we seen them go to a club?"

"A couple of times."

"And each time we've seen them leave with some guy. Right?"

"Yeah, sure."

"And what about their driver? That big dude's gotta be Russian."

"Could be."

"I'm telling you that it all fits. Now do you mind if I continue?"

Wilson sighed. "The floor's all yours."

"Thank you. Now where was I? Yes. Webb is supplying the Russians. Dragan Millovic tries to muscle in on their operation and gets burned. Goran hears of his big brother's demise and decides to get revenge. Webb gets wind of the whole gangland killing thing and gets nervous. The police file doesn't give him much, so he gets us on the case to find out if he really has something to worry about."

"You have one fertile imagination, Allan," said Wilson, shaking his head.

"Well, do you have a better idea?"

"You ever think that maybe Webb is a crackpot who actually believes in the whole alien-virus thing?"

"That still doesn't explain Strajinski or Millovic. How are they connected?"

"I didn't say it had to. Maybe us seeing Millovic at the church was a coincidence. Yes, he has a connection to Strajinski, but that doesn't necessarily mean that either are connected to Webb."

"So why are we continuing to tail Millovic then?"

"Remember what you said about synchronicity?"

"Yeah, and..."

"And nothing," said Wilson. "But running into Millovic has to mean something. Whatever that something is, I'm betting it'll give us answers on Webb. And until we find a better lead, I say we keep on Millovic. Agreed?"

"Agreed," said Clark. "But I still say I'm right about the little prick. It's drugs and the Russian mafia."

"Let's stick with what we know for now," replied Wilson, looking down at his watch. "We'd better get back before Jenkins reams both our asses."

Clark picked up his cup and drained the last of the coffee with relish. "After you," he said.

24

Hunt night. The nightclub appeared no different to countless others she'd prowled. Meredith knew she should feel the excitement of it—to lure him in, sate her lust, and finally feed on his life essence. Sex and death. An intoxicating cocktail. But as she sat and watched the revelers on the dance floor, she felt strangely indifferent.

What was different? The more she thought, the more she realized she had no answer. Losing the fight had not upset the social dynamic as she had feared. The other acolytes still looked to her for leadership. They still responded to her whims and laughed at her every dumb joke. Faith had not challenged her position, and most importantly Anastasiya did not appear to hold her in any less regard. In short, everything was as it had always been. On the surface at least. Perhaps that was the issue. Nothing had changed. Everything was as before.

It was as though the fight and her defeat never happened. Or perhaps an embarrassing subject to be avoided? In the end, she had been left to deal with her fractured ego. She felt alone. A girl lost and drifting on the shifting sands of her emotions.

"Hey there. You've obviously never been here before," said a husky voice behind her.

Meredith turned to face the man who'd spoken. He had the typical look of a nightclub Lothario—tight, well-tailored clothes, athletic build, smooth olive skin, jet black hair. In that instant, Meredith realized she knew him. Hernando Velez. Drug dealer and part-time pimp. Hernando, the man who'd introduced her to heroin. And then finally, when she'd run out of money and begged him desperately for that next hit, the man who'd forced her into prostitution. She wondered if he recognized her.

Hernando leaned in close. "I said, you've obviously never been here before because if you had, I'd..."

"Let me guess, because you'd have noticed me?" she said.

"That's right. I'd have noticed for sure," said Hernando. "You mind if I sit?"

He pulled out the chair next to her and sat down before she could answer.

Meredith couldn't tell why she felt annoyed. Was it his arrogance or his failure to recognize her? The virus may have changed her physical appearance, but now she saw he wouldn't have recognized her either way. The realization hit a nerve. She was nothing more than an object to him. A sex toy to be used then cast aside. Another in a long line of used-up junkie whores.

"Whoa there, stud," she said, raising her hands in objection. "I didn't say you could sit down."

"Oh, I'm sorry. I assumed you wouldn't't mind. You, being this knock-out gorgeous woman, and me being, well, me." He smiled seductively.

"Well, aren't you the man."

"My friends like to think so. But me, I leave it to the woman to decide."

"You sure you want to do that? I can be pretty demanding. You might find you fall way short of what I want in a man."

"I think you'll find me up to the challenge, mi chica bonita. The very best. My name's Hernando, and yours?"

"Meredith."

"Meredith. That's a pretty name."

"I bet you say that to all the girls."

"You can't blame me for trying. Say, you wanna dance?" He held out his hand.

"Lead on, handsome." She took his hand.

She allowed him to lead her through the crush of revelers onto the dance floor.

They danced, joining their fellow worshippers in a sympathetic union forged by the hypnotic beat of the music. The rhythmic sea of bodies surged and receded under the pulsing techno lights. Humanity enslaved in an artificial state of flux.

Hernando was as good as she remembered. The way he moved betrayed his cocky bravado. He was supremely confident in his world. She responded, her dance a sensual mirror of his own. She wanted to entice him. She wanted to enflame his lust so that he'd agree to whatever she wanted.

He moved close and pulled her to him. She could feel his heart beating, his sinewy body hard against hers. She moved her hips, stoking his desire. He kissed her then, his tongue seeking hers hungrily. She teased out the kiss, pulling back slowly with his lower lip between her teeth then delivered a playful nip that drew blood. Her nostrils flared at the scent.

"Hey!" he gasped with bemused surprise.

She leaned close. "Got any E?" she said, her cool lips pressed to his ear.

He smiled. "For you, baby, anything. You wanna go out back?"

"I thought you'd never ask."

He steered her through the nightclub to a passage that led to an emergency exit door. He'd obviously used this way many times before, she realized. Hernando pushed down on the panic bar and the door swung open.

"After you," he said with a flourish.

Meredith stepped into the cool night, and he followed, closing the door behind them. She looked around. The alleyway was dark and empty. He pulled her to him, eager to resume where they'd left off on the dance floor. He pushed her up against the wall, and she submitted to his groping, allowing his hands to move down her body to the hem of her dress. He eased the dress above her hips and slipped one hand into her panties.

She responded with a feral growl, and he quickly found himself pinned against the wall, her hand about his throat in a vice-like grip. He attempted to shout, but she tightened her grip, and all he could utter was a rasping gasp.

"Pathetic fuck!" she snarled contemptuously. "Did you really think I'd let you mount me?"

She squeezed a little harder. Hernando clawed desperately at her hand but was unable to loosen her steel grip. In a panic, he kicked out, but she appeared unfazed by his blows. She laughed and exposed her pointed canines with a satisfied grin. His eyes widened, and a surge of adrenalin intensified his struggles. He lashed out with his fists, but she easily countered with her free hand, grabbing his arm and snapping it across her raised knee. He cried out as his shattered forearm bones pierced the fabric of his coat. Meredith laughed. A cruel, soulless chuckle that echoed against the cold dank walls of the alley.

"I'm going to drain the life from you, like you drained the life from all those girls," she snarled, her face inches from his. "Then I'm going to rip off your head. Your body will crumble to dust, and it'll be as if you'd never existed. No one will remember you!"

The air stank of his terror, and it aroused her more than anything ever had. She clamped her hand over his mouth then sank her fangs deep into his neck. She drank deeply, relishing every drop. The emergency exit door suddenly swung open, and light spilled into the alley, illuminating the vampire latched to her struggling victim.

"Meredith! What the fuck? What are you doing?" gasped Jennifer, closing the door quickly.

Meredith stopped feeding and turned to look at Jen, her mouth and chin red with blood.

"What does it look like? I'm feeding," she drawled.

"But you can't! Not here. We're not allowed."

"Oh, but I can," said Meredith with a laugh. "Try and stop me!"

"But it's the rule. What will Anastasiya say?" Jen stepped towards Meredith and her victim.

"Don't even try, bitch! This one's mine! Him and every other motherfucker like him. I'm going to kill them all. It's what they deserve!"

Hernando groaned weakly. He'd lost too much blood to offer any resistance.

"Meredith, please leave him, and let's get out of here," said Jen, stepping back. "We can figure out what to say later."

"Oh, I think we both know it's too late for that, Jennifer. Come, sister, join me," said Meredith, nodding to the dying man. "Come, drink with me."

"No, I can't. It's not allowed."

"No? What then? You think you'll be able to run back to the countess and tell her? And when you spill your guts to her, what do you think she's gonna say? Do you really think she's gonna reward you? You'll be condemned the same as me."

"I'm not going to say anything! I promise. Let's go before somebody sees us."

"Join me, sister, and let's finish him," said Meredith, extending her hand in invitation.

Jen hesitated. She looked around, but there was no one else to make the decision for her.

"What's it to be, Jennifer? Death? Or life?"

Meredith pulled her victim away from the wall and pushed him towards the indecisive girl.

"Drink, sister! Drink deep."

When Jennifer tried to analyze her actions later, she found she couldn't remember how it was that she came to feed on the man. He'd fallen against her, and then she found herself pinning him to the ground, her fangs deep in his jugular. Meredith quickly joined her, and together they drained Hernando. Jennifer sat up. She looked surprised, as though she still couldn't quite figure what had just occurred.

"What are we going to do about his body?" she asked.

"First, I'm going to take his head." Meredith reached over to rip off the dead man's head. "We don't want his undead corpse to go wandering around, now do we?"

She stood up with the head and strolled over to the wall.

"Then I'm going to make identification difficult," she said, smashing the head against the wall until it was pulp. She dropped the crushed skull to the ground and walked over to the body.

"Next, we go through his pockets and take his wallet and anything else that'll ID the fucker," she said, kneeling next to the decapitated corpse.

The girls proceeded to rifle the dead man's pockets and removed his wallet, a butterfly knife, a pack of gum, and a set of car keys. They stood up, and Jen handed over what she'd taken. Meredith walked over to the nearby dumpster. She wiped the knife clean of fingerprints then tossed both knife and gum inside.

"I'll get rid of these later," she said, waving the keys and wallet at Jen. "See, the virus is already at work. Soon there'll be nothing left but a dried-out husk of bones and papery skin. Let the cops try to ID that."

"What do we do now?" asked Jen uncertainly.

"What do you mean?"

"We can't go back to the house empty handed. I mean, won't they ask us why we didn't get anyone? What do we say then?"

"It's simple really. We go back to the car, and I tell the big dope this nightclub's a bust. He takes us to another club, and we pick our man."

"So it's happened before?"

"If by it, you mean this," said Meredith, pointing at the corpse, "then no. But failing to net our prey does happen from time to time. I tell you what, you can pick up the guy this time. Who knows, maybe you'll be luckier than me." She chuckled.

"You think we'll be in the clear?"

"Sure, we'll be in the clear."

Meredith walked over to the emergency exit door and casually punched a hole through it near the panic bar. She reached in and pushed down on the lever. The door swung open, and she ushered Jen through. She was about to follow then stopped. She looked back up the alleyway, her keen eyes scanning the shadows. Had she heard something? A shoe scraping against the pavement perhaps? She cocked her head to the side and listened carefully. There! A heartbeat?

"Meredith," pleaded Jen, "let's get out of here."

"Wait," she said, "I think I heard something."

"Come on! I wanna get outta here now before somebody sees us," said Jen, pulling Meredith inside by the hand.

The damaged emergency door swung shut behind them. Meredith deliberated at the door for a moment then followed Jen back through the bustling nightclub. The night was young, and they had prey to snare.

◊ ◊ ◊

Goran remained hidden in the shadows a few more minutes. Only once he was certain the creatures had gone did he move from his hiding place. He pulled out his Glock 9mm and held it at the ready as he moved carefully down the alley towards the shriveling corpse. He looked down at the desiccated remains with interest. His grandmother had never mentioned this in her story.

He glanced at the damaged door and decided against following. This was not the time or place. He retreated back up the alleyway, holstered the Glock, then slipped quietly into the street beyond.

25

"Here it is," announced Dr Advani triumphantly, pulling back the sheet.

Dr Webb stepped forward to inspect the desiccated corpse. It appeared to be devoid of all muscle tissue, the shriveled brownish-yellow skin left stretched over the remaining skeleton much like an Egyptian mummy.

"Have you identified the body yet?" he asked.

"I'm afraid not. The condition of the skin has made fingerprinting impossible."

"Impossible?" said Webb, reaching out to touch the body. The surface of the parchment-like skin disintegrated to powder under his latex-covered fingertips. "Ah, I see what you mean. Interesting."

"Yes, quite unlike anything I have ever seen. The condition of the skull has made both physical identification and checking dental records impossible. What we do know is that this is an unidentified male of medium build, five ten in height, with an expensive taste in clothes."

"Where was the body found?"

"In the alley at the back of a downtown nightclub."

"The condition of the body will have made determining time of death impossible, I suppose."

"That is correct. The police have questioned the staff at the club. Someone generally takes the garbage out in the early hours. The body wasn't there a day earlier. That much was confirmed."

"Perhaps the body was dumped."

"I had thought of that," said Advani. "The police have sent the clothes away for analysis — fibers, hair, etc. And they are checking footage of nearby street surveillance cameras."

"Have they found anything yet?"

"No. Apparently the camera in the adjoining street was faulty, so they're looking at footage from cameras located further away."

"Did your autopsy determine a cause of death?"

"At this stage, no. The extreme desiccation of the internal organs, muscle tissue, and skin has made it all very difficult. I found no blood or urine to test, and some of the internal organs disintegrated when I attempted to handle them. I cannot even say whether the decapitation was post-mortem or not."

"Perhaps a virtopsy would have been a better approach. A CT or MRI scan of the body would have meant no incisions," said Webb.

"In hindsight, perhaps," conceded Advani. "I, however, did note small puncture wounds on the neck."

"Puncture wounds?" said Web, his interest piqued.

"Yes, see over here." Advani leaned over the body to indicate the small, blackened holes in the skin. "And here, a second set of marks on the inside of the right wrist."

"Yes, I see," said Webb. "Interesting."

"I was thinking that perhaps these were caused by some type of animal. Note the discoloration," said Advani, pointing to the blackened edges. "Perhaps this is an indication of an infection."

"Perhaps. I assume you've taken tissue samples for analysis."

"I'm afraid not," admitted Advani sheepishly. "The body was only brought in the day before yesterday. In any case, I thought you were here for that. Agent Wilson made it quite clear."

"Good," said Webb.

He proceeded to pack out sampling equipment from his case. He stopped when he realized Advani was still behind him. He turned and glared at the coroner.

"I'll let you know if I need anything," he said.

"Oh, I thought perhaps I could assist you. It is a very intriguing case after all," said Advani, looking disappointed.

"Doctor Advani, I've been stuck in traffic for the past two hours. Add the five-hour flight and twelve-hour shift I worked yesterday, and you'll understand that I'm in no mood for drawn-out explanations. Suffice to say that this is a priority case, and the need for discretion is imperative. I should not have to say more."

"You mean, there's been more than one case such as this?"

"One other case, yes."

"Did that also occur here?"

"That I cannot say. The investigation is still at an early stage. As I said before, discretion is imperative."

"But two corpses with identical wounds. Could we be dealing with a serial killer?"

"There'd need to be more than two deaths for that to be the case," said Webb, raising his eyebrow derisively. "Now, if you don't mind, I need to get on with my work."

"Yes, I apologize," said Advani, turning to leave.

"Oh, Doctor," began Webb imperiously, "I don't think I need remind you of the need to be discreet about this matter. The last thing we need is the press trying to sensationalize the whole thing. That would make our investigation more difficult and excite the public unnecessarily, don't you think?"

He peered owlishly through his thick spectacles at Advani.

"Yes, of course. I do know the protocol, Doctor."

Webb waited until Advani had left the room before continuing. He walked over to the room's camera and recording device and switched them off before returning to the table. Then he pulled a small tape recorder from his bag, switched it on, and placed it on the bench top. He didn't bother noting date or time. This was strictly off the record. Picking up his magnifying glass, he leant over the corpse to study the small holes in the neck.

"Puncture wounds are located on the jugular," he noted aloud. "Approximately an inch-deep and..."

He put aside the magnifying glass, picked up a measuring tape, and proceeded to measure the distance between the wounds.

"Two inches apart. Most likely an animal of some kind. In that case, there should be at least two sets of puncture marks, one set each for top and bottom jaw. Also, there appears to be a second set of puncture wounds on the ulnar artery near the wrist. I can't find any other marks, so this doesn't appear to be some run of the mill mountain lion, but something a little more exotic. Wounds are too wide for a spider, so perhaps a snake. Plausible, I suppose. Will need to run a toxicology screen to rule out poisoning. Somehow though, I don't think anything will show up. No, this is something else entirely."

Webb reached over for his camera and proceeded to take some photos. He knew that Advani's autopsy report would include plenty of visual evidence but preferred to be certain. Once satisfied he'd taken enough, he put down the camera and picked up a scalpel.

He sliced into the brittle tissue as carefully as possible and proceeded to cut out a rectangular section that included the holes. He placed it in one of his formalin-filled sample jars then screwed down the lid. He repeated the process at other places on the corpse and then again on the internal organs that had previously been set aside.

Once he'd placed the last jar in his case, he stepped back from the table and looked at the headless corpse. The body had not been dumped in the alley, he decided. After all, if that were the case, why not dispose of the head somewhere else? Perhaps the head had been removed from the body for another reason. But what would that be? Perhaps some sort of gang-related signature? That still didn't explain the bacterial infection.

The two had to be related, he decided. What did the head having been removed have to do with the infection? It certainly wasn't an attempt at a cure. The thought of a headless chicken running about suddenly popped into his head, and he snickered. He was certain the pathogen wasn't airborne, so it obviously hadn't been done to stop the infection from spreading.

Then it occurred to him. To prevent the infection from spreading, one would need to neutralize the infected host. The easiest way to do this would be to destroy the command center of the body—the brain. A creature intelligent enough to understand this could only mean the killer had to be human. But this still did not provide an answer to the question of how the victim had been infected in the first place. There appeared to be only one answer—the killer and vector were one and the same. Webb shook his head. It seemed ridiculous.

He stood in front of the table with its grizzly display and deliberated. Why would this man go into the alley in the first place? To buy drugs perhaps? It was possible, he supposed, but most times deals went down in clubs, not the back alley. If not drugs, then what had enticed the man to go into the alley? He smiled. Of course, sex.

The man had been lured into the alley with the promise of sex. He stepped forward and ran his gloved fingers over the neck where he'd removed the puncture-wound sample. The wounds did look as though they'd been caused by a bite, he thought. But not a bite inflicted in the heat of passion or anger, he decided. No, the bite had been deliberate. As had the one on the wrist. That led him to the most obvious conclusion.

The killer's motivation had been to feed.

Webb smiled. He was back in territory he understood—a parasite that infected its host. Or more precisely, a viral infection that caused the host to become a parasite driven by the need to feed on what, blood? He laughed out loud at the ridiculous idea. And yet the more he considered it, the more plausible it appeared. Somewhere out there was a man or woman, infected by some exotic new virus, feeding on people and then killing them to eliminate the chance of the disease spreading. To a man like Webb, who'd dealt with all manner of exotic bugs over the years, the idea appeared quite reasonable. The problem now was how to locate the infected individual or individuals.

The door to the room opened, and Advani peered in.

"Excuse me, Dr Webb, I wondered if you were..." he began.

"I'm not quite finished, Dr Advani. A few more minutes, if you will," said Webb brusquely.

The door closed, and Webb was left to his musing once more.

The two cases had to be connected, he decided. The question was how.

"If only you could talk," he said, looking down at the dried-out husk that had once been Hernando Velez.

He shook his head in frustration and pulled off the latex gloves. Everything he'd learned thus far brought him no closer to finding a live specimen. He dropped the gloves into the waste disposal, picked up his case, and strode disconsolately from the room.

"Thank you for your cooperation, Dr Advani," he said quickly before the other man could speak. "I will keep you informed of any developments. For the time being, I would recommend cremating the remains of our John Doe. We have, after all, collected all the physical evidence we require, and I would prefer avoiding any unnecessary risk."

"Risk? You mean of infection?" Advani appeared concerned.

"A remote possibility to be sure, but I wouldn't want to chance it, would you?"

"No, of course. Thank you, Dr Webb."

"Good day, Dr Advani," said Webb before turning to the two men waiting silently in the hall. "Gentlemen, I think it is time to go."

Advani watched the three men leave before returning to the corpse lying mutely on the stainless-steel table. He saw where Webb had removed the samples and then walked over to the room's recording device. He noted without surprise that the equipment had been turned off. They obviously wanted to hide something. The question was what. More importantly though was whether he felt the need to investigate further.

The CDC, the FBI, or possibly one or more faceless government agencies appeared to be involved, which left him contemplating whether he wanted to jeopardize his green card or not. In the end, the decision was simple and made in a heartbeat. As Webb suggested, the body would be cremated. Advani felt a weight lift from his shoulders as he walked from the room. He began humming a little tune. The mummified corpse in the room beyond was no longer his problem.

◊ ◊ ◊

"Goddamn this traffic," grumbled Clark as they slowed to a sedate crawl.

"Did you expect anything less this time of day?" chuckled Wilson.

He turned to Webb, who'd been sitting silently in the back of the car.

"So, Doctor, you get everything you wanted?"

"Yes and no. Obtaining physical evidence is only a part of my investigation. I still require the source of this virus."

"Don't you mean bacteriophage?" quipped Clark casually over his shoulder.

"It hardly matters at this point, don't you think?" said Webb, glaring at the back of Clark's head. "What I really require is some sort of connection."

"Connection?" said Wilson. "You mean between this corpse and the two found at the house?"

"Yes, that or something else. These people were all infected with the same virus, and each occurred in this city. There simply has to be a connection. And you need to find it."

The Millovic brothers popped into Wilson's head.

"We'll make some enquiries," he said, poker faced.

"Good, and the sooner the better. Need I remind you I'm on a tight schedule, and so far all my investment in you has netted me is a few dead tissue samples."

"That may be, but still tissue samples you wouldn't have had if not for us," observed Clark.

"Tell you what, we find the connection in the next, say, twenty-four hours, and you pay us a bonus. Make it an extra five grand?" said Wilson.

"I don't appreciate extortion, Mr White," retorted Webb, calling the agent by the fake name Wilson had given him at their first meeting. "But under the circumstances, I don't see I have much choice. Five thousand dollars, but then you must deliver."

"A deal it is then." Wilson grinned.

Webb shifted uncomfortably in the back seat and eyed the two men suspiciously. Mr White seemed very sure of himself, he thought. He'd always suspected the two men to be linked to law enforcement in some way or other, but now he wondered what else they weren't telling him. Worst still was the idea that perhaps they really knew nothing and were intent on stringing him along to get more money. Still, five thousand was nothing compared to the millions he'd make if he delivered what he'd promised his backers. But what if they couldn't deliver? His stomach turned at the thought.

"Come on already!" shouted Clark, hitting the car's horn. "If this traffic doesn't ease up soon, you might end up missing your flight."

"No matter, there's always another," said Webb, looking gloomily out the window at the cars crawling up the motorway.

He guessed it would take two or three hours more before they got to the airport. Add a couple of hours waiting in the departure lounge and another five-hour plane trip and finally he'd get to the end of what was turning out to be a very long day.

26

I t was night. Faith sat on her bed with her back against the wall and her legs drawn up as an impromptu book rest. She pretended to read but was really watching Jen. The girl had been staring silently out the window for the past hour. Something or someone had upset her friend, and Faith was convinced Meredith was to blame. Could it have something to do with the hunt Meredith and Jen had been sent on a few nights before? It seemed the only explanation to account for her friend's sudden mood swing.

She hoped Jen would talk, but the girl remained stubbornly withdrawn. She couldn't decide what upset her more—that she was annoyed at Jen because she wouldn't confide in her or her concern for her friend's wellbeing.

"Is everything okay, Jen?" she asked, closing the book.

Jen turned to look a Faith. Her eyes were wide, like a rabbit caught in the headlights.

"What?"

"I asked whether you were feeling okay."

Jen attempted a smile. "Oh, yes, sorry," she said. "I was miles away."

"Miles away? No kidding. You've been like this ever since the other night."

"Other night? What night would that be?"

"Seriously? Okay, if you wanna play it that way, the night you went out with Meredith."

"Oh, that night."

"Yes, that night. Usually, you don't stop talking, but you've not spoken a word about it."

"Nothing happened."

"Look, if something went down, tell me. You know I won't repeat anything you say, right?" said Faith, searching Jen's expression.

"I really don't know what you mean, Faith. Why would you even say that?"

"Come on. You and I both know you're far from okay. Something's upset you, and odds are its connected to the hunt you went on with Meredith."

"Nothing's upset me, really," said Jen. "I mean, can't a girl have a bad day? Like, what do you want me to say? We can't all be like you, you know."

"Can't be like me? I don't understand," said Faith.

"Right, you don't understand. So maybe you should butt out and let things be."

"You know I can't do that, Jen," said Faith, putting the book aside. She stood up and walked over to Jen. "I'm your friend, and friends don't butt out. Not if they really care."

"Please, leave it be, Faith. There's nothing you can do anyway."

"Leave what be?" said Faith, taking Jen's hands in hers. "What don't you want me to do?"

"Nothing, I want you to do nothing. Stop asking me, okay?"

"What happened the other night, Jen? You can tell me."

"Meredith, she..."

"No," said Faith, placing her finger to her lips. "Not here."

She'd always suspected their rooms were bugged and suddenly feared Jen might confess something that would make Anastasiya decide to terminate her friend.

"Let's go for a walk. We can talk then," she said.

The pair slipped quietly out of the house. Though Anastasiya had forbidden venturing outside at night, she was aware that most of the girls did so from time to time. She'd turned a blind eye to it, realizing perhaps that it served as a kind of pressure release from the extended periods her acolytes spent within the walls of her mansion. After all, a cage was still a cage no matter how much gilding on the bars.

Jen followed Faith through the dark to a secluded area of the garden. Faith looked around before turning to her friend.

"We can talk here," she whispered.

"What's the problem?" replied Jen. "You mean our rooms are bugged?"

"Honestly, I'm not sure. I figured you wouldn't want anyone overhearing you. I mean, one of the others might walk in or be standing outside the door."

"You're right, I suppose," said Jen.

"You were telling me about Meredith."

"Oh... Yes, I was," began Jen hesitantly. "I don't know. I don't want to get you into trouble or anything."

"Don't worry about me, Jen, I'm a big girl. Tell me what happened. You'll feel better for it, trust me."

"I don't think anything's gonna make me feel better, Faith. Not after what Meredith did."

"Okay, what did she do?"

"The other night at the club, she took a man into the alley out back and fed on him."

"How do you know that?"

The answer was obvious of course, but she wanted Jen to say it.

"I walked in on her. I'd lost sight of her before in the club.

One moment she was talking to this guy and the next thing they'd disappeared somewhere. I was worried. I mean, we're supposed to remain in visual contact, and somehow I..."

"It doesn't matter, Jen. Tell me what happened," said Faith, placing a reassuring hand on her friend's shoulder.

"She was angry. I mean, really angry. I think she knew him, you know, from before."

"What did she do when she saw you?"

"She'd drunk a lot of his blood by then. I told her to stop. I told her how much trouble she'd be in. But she didn't care. She laughed and said I'd be in as much trouble as her. Then I thought about what the countess would do to us. I couldn't risk that, Faith. I stood there, but then Meredith forced me to join her."

"You fed on him?"

"Yes," replied Jen softly. "Once I tasted his blood, I couldn't stop, and when we'd drained him, she ripped off his head."

"To stop him from turning."

"What?"

"Shit, Jen, didn't you ever wonder about what happens to all the bodies?"

"No, I thought Lotho took them away and cremated them. You know, to hide the evidence."

"We infect those we feed on, Jen. They don't simply die. The infection does something to them. After a time, the dead body sort of reanimates."

"You mean like some kind of zombie?"

"I guess. Anyway, that's why she did it. It wasn't a sadistic revenge thing, if that's what you were thinking."

"But she smashed the head against the wall," said Jen, her voice trembling. "She smashed it till you couldn't tell what it was anymore."

Faith couldn't help wondering why Meredith's action had upset Jen so much. After all, was draining a man of his life's blood any less horrific? It occurred to her then that the virus might be doing more to them than only changing their physiology. Perhaps it altered their personalities as well. Or tweaked them enough to become indifferent to the suffering of their prey. Just how much of a puppet to the virus was she then? She pushed the chilling thought from her mind. She was in control. Always. She was sure of it. Or was she?

"What happened then?"

"She cleaned out his pockets. She said there'd be no evidence. But I can't help thinking about if the countess finds out. What will she do to me?"

"Somehow, I don't think she will find out. Meredith has as much to lose as you," said Faith. She placed her hands on Jen's shoulders and looked closely at her. "What you need to do now is calm down and get your head in the right space. If you don't, Anastasiya might begin to suspect something. You understand me?"

"Yes, you're right. I know you are but it was so horribly real. So brutal. I know this sounds kinda stupid, but when we bring them back here, it doesn't seem so bad. It's like I said before, it sorta feels like a religious ritual or something. Like they're offering themselves up to us. It's like they want to give up their lives so that we might live. You know what I mean?"

"Yeah, I do, believe it or not."

And even though on some level she did, she also felt annoyed at Jen's naivety. The girl refused to give up her fairy tale view of the world, and it would be the death of her in the end. There'd always be a bitch like Meredith Young ready to stick the knife in.

"Don't you feel better now you've got that off your chest?" she said.

"Thanks, Faith. I suppose I'm lucky I've got you as a friend."

"There's no suppose about it, girl. You better believe it. Let's get back to the house before someone misses us."

The girls headed back, and though Jen felt relieved, Faith was more worried than ever. A showdown between her and Anastasiya seemed more inevitable than ever now, yet she seemed unable to avoid it.

27

Later that night, a black sedan pulled up to the curb one street away from the school. Goran picked up the tablet from the passenger seat and proceeded to activate the hidden drone he'd left perched on the conservatory rooftop. He tapped the screen to download the recorded surveillance data. He'd set the drone's programming to take a photo every fifteen minutes with the time and date appearing on each. He glanced casually in his rearview mirror as he waited for the download to be completed. The agents were back, he noted idly. They'd not tailed him the past few days, yet tonight the pair had suddenly reappeared.

More telling though was the fact that they'd not followed him from the motel but had apparently known exactly where he'd be. That meant there was tracker fixed to his vehicle. A muted ping alerted him that the download was complete. He proceeded to scroll through the photos and before long found the pattern he'd hoped for. It was the class Anastasiya presented each morning. Like clockwork. He pulled out his cell phone and placed the call.

"It's me. My consignment, it is on schedule?" he asked. "Good.

I will confirm time later. Goodbye."

He slipped the cell back into his pocket and glanced in the rear-view mirror again. He needed to get back to the lock-up where he'd installed a rudimentary but effective workshop. This would require losing the agents tailing him. He started the car and pulled away from the curb. He eyed his rearview mirror and noted the pair of headlights following cautiously behind. His plan was simple. Early tomorrow, he'd drive to a convenient shopping mall and dump the car. He reasoned evading the agents from then on would be a simple affair as he wouldn't be going back to the motel. The school, of course, was another matter, but then he only needed to return one final time, and then no one would stand in his way.

◊ ◊ ◊

The vehicle carrying Agents Clark and Wilson followed Goran's black sedan at a discreet distance through the quiet suburban streets.

"You reckon he's made us yet?" enquired Clark.

"I'm not sure. If he has, then either he doesn't give a shit or he's planning to give us the slip when he's ready," said Wilson. "I guess we'll have to see which."

"Well, if he hasn't, then he's a dumb shit. There're only two cars on the road right now. A fucking blind man could see us!"

Wilson smirked. "A blind man? How's that possible?"

"You know what I mean. You think he's going back to the motel?"

"Probably," said Wilson, reaching over and punching the quick dial on the hands-free cell.

"You, calling Webb?"

Wilson nodded and grinned broadly.

"Hello?" a sleepy voice answered.

"Doctor Webb, it's Mr White."

He winked at Clark.

"Mr White?" repeated Webb struggling to shake off the fog of sleep. "Do you know what time it is here?"

"Yes, but I figured you'd want to hear that we got that lead you've been wanting. Of course, if you're not interested, I'll call you in a day or so. Perhaps we can discuss it then after you've had your beauty sleep."

"Lead?" said Webb, his interest quickening. "What lead?"

"Remember the house where the first bodies were discovered?"

"Yes?"

"My partner and I were following up a lead on who'd owned the property when we discovered a man named Goron Millovic snooping around. He's a hit man also wanted for war crimes committed during the Bosnian war. He's also the brother of Dragan Millovic, one of the decapitated corpses identified at the house."

"You have my attention, Mr White. Go on."

"Well, we figured he was searching for the people who killed his brother, and as they're probably the same people you're interested in, we decided to keep tabs on him. Long story short, he's been observing a school. The Whitby Foundation Finishing Academy for Girls. It appears to be some sort of exclusive finishing school rich folks send their daughters to after high school."

"I assume you've looked into this school."

"Yes, we have. But there's not much to go on, I'm afraid. The school's headmistress is an Anastasiya Strajinski. The school's finances are managed by an old law firm out of New York."

"This Strajinksi woman—her name sounds foreign. What have you got on her?"

"Nothing thus far, but we'll keep digging."

"I still don't see the connection to the desiccated cadavers, Mr White. I certainly hope you're not expecting five thousand for this trifling bit of information."

"I haven't finished what I have to say."

"I'm listening."

"Well, he's been watching the school every day as far as we know.

He also followed a black limo that left the school on one of the nights we were tailing him. The limo took two of the girls from the school out clubbing. It struck us as kinda strange at the time, but we figured it was a reward for something or other." Wilson thought it better not to mention Clark's prostitution ring theory. "Anyway, the latest body was found near a nightclub, so we figured there had to be a connection. We've been reviewing footage from street surveillance cameras and..."

"I thought the street surveillance camera wasn't working," interrupted Webb.

"The one with a view on the alley wasn't, but there are other cameras in streets nearby. We've been reviewing footage, and sure enough Millovic was in the area the night before the body was found."

"And?"

"Let's review what we've got so far, Dr Webb," said Wilson. "An apparently elite, well-to-do finishing school that doesn't advertise itself is headed by a school principal who has no driver's license, no social security number, or any other record for that matter. Then there's a foreign national obviously investigating the death of his criminal brother and who also happens to be a wanted hit man. Not only has this man risked his freedom by sneaking into the U.S., but he's also invested a lot of time watching the aforementioned school. And we have a black limo leaving the school grounds at night, probably on more than one occasion. Finally, we have a decapitated corpse in much the same mummified condition as his brother, found in the alley behind a well-known nightclub we now know Millovic was seen in.

"If I were a betting man, I'd say Goran Millovic has discovered either something about that school or someone from there linking the death of his brother and the deaths of these others. I reckon the starting point of this infection, that vector you keep talking about, is at that school."

The two agents waited for Webb's response but were met instead with a prolonged silence.

"Dr Webb?" Wilson asked.

"I'm still here, Mr White," said Webb. "I've been considering your points, and it does appear you might be onto something. Or should I say, the hit man Millovic appears to be onto something. Tell me, have either of you ever been big game hunting?"

Wilson looked quizzically at Clark, who raised his eyebrows in return. Neither could figure what Webb meant with that comment, but they knew they soon would.

28

Tammy Sloane pulled into the parking lot of a remote motel about the same time Wilson and Clark watched Goran turn into the Gateway Motor Inn. The word "vacancy" flickered fitfully below the big red neon sign that read "Motel Here". The light in the last letter had died, and the sign boasted zero stars, which pretty much summed up the run-down look of the place.

She parked the car, turned off the ignition, and looked over at the long single-story building. The rooms were set side by side so that either each room's door or window paired with the next room on. Dull light shining through the curtains of a window here and there indicated a few were occupied. Her eyes followed the room numbers painted on the front of each door until she found the room she was looking for. No 15. The light was on. The queasy feeling in her stomach returned. She reached out and placed a nervous hand on the black briefcase on the passenger seat alongside but made no move to get out of the car.

The stress of the past week had been unbearable. Getting her hands on the money Holland demanded had consumed her every waking moment. It had also been the first time she'd thought about her daughter, Faith. She knew she should feel some maternal love for the girl, but she didn't. Faith was part of some other life. The woman from that life did not exist. She had simply disappeared, locked away deep in the psyche of the woman known as Tammy Sloane. Tammy was real, and that woman was not. She'd destroyed the photo of Faith the night she'd taken it from Don's apartment. It was the same night she'd poisoned him. Her new life, the one she'd worked so hard to create, was all that mattered.

Tammy stiffened as the door to one of the rooms further along opened. Light spilled onto the concrete porch, and a heavyset man in shorts and t-shirt appeared. He yawned, gave his crotch a good scratch, then ambled over to the Coke dispensing machine situated three doors down. Tammy sank down in her seat even though the man probably wouldn't have noticed her. He presented his offering to the glowing machine then stood back expectantly. There was a grating hum before the mechanical cornucopia grudgingly relinquished two cans with a metallic clunk. He reached down, retrieved his booty, then turned and walked back to his room without even a sideways glance.

She was alone again. She looked back at the door of No 15. He was there, waiting for her. There was no way of avoiding what she had to do. Tammy opened her handbag and pulled out the small silver .38 revolver. She pushed the cylinder out and checked the chambered rounds for what must have been the tenth time. Satisfied, she locked the cylinder back into position and slipped the handgun into her designer bag.

Tammy looked around one final time and then, with bag and briefcase, exited her vehicle and walked quickly over to the motel room door. She knocked hesitantly. After what felt like an eternity, the door opened.

"You're late," observed Jack Holland, peering round the door.

"I got lost," said Tammy, stepping quickly into the room.

"You expect me to believe the krauts didn't install GPS navigation in that fancy sports car of yours?"

He closed the door.

"It's not working," lied Tammy.

She took a few tentative steps further into the room.

"You brought the goods?" asked Jack, eyeing the briefcase.

"Right here," she said, holding up the case.

"Put it on the bed."

Jack took a step back and watched as she placed the case on the bed.

"Open it."

Tammy opened the case and turned it round so that he could see its contents.

"It's all there," she said.

"I didn't expect anything less," said Jack, reaching down to pick up a wad of Benjamin Franklins. "Still, I'll count it all the same."

"Can I go now?"

"Not till I've finished counting. Why don't you sit down? This might take a while," he said, flicking through a wad of bills.

"No thanks, I'd prefer to stand," she said, clutching her bag tightly.

"Suit yourself."

Jack picked up another wad of bills. He resumed counting then stopped. He put the bills to his nose and sniffed. His nose wrinkled at the faint chemical odor.

"Where'd you get the money?"

"Does it matter?"

"That depends. You got the money pretty fast. Maybe you robbed a bank. Or maybe you've gone into drug dealing and I'm handling the illicit proceeds right here. Or maybe you took my advice and hit the strip, hard."

"I took out a couple a cash loans across town, if you must know. Nothing illegal in that."

It was a lie of course. Tammy had drawn the money from her own private bank account she kept under an assumed name.

"Course not," chuckled Jack, who resumed his counting.

Tammy watched him intently, her hands fidgeting with her bag. The detective finally finished counting the money. He placed the last wad of bills back into the briefcase, closed the lid, and snapped the locks shut.

"Okay then," he said. "I'll be on my way. You can leave here half an hour from now."

He picked up the case and walked over to the door.

"Now you've got your money you're gonna leave me alone, right?"

"That depends," he said, opening the door.

"Depends on what?"

"On how far this fifty stretches. Colleges are real expensive places these days. I think Stacey deserved only the best, don't you?"

"You bastard," she snarled.

Jack laughed. "Goodbye, Ms Sloane," he said and closed the door.

Tammy walked over to the window and parted the curtain enough to see the detective walk over to his car. Her face betrayed a studied malevolence as she looked on. She watched Holland's vehicle leave the motel parking lot and smiled grimly to herself.

29

Anastasiya awoke. It was morning. She stretched languorously, turned onto her side, and looked into the vacant eyes of the dead girl lying beside her. The girl's pallid face wore a faintly hopeless expression. It was as if, at the moment of her death, she finally understood the full sum of her fruitless existence. Anastasiya's gaze drifted down the naked corpse, noting the blackened veins and the discoloration of the limbs—changes wrought as the virus took hold. Soon the girl's corpse would rise, reanimated as the virus seized control of the brain's most basic functions.

She had never really attempted to understand the nature of this. Was it the natural progression of the infection? Or did the virus, on a fundamental level, realize being trapped in this rotting body meant its death unless it could find a new host? Either way, of what possible benefit was knowing which. That was a human concern. She was above it all. She alone had evolved into something more than human, superhuman even. But that was no longer entirely true. Faith had achieved the same. Anastasiya scowled.

The thought was like a nagging toothache that refused to go away. An obvious solution was to remove the tooth. Eliminate the girl and be done with the problem. Once and for all. But even though she'd oft contemplated it she found herself unwilling to take the final step. Why was this? Did part of her seek an equal? Someone who could finally understand what it was to be her? Or was she curious to see how Faith would cope with her power? But curiosity had its limits and entertained for too long could prove deadly. What was it to be then—eliminate the risk now or wait to see how things evolved. She still did not know which.

A tremor ran through the girl's corpse. It would not be long now. Anastasiya rose from the bed, pulled on her silk robe, then walked over to the small intercom on the wall. She pressed the button.

"Lotho, you are required now," she said and left the room.

She made her way through a number of corridors and entered the inner sanctum of her underground complex—that part only she had access to. She sat down in front of the array of monitors connected to cameras in each of her acolytes' rooms. These had been installed after the trouble with Bethany. It had become part of her morning ritual to scan the video recordings from the previous day. Tapping the PC screen to access the video log, she scrolled through the list until she located the file to Faith and Jennifer's room.

It was the obvious place to start. She tapped the screen again to access the file then fast-forwarded in vision. She watched as Faith and Jennifer jerked back and forth across the screen like agitated marionettes until something in the way they talked caught her eye. Anastasiya tapped the play button. Jennifer looked upset.

"What happened the other night, Jen?" said Faith. "You can tell me."

"Meredith, she..."

"No, not here," said Faith with an almost imperceptible glance at the hidden camera. "Let's go for a walk. We can talk then."

Anastasiya watched them leave the room. She tapped the screen to access the file of another camera located outside and watched the girls walk through the garden. Faith appeared to be guiding Jennifer. The girls turned suddenly, stepped through a gap in a hedge, and were lost from view. She frowned and began tapping the screen to access other cameras located around the mansion's grounds. The girls were nowhere to be seen. Coincidence? Or did Faith know about the surveillance?

Anastasiya looked across to the monitor linked to the camera in Faith and Jennifer's room. The girls were getting dressed. Nothing in the way Faith was acting now betrayed she knew they were being observed. The video from the night before, however, suggested otherwise. It was inevitable, she supposed, that in this technological age her acolytes would be more aware of such things. More surprising then that the others appeared not to be. Then again, perhaps they were but were better at hiding their knowledge. Not that it mattered in the end. The unwritten contract she had with them all was simple—she had bestowed on each the gift of life, and they had become hers to command.

She studied the girls on the screen, her long fingers tapping a measured tempo on the chair's armrest. Something had occurred between Meredith and Jennifer. Something that involved the night she'd sent the pair hunting. This presented a dilemma. Confronting these girls meant revealing her surveillance to the rest of her acolytes. But not knowing what Meredith had done vexed her more. Was it something that placed the school at risk? Or was it something altogether less serious? Perhaps a case of Jennifer overreacting to some imagined slight? Anastasiya slammed her fist on the desk and spat out an expletive. She, their all-seeing, all-knowing god, was not so omniscient after all, and it stung.

◇ ◇ ◇

The afternoon fight training started as always with Meredith leading them through the warmup. Then they moved on to the monotonous repetition of punches and kicks. Anastasiya entered the room silently and stood behind her acolytes and watched.

She signaled Meredith to stop the class then stepped onto the mat and walked amongst them.

"It is said that all life is a struggle for survival," she began. "A battle of wills that decides who will live and who will die."

She reached the front of the class and turned to face her acolytes before speaking.

"Meredith, return to your place."

Her acolytes looked at her curiously. She had never interrupted a class before.

"All of you, off the mat!" she barked.

The girls began to move.

"Jennifer!" she snapped. "Stay where you are."

Jennifer stopped and turned apprehensively to face her.

Anastasiya walked over to the weapons rack and pulled off a pair of naginatas. She tossed one at Jennifer, who caught it. The girls had been trained in the use of the polearm with its curved blade and were familiar with the fighting technique.

"This world is the will to power and nothing besides," she said then darted forward to thrust her naginata at the unprepared girl.

Startled, Jennifer managed to parry the strike before stumbling back but then found herself driven backward as she desperately attempted to block her assailant's unrelenting assault. Anastasiya's whirling blade soon found its mark, slicing deep into Jennifer's left leg. The girl gasped in pain but found no respite as Anastasiya continued to press the attack. Jennifer gamely attempted to block and counter, favoring her good leg as she did.

But Anastasiya contemptuously pushed the incoming blade aside with her naginata and struck again, opening a red gash in Jennifer's side. The cut was to the bone, and the girl cried out. She used the shaft of her weapon to deflect the next downward strike but was a fraction too slow to block the follow up as Anastasiya dropped to one knee, flicked her naginata up and pierced Jen's stomach with the sharpened butt of the naginata. Jen's agony was plain as she bent over, clutching at the gaping wound. She shuffled back using her weapon for support, her face contorted with fear.

"I am disappointed in you Jennifer," said Anastasiya. "I had assumed you would have learned more in your time with us, but it appears this is not so. Why is this?"

"I... I don't know, ma'am. I thought I was."

"You thought you were doing enough? What does that mean? You should know to merely exist is never enough. You must always do more. The gift I gave you demands it. See, even now, your wounds heal. Given the time, you would heal completely, and perhaps this very strength is your weakness. You think you have time, and this has made you..." She turned to look at the others. "This has made all of you complacent."

She turned back to Jen and assumed an attack stance with her naginata.

"The fact is we never have enough time. To merely exist and to be content with that is to invite death," she said. "And now, Jennifer, how much time do you think you have?"

She attacked before Jen could answer, the blade of her naginata sweeping viciously through the air. The blow glanced off Jen's weapon and forced her back, but Anastasiya sprang forward before the girl could recover and delivered another cut, reopening the wound on her leg. The darting blade found its mark again and again as Anastasiya advanced relentlessly.

Jen attempted desperately to block each attack but soon weakened as the toll from her wounds began to tell. The virus could not heal her fast enough to counter Anastasiya's calculated onslaught. Inevitably, she could do no more and sank to her knees. Blood streamed from a multitude of deep wounds. She watched helplessly as her antagonist advanced and weakly raised her weapon in defiance. Anastasiya flicked Jen's naginata contemptuously from her grasp and raised her own blade for a killing blow.

"Stop!" yelled Faith.

"You dare to challenge me, girl?" growled Anastasiya, turning to face Faith with her naginata raised.

"If that's what it'll take to make you stop, then yes," said Faith, her fists clenched.

There was an audible gasp from some of the others, but her anger had driven her beyond the point of caring. She stepped onto the mat.

"Very well, we shall see if you can do any better," said Anastasiya. "Pick up the weapon."

Faith walked across and picked up Jen's discarded naginata, her eyes never leaving her opponent. The two women circled each other warily, each looking for an opening.

Anastasiya attacked first, moving in quickly to deliver a murderous downward cut. Faith blocked it easily, her prescient ability allowing her to also anticipate Anastasiya's vicious follow through with the naginata's spiked end. She twisted her hips to evade the sharpened spike before delivering a counter strike that opened a red gash on Anastasiya's forearm. The wound elicited another gasp from some of the girls.

Faith skipped backward, her naginata at the ready. Anastasiya shot her a look of ice-cold fury as she skirted round looking for another opening. She struck suddenly, unleashing a dazzling combination of thrusts and cuts designed to overwhelm her opponent. But Faith blocked each before finally delivering her counter thrust, piercing Anastasiya's thigh to the bone. Anastasiya shuffled back, attempting to keep weight off her damaged leg whilst keeping her naginata levelled. Now it was Faith's turn to strike. She darted forward and delivered a traditional overhead strike. Anastasiya parried but found there was no time to counter as Faith followed through, spinning her weapon to deliver a cutting blow. Only Anastasiya's experience saved her from another wound as she sidestepped. Again, she attempted to counter, but Faith was too fast, the tip of her blade grazing Anastasiya's cheek.

The two women circled each other, Faith appearing the more confident. She switched quickly to a left-handed grip then delivered a barrage of slashes and jabs that forced Anastasiya back, desperately parrying each attack. The result was another deep cut to Anastasiya's body. Faith danced away, her arms to her side with weapon resting comfortably in her grip. She glanced at the faces of the other girls and the anger and fear she saw caused her to pause. At once she understood why they felt that way. She was a threat.

Anastasiya had been their savior. The one who'd rescued them from the terrible circumstances of their lives and given them a new meaning, but she was also their only means of survival. Without her, they would cease to be, and though the devil in Faith wanted to destroy it all, she knew she could not. Who was she to decide the other acolytes' fate? She glanced at Jen and saw the anguish in her face. She knew then she'd have to lose the fight. The problem was that Anastasiya might use the opportunity offered to eliminate her. Faith took a defensive stance as her opponent circled once more. She noted with begrudging admiration that the woman's movements betrayed no hint of uncertainty. It was as though her entire being exuded nothing but a single-minded determination. The trick now was to allow Anastasiya the upper hand and not get killed in the process.

Anastasiya darted forward, feinting with a high jab before spinning her naginata to thrust the spiked end at her opponent's thigh. Faith slowed her block enough to allow the weapon to pierce her flesh. She winced at the sharp pain and stumbled backward. Anastasiya seized upon her opponent's apparent lapse and struck again, launching a one-two-three combination that found its mark. Faith limped backward, blood streaming from her side. She deftly parried Anastasiya's next attack and countered, nicking her arm.

No need to make it too easy, she thought to herself.

The fight continued, Faith slowly allowing her opponent to gain the upper hand until Anastasiya finally succeeded in disarming her. Despite her wounds, Faith dodged the whirling blade but succumbed to a leg sweep that brought her to the floor. She fell on the bloodied mat, her opponent's blade at her neck. There was a long pause as the two women glared at each other.

"In the end, there can be only one victor," growled Anastasiya.

She pressed the blade of her naginata against Faith's neck, drawing a trickle of blood. Then she lifted the weapon and turned to the class.

"You will all do well to learn from this."

She turned and looked down at Faith.

"You are fortunate, girl, that I have decided to ignore your apparent lack of self-control. Now, get up and join the others."

Faith got to her feet slowly and painfully. She limped dejectedly from the mat to rejoin her fellow acolytes.

"Now, you may return to your rooms," said Anastasiya.

She watched her acolytes file obediently from the room. Once alone, she walked over to the other naginata still on the floor and picked it up. She cleaned the blood off each blade in turn before placing them back onto the weapons rack. It was a task she'd usually have given one of her acolytes, but she needed the time alone to think. She reached over and took a katana from its stand at the top of the rack. She unsheathed the weapon slowly, admiring the simple beauty of the forged blade. The polished steel glinted malevolently in the muted light of the training room. Form and function in perfect union. She sheathed the sword. It was decided. The girl had to go. The question was how and when best to achieve this.

◊ ◊ ◊

In the evening, Anastasiya called her acolytes to blood communion, the ritual in which she allowed them a small measure of her blood. Rather than as a means of allowing her followers access to the blood they needed to survive, the intended aim of the ritual was to bind them ever closer to her. Observed every seven days, she'd called them to this communion a day early. If any of the girls wondered at the reason, none chose to question.

She mounted the small dais and took a small ornamental knife from inside the sleeve of her robe. Then she held her arms outstretched.

"This is my blood, given so that you may share in the gift of eternal life. When you drink, let it be a reminder of the lasting bond that unites us and of the trust that I have placed in each of you," she said solemnly before cutting her left arm.

The blood trickled into an ornate silver bowl placed on a stand before her. She looked down at the girls as the blood flowed, searching their expressions for any sign of dissent or doubt. Her acolytes gazed serenely back at her. Even Faith wore a conveniently compliant expression. How many of them truly believed in her now? There was no way of knowing for sure. At that precise moment, she couldn't tell which angered her more—that Faith had challenged her or that none of the others ever had.

Her wound had healed by the time the bowl had filled. She handed the bowl to Meredith and looked on as each acolyte drank in turn. The girls sank into the usual trance-like state as Anastasiya's blood reacted with the virus in each. She watched as the kneeling women lost themselves in the temporary stupor, swaying from side to side, and could not help but feel disappointed. The world she'd created for herself suddenly appeared hollow, devoid of any real meaning. A world of shadow and masks. Anastasiya tried to shake the feeling but could not. She waited patiently for the girls to surface from the trance.

"You may go to your rooms. There will be no hunt tonight," she said, dismissing them curtly.

The bemused young women looked round at each other. They were unused to seeing their mistress agitated, and it unsettled them. They exited the room in silence, leaving Anastasiya to brood.

30

Faith lay on the bed staring up at the ceiling. It had been nine hours since she'd challenged Anastasiya. Nine hours of working through the potential repercussions of the fight and still she could not fathom the outcome. She glanced across at Jen and felt a stab of annoyance. The girl would be the death of her. But what choice had she but to intervene? It was not in her nature to stand by and watch her friend suffer and not do anything. Every fiber of her being had demanded she act, no matter the consequences.

So much for the instinct of self-preservation. You've really got yourself in a pickle this time, girl.

"Is everything okay?" asked Jen.

She'd been attempting to get Faith to speak to her for the past hour without success.

"Yeah, I told you that everything's fine," said Faith.

"You sure? I mean, the fight and everything. You and the countess, and me. I don't know why I got her so mad, and I'm sorry if it got you into trouble. I didn't mean to. I mean, it turned out okay in the end, didn't it?"

"Look, Jen, don't sweat it. It's over now. Anastasiya was using you to prove a point. I butted in, and then she beat me. Case closed."

"You sure you're not mad at me?"

"Look, I'm not mad at you, okay?" sighed Faith. "Let's leave it alone already."

An uneasy silence settled on the room. Faith closed her eyes to concentrate but could feel Jen watching her. She sat up and slid off the bed.

"Where are you going?" asked Jen.

"Training room," said Faith, walking over to the door.

"Oh. You mind if I come along?"

"Look, Jen," said Faith, opening the door, "don't take this in a bad way or anything, but I need some time alone, okay?"

"So you are mad at me."

"Oh, for crying out loud!" snapped Faith, turning to face her friend. "This isn't about you. I need some time to think. Can you at least give me that?"

"Faith, I'm really sorry. I want you to know that, okay?" said Jen, wringing her hands. "Everything that happened. It was all so full on. You say she was trying to make a point, but I think there's more to it than that. Maybe she suspects what I did. Maybe that's why she hurt me like that. Maybe she was punishing me, and I'm sorry I got you involved. I don't want you to think I caused all this. I mean, what I'm really saying is I don't want to lose you. You're the only friend I have. Please..."

"It's okay, Jen. We'll talk about it later. Right now, I need to clear my head," said Faith, stepping into the hall. "I'll be back soon."

Faith offered a faint smile and closed the door before Jennifer could answer.

She stood in the center of the mat holding her naginata firmly. She'd spent the past hour going through various katas. The defensive blocks and counter strikes that formed each kata were meant to simulate the parry and attack of actual combat and she executed them with deadly efficiency. Yet her thoughts remained troubled. Perhaps it'd been a mistake to come to the training room, of all places, to clear her mind. Why had she chosen this weapon? She looked down in surprise at the naginata as though realizing only now she held it. Was it because she wanted to revisit her failure and so understand what could have been? It had been so close. Did hesitating at the brink betray weakness or strength? She couldn't decide. She readied herself for the next kata. Forcing her mind to concentrate on the set movements of the kata was easier than thinking about everything else.

"Look, she enjoyed getting her ass kicked so much she's trying to relive the whole thing!"

Faith turned to face the source of the mocking voice. Meredith stood with folded arms and regarded her from the edge of the mat. She was flanked by Judith and Mia wearing the same contemptuous expression. Lily and Cass hovered in the background.

"Not the way I look at it, but you can choose to see it that way if you want," said Faith.

"Oh? So how do you see it then?" snorted Meredith and winked at the other girls. "No wait, let me guess. You didn't want to embarrass the countess, so you let her win. Is that it? You really want us to believe a crock of shit like that?"

The other girls chuckled nervously.

"Maybe I did, and maybe I didn't. But you'll never know, will you?" said Faith, spinning the naginata around nonchalantly with a smile. "You know what, we could find out right here and now. You girls and me."

"What do you mean? By fighting you?" retorted Judith incredulously. "The countess is better than any of us. How is fighting one of us supposed to prove anything?"

Faith flicked the naginata high into the air. She caught it one handed then spun it casually about her body before answering.

"She's better than any one of you, yes. But what if, say, I fought all of you at once?"

Meredith snorted derisively. "You really think a lot of yourself, don't you?"

"You're not answering my question," replied Faith.

"You're so full of shit," said Judith, folding her arms.

"Still not answering my question," sighed Faith. "So here I am, alone. Me and the five of you."

She spun the naginata round again. The girls stood silently watching her. Faith took a few steps towards the group and smiled.

Go on. Destroy it all. Pull the pin and be done with everything.

She turned her back to them and walked slowly back to the center of the mat. She faced them.

"What? Still no takers? I'm disappointed. I thought at least one of you would have the guts."

"Fuck you!" yelled Meredith.

"Oh, I don't think so, Meredith. I think it's you who's really fucked," said Faith. "Shall I tell your friends why, or will you?"

The other girls looked questioningly at Meredith, but she didn't respond. Faith could see the fear in her eyes.

"When you and Jennifer went on that hunt the other night, things got a little interesting, wouldn't you say? You want to tell your friends about the man you fed on out back of that nightclub?"

"What's she talking 'bout, Meredith?" asked Mia, frowning quizzically.

"She's lying," said Judith, looking around at the others for agreement. "She's gotta be. There's no way Meredith or any of us would break the countess's rules."

"Shut up, Judith. I can speak for myself," snapped Meredith, stepping towards Faith with her fists clenched. "Is that what that whiny little bitch told you? That I fed on some man? And you actually believed her?"

She laughed and turned to the others shaking her head.

"It's not what I believe you should be worrying about, Meredith. It's what Anastasiya believes. There's a reason she went after Jen today. Who knows what she'll do tomorrow? Or who she'll do it to."

"She went after Jen because Jen is weak. She was teaching that stupid bitch a lesson. It's as simple as that. Why don't you go back and tell that lying little cow she better watch her back from now on."

Faith responded with lighting speed, the blade of her naginata nicking Meredith's cheek. The strike drew a collective gasp from the others as Meredith flinched, blood trickling down her cheek. She glared fearfully at Faith.

"You're the one who's weak, Meredith," said Faith stepping towards the others with her naginata held low. "I'm only gonna warn the rest of you cunts once. Anyone here touches Jen, and they'll have me to deal with. Is that understood?"

No one moved. Judith and Mia glared at her, but Faith could tell they were afraid.

"I'm gonna take that as a yes."

She smiled grimly and strolled over to the weapons rack and replaced her naginata. Then she turned and walked from the mat, ignoring Meredith and the others as she passed. She glanced up at the hidden camera as she left the room and wondered what Anastasiya would make of everything. And then she realized she no longer cared.

31

Tammy sat at the breakfast table, a copy of the LA Times spread before her. It'd been two days since her rendezvous with Jack Holland, and the article she was hoping for had not yet materialized. Her husband walked in.

"What's with the sudden interest in the papers, babe?" he asked, noting the pile of early editions at her elbow. "Did I miss something important, or is there a big jewelry sale you wanna beat the other hens to?"

He chuckled derisively.

"It's good to keep up with the latest news now and then, George. You should try it some time," said Tammy. "Oh look, Councilman Sherman has been arrested."

He blanched and stopped midway through putting his coat on. "What?"

"Yeah, it says here he was involved in illegal land rezoning. Apparently, the rezoning benefits some of his family and a local real estate magnate. I wonder who that could be."

"Let me see that," he said, craning his neck to view the article, his coat still halfway on.

"Oh, I'm sorry," said Tammy, pulling the paper out of reach. "What I meant to say is, he's been applauded."

"That's hilarious," he said, buttoning his coat. "Did anyone ever tell you that you have a sick sense of humor?"

"All the time, honey. I married you, didn't I?"

"Careful, babe, I might have to spank that tight ass of yours again."

He leant forward to nuzzle her ear, his hands sliding round to fondle her heavy breasts through the short silk kimono robe. Her nipples stiffened under his working fingers, an involuntary response to the unwanted tactile stimulation.

"I thought you were going to work?" she said.

He chuckled seductively. "Hmm, I could be tempted to stay a few more minutes. What ya say, babe? A little morning roll in the hay?"

His fingers continued their exploration.

"You really think Mitch can run the office?" she said and felt his hands pull away.

"You sure know how to kill the mood," he muttered and looked at his watch. "Suppose I better get going."

He kissed her on the cheek and left. Tammy resumed reading and was rewarded a few pages in.

"DECORATED DETECTIVE DIES IN AUTO CRASH."

She smiled as she read the title.

"Los Angeles—Detective Jack Holland was incinerated in a fiery auto accident late Tuesday night. The decorated detective appears to have lost control of his vehicle on the San Bernardino freeway outside San Gabriel. The automobile rolled down an embankment and hit a tree before bursting into flames. It is not clear at this stage why Holland lost control of his vehicle. The investigation is ongoing."

Tammy sat back, the tension of the past few days melting away. She smiled. The whole thing had worked out better than she could ever have planned. The money had probably been destroyed in the fire. Not that it mattered. She was sure the cash was untraceable.

She also doubted the police would ever discover the reason Jack Holland had lost control of his car.

This time, she'd used Aconite extracted from the crushed roots of the Monkshood plants grown in her green house. She'd blended the highly toxic juice with alcohol and carefully soaked each of the hundred-dollar bills in the solution. She knew Holland would want to check the money before letting her go. In fact, she'd counted on it.

He'd sealed his fate the moment he touched the first bill. It would have taken some time for the poison absorbed through his skin to take effect. Had he realized what she'd done in those final moments before losing consciousness?

"And I didn't even have to get on my knees and give you a blow-job," she said aloud.

She glanced up at the clock on the wall. She still needed to get ready for her exercise class. She closed the newspaper, folded it, and placed it with the others. Maria could throw them out with the trash later. It was going to be a busy day. Rush back home from the gym. A light meal, then off to her two o'clock hair appointment. After that it was the nail salon. And then George was taking her to some fancy new French restaurant for dinner. The slob probably thought giving her the five-star treatment would get him sex. She smiled. Maybe he'd be in luck tonight. It had been some time since she'd felt this good about life.

◊ ◊ ◊

The sound of a thousand angry bees filled the morning's air. Then as of one mind, the six large drones lifted off, rising steadily into the sky until they hovered a hundred feet above the Earth, like giant alien insects ready to conquer the planet.

"They are still noisy," observed Goran.

"I did warn you, though the brushless motors do help cut the decibel level somewhat," said Tony, his eyes on the tablet screen as he pushed the joystick gently.

The drones moved to the right in unison and then hovered obediently.

"See, centralized control, like you asked," he said.

"GPS?" asked Goran.

"Of course. You input the destination by touching the point on the satellite map like so," he said, tapping the screen. "And these babies will get there. I've programmed it so that you can set any number of waypoints, and the drones will fly to each as per the input sequence. Neat, huh?"

To make his point Tony tapped the screen, and the drones moved off a few hundred feet.

Goran looked up at the flying insects. "What is range?"

"That depends. The more weight, the more drain on the batteries. You've also got to consider flying time, wind velocity, amongst other things. All things being equal, I reckon you should get at least twelve miles or so."

"Good," said Goran and held out his hand for the controls.

"I take it the balance owed will be deposited today?" he enquired and handed Goran the controls.

"Da, you will get money."

Goran gave the left joystick a tentative nudge, and the drones rose higher. A push on the right stick sent the drones back another twenty feet.

"The control, it commands all of drones?" he asked.

"Not exactly. The signal is sent to the lead drone, which then relays it to the next in the chain and so on. It all happens very quickly. You could say instantaneous really. The bottom line is there shouldn't be any noticeable delay in response. Each drone also has an in-built situational awareness, so they adjust to the position of the others."

"What if main drone is destroyed?"

Tony grinned smugly. "I've programmed in a multi-directional chain of command. The lead drone goes down, another takes its place.

One of the others goes down, the others move up or down the chain as needed. It's all very simple really."

"Each drone will carry twenty pounds?" asked Goran as he moved the joysticks to bring the flight of drones in close.

"As you ordered."

"Good," said Goran, allowing the drones to gently descend to earth. "You have boxes for drones?"

"Of course. They're in my van. Let me get them for you."

Tony walked over to his vehicle, opened the side doors, and began taking out each case.

"You know, if I didn't know any better, I'd say what you got there is a bunch of attack drones," said Tony casually over his shoulder. "But it's not really my business what you do with them, is it?"

Goran stepped up to the van, pulling a silenced pistol from the shoulder holster beneath his coat as he did. He raised the weapon.

"You are correct. It is not your business," he said and fired before Tony could turn around.

The shot echoed in the open air, and Tony fell forward, overturning the stacked cases. Goran looked around then calmly dragged the corpse over to the open door of the van. He hoisted the body over his shoulder and tipped it unceremoniously into the van before closing the side door.

It took him another half hour to pack each drone into their respective cases and then load these into his own black van. He looked over at the other van and thought about setting it on fire but then decided the black smoke created might increase the chance of the body being discovered. It didn't really matter either way. By tomorrow evening, his brother would be avenged and he'd be gone. Goran turned the ignition, looked around a final time, then slowly turned the van back onto the dirt track he'd used on the way in.

◊ ◊ ◊

Wilson and Clark looked at Webb in stunned silence.

Clark leaned forward so that his large frame appeared more intimidating. "You want us to do what?"

"I want you to obtain a test subject for me," repeated Webb.

"No, that's not what you said," interrupted Wilson with a contradictory shake of his head. "What you said was you'd like us to kidnap a teenage girl, bring her to you so that you can perform some kind of bullshit experiment on her."

Webb responded with a perplexed frown. "Really, gentlemen, I don't understand your sudden hesitation."

"Oh, you don't? Tell me, Doc, anyone ever accuse you of being insane?" said Wilson. "What in hell's name made you even think of something like this?"

Webb pointed a chubby finger at Wilson. "You did, Mr White."

"How so?"

"You quite correctly identified the source of the infection as being from that finishing academy. My study of the corpse found outside the nightclub confirms the victim to have been infected by bites he sustained. The position of the two sets of bite marks appears to be calculated. In other words, not something one would expect in a random violent attack. Both are located on arteries thus it is logical to conclude that the intention was to feed on his blood."

"Hold on a minute there," said Clark, raising his hands in protest. "I can't believe I'm about to say this. What you're saying is the man was attacked by vampires?"

Webb responded with a shrug. "Perhaps. But I prefer to think what we're facing is something a little more exotic than that."

Clark snorted. "More exotic? What? You mean more exotic than vampires? You gotta be kidding."

"Yes," said Webb, choosing to ignore the remark. "What we have here is something more than the cartoon character of legend. What we have is a human being or beings who appear to have somehow been altered by this viral infection and in so doing require constant infusions of fresh human blood."

Wilson took a step back from Webb as though the idea itself was infectious. "Are you saying this virus turns us into vampires?"

"Not exactly. I'm saying the genetic makeup of only a few allows the virus to adapt them to its needs. For the great majority, the likes of you and me for example, the prognosis of this infection would be death. The fact the head of the victim was removed post-mortem proves to me that whoever attacked him knew how to eliminate the risk of the infection spreading."

"Why would they bother? I mean, you said the infection causes death for the rest of us."

Webb placed his hands behind his back as though he were addressing an auditorium of students. "Eventually, yes. But then one must ask: how long does it take for the infected host to die? Then there is the question of how this infected person would react in that time. My theory, and it is only a theory, is that the infected victim is driven by the virus to feed on human blood. Why, I'm still not entirely sure. Although, it might have something to do with the initial bacterial infection. In any event, allowing the infected victim to roam about attacking people would serve only to draw attention to their own existence. That, I would presume, is the last thing they would want. Wouldn't you say?"

Wilson folded his arms across his chest and eyed the doctor suspiciously. "Okay, Webb, let's say you're right about all this. And assuming these things need to feed every so often, that would mean killing and disposing of a whole lot of people."

"A whole lot," repeated Clark, raising his eyebrows.

"Perhaps the bodies are disposed of at the school. Considering the desiccated condition of the remains, it would be relatively easy," said Webb.

"Relatively easy?"

"Well, one could find the means to crush the dried remains to a powder and then either use the resultant material as fertilizer or flush it away as waste."

Wilson shook his head. "I don't think you quite understand what you're proposing, Webb. Let's say they feed on one person a week. That's one body every week. That's fifty-two a year. That school's been around a long time. You do the math. The sheer number of murder victims makes even our worst serial killers look like amateurs. I don't buy it."

"I understand your skepticism, Mr White, but do you have a better explanation?"

"The whole thing could be a coincidence," said Wilson.

"What of the presence of the hit man, Millovic? Is that also a coincidence? Come now, you don't expect me to believe that, do you? There is no such thing as coincidence in my line of work. And I would think the same of yours too."

"Not as much as you seem to think," said Clark.

"On the contrary. Cause and effect, action and reaction," said Webb, clapping his hands together to stress each point. "Whatever you prefer to call it, it still comes down to the same thing. There is always a reason for everything that happens in this world. Not some of the time but all of the time."

He picked up the metal case at his feet and placed it on the table. He snapped back the locks, opened the case, and turned it round to show the agents. Two tranquilizer dart guns were imbedded in the foam packing. A case of tranquilizer darts was beside the guns.

"Now, are you two gentlemen going to carry out my request or not?"

Clark laughed out loud. "Jesus Christ, you're crazier than I thought!"

Webb shot him a look of studied contempt. "No, Mr Black, I'm not crazy. I'm a man who always acts on the strength of his convictions. I'd presumed you were both of similar character, but perhaps I was wrong."

Wilson took a menacing step forward. "My associate and I don't take kindly to being insulted, Webb. Acting on a theory is one thing, but we only deal in hard evidence."

"Hard evidence is what I hired you to find in the first place, isn't that so, Mr White? But at this late stage of the proceedings, I suppose that is a moot point. Now, I have a strict deadline to keep, so I'm going to make this easy for you. I'll pay an extra ten thousand dollars if you deliver the goods in the next five days."

"Thirty thousand, and it's a deal," said Clark.

Wilson shook his head. "We'll have to think about it."

"Twenty-five and you deliver the subject in four days," said Webb.

"I said we'll think about it," said Wilson.

"You do that, Mr White," said Webb, reaching for his coat. "But remember, I'm working to a deadline. I need an answer in the next twenty-four hours."

Webb slipped on his coat before opening the door of the dingy motel room they'd selected for the meeting.

"Good day, gentlemen," he said with a nod and left, closing the door behind him.

The case with the tranquilizer guns and darts remained open on the small table between the two men.

"What's the deal, Nate? He's offering another twenty-five thousand and you suddenly grow a conscience?" said Clark.

"A couple of thousand dollars and you suddenly think it's okay to kidnap some schoolgirl? What the fuck, Allan? Where the hell do you draw the line?"

Clark threw up his arms in disgust.

"Ah, come on, Nate!" said Clark, throwing up his hands in disgust. "You know as well as I do something's going on at that school. Circumstantial though the evidence may be, but you've got to admit it all stacks up."

"It still doesn't give us cause," said Wilson stubbornly.

"Look, whether the school's a front for some drug cartel or a crazy blood-sucking cult, those girls have gotta be involved."

Clark walked over to the case and picked up one of the tranquilizer guns to inspect it.

"Worst case is we end up darting some chick who turns out to be either drug mule or dealer," he said, aiming the gun. "Then again, we might nab us a real live blood-sucking vampire."

Wilson snorted. "You really believe that vampire bullshit?"

"It's not what I believe that counts, Nate. It's that I think it's worth taking a shot. No pun intended."

"It's noon," said Wilson, looking at his watch. "Give me the afternoon to think on it, okay? I'll call you tonight with my decision."

"You do that, Nate. I'll hold onto these babies for the time being," said Clark, placing the tranquilizer gun back on its foam bed and closing the case. "See you back at the office."

Clark left Special Agent Nathaniel Wilson to ponder, as Webb had put it, 'the strength of his convictions."

32

The large black automobile purred along the quiet two-lane road, its headlights picking out the line of cat's eyes glinting in the darkness ahead. Every so often, a set of headlights would appear in the distance. The lights would grow steadily larger as the cars sped towards each other, shimmering specters flying through the dark. For the briefest of moments, the cars would be illuminated in a glare of light as they flashed by, a snapshot in time, and then the blackness would envelope them again.

Faith sat staring out the window of the limo. She turned from the window and looked at the back of Lotho's large dome-like head through the plate glass separating driver from passengers. Not for the first time, she found herself wondering how he'd come to be in Anastasiya's employ. He appeared content in his role, although it was impossible to tell really. The only expression he seemed capable of was a stony-faced aloofness.

Did he view Anastasiya's followers, she wondered, with the same apparent indifference? Perhaps he thought of them as serving no other purpose than that of amusement for his mistress and his role as a detached facilitator of sorts, driving them to and from nightclubs, disposing of their victims' remains, and so on. Her body swayed as the limo pulled off onto a side road, and she turned to look out the window again.

Strange, tonight he appeared to be taking them to one of the more out-of-the-way nightclubs. This was not unusual, but the route he'd chosen felt unnecessarily circuitous to her. Still, the man knew what he was doing, she supposed.

Faith stole a glance at Meredith, who sat diagonally across from her. The girl continued to stare resolutely out the window in what was an obvious attempt to avoid conversation. Why did Anastasiya insist on pairing them together tonight? She must sense the obvious animosity between them, surely. Did it not concern her that this antipathy might spill over during a hunt? Was she prepared to deal with the possible consequence of that? Faith speculated briefly on an answer to these questions, but there was no way of really knowing for sure. Anastasiya was as unfathomable as ever.

She pushed the thoughts from her mind. Too much had happened in the past few days, and Faith decided right now she didn't really care to overthink the situation. Besides, she could feel the hunger growing within her, and with the hunger came the thrill of the coming hunt, a tingling excitement that spread through every fiber of her being. Perhaps sending her on a hunt was Anastasiya's way of getting her to refocus. As much as she wanted to believe that, she knew deep down it wasn't true.

Fuck it. Relax and enjoy the music.

She flopped back against the cool leather and allowed the song to drift over her. She closed her eyes. Her body swayed as the limo turned again. She heard the gravel crunching under the limo's tires and opened her eyes. Where in the hell were they going? She looked at Meredith and realized she too had no idea.

Vents in the limo's floor suddenly opened, and a cloud of gas began rapidly filling the sealed passenger compartment.

"Oh my God, no!" screamed Meredith, turning to smash at the plate glass with her fists. "No, please, no!"

Faith joined Meredith and lunged at the glass, striking with her fists and forearms as they struggled to break out. They yelled and cursed at the silent chauffeur through the glass, but he ignored them. The limo slowed to a halt. Lotho turned to watch their struggle. He smiled.

"Please don't do this!" begged Meredith. "Please, let me talk to Anastasiya! Tell her I won't do it again."

He turned away.

"Let us out, you fuck!" she screamed.

Meredith's panic made Faith more determined not to give into her own fear. She tried to focus her attack on one part of the glass barrier, smashing her fists again and again into the unyielding surface. They started coughing as the acrid vapor reached their lungs. Their attacks became more desperate, blood smearing on the glass as they split their bare knuckles against it. Meredith bent over and retched. It was difficult to breathe now.

Faith turned her attention to the passenger door, lying back on the seat to kick at the window with her heels. Her head started spinning, and she became dimly aware that Meredith's struggles had ceased. She pulled herself half upright and saw Meredith slumped across the seat opposite. Faith tried to focus, but the limo's interior seemed to lurch from side to side. She sensed rather than saw Lotho observing her through the bloody plate glass.

The effects of the gas took their inexorable toll, and Faith finally succumbed, sliding down in her seat as Lou Reed crooned on.

Lotho waited another five minutes before flicking the switch to flush the gas from the passenger compartment. He pulled on a military-grade gas mask, yanked the lever to open the boot, and exited the limo. He removed a large plastic groundsheet from the boot and spread it neatly on the ground immediately behind the car. Satisfied with his handiwork, he walked over to one of the passenger doors.

Another quick look through the window convinced him the girls would offer no resistance. He opened the limo door, grabbed Meredith by her ankles and pulled her unceremoniously from the vehicle. Her head hit the gravel with a sickening thud as he dragged her onto the plastic sheet.

Lotho looked down impassively at the comatose girl sprawled out like a rag doll, her summer dress crudely hiked up around her waist by the force of his actions. He reached back into the boot, retrieved a katana, and unsheathed it with a metallic rasp. Meredith stirred weakly. The big man reached down quickly and grabbed her by the hair. He yanked her body half upright, swinging the katana in a deadly arc as he did.

The blade sheared through Meredith's extended neck with deadly efficiency. Her body dropped back, and he stood upright, holding her severed head by the hair. Flicking the excess blood from the blade, he casually dropped the dead girl's head onto the plastic sheet. He then proceeded round to the other passenger door. He opened the door, reached in, and grabbed Faith by the hair. She moaned in protest as he pulled her from the car with a violent jerk.

He dragged her round onto the slick plastic sheet. She tried to reach up and loosen his grip, but she was still too weak. The big man knew he was running out of time. He yanked her head up and drew the katana back for the final cut.

"FBI! Freeze!"

Lotho stopped in mid action and turned to see two men advancing towards him, their pistols raised.

"Don't even think about it, buddy!" yelled Special Agent Wilson. "Let the girl go and drop the sword."

Lotho hesitated, the deadly blade still raised. He could feel Faith coming around, her movements becoming stronger with every passing second. In that moment, he felt torn between the mistress he worshipped and the instinct of self-preservation. The big man bowed his head in resignation.

"Drop the blade, motherfucker!" shouted Clark.

He approached cautiously, his gun trained on the big man. Lotho exploded with a speed that belied his size, hurling the sword at Clark and reaching for the pistol at his hip in one fluid motion. Wilson fired two rounds in rapid succession, hitting the big man square in the chest. Lotho grunted and stumbled backward, letting go of Faith as he did. He steadied himself and raised his pistol but was hit again as the agents opened fire. The pistol spilled from his hand as he fell back onto Meredith's decapitated corpse. He writhed there ripping the gas mask off to get more air into his shattered lungs. The agents hesitated as they watched him struggle to sit upright. Neither of them had killed before.

An inhuman howl of rage pierced the night air, and Faith leapt upon Lotho. He screamed as she sank her canines deep into his neck. Then she tore out his throat with an unceremonious jerk of her head. A tranquilizer dart hit her in her back. She turned with a hiss to face the agents with her bloody fangs bared. Another dart hit her in the chest. She pulled the dart from her body. She attempted to stand but found her limbs unresponsive as the powerful narcotic took effect. Hissing impotently at the two men, she fell back unconscious as another dart found its target.

"Jesus Christ! Jesus fucking Christ!" exclaimed Wilson.

The two men moved cautiously towards the prostrate girl, dart guns reloaded and ready. But the effects of both gas and tranquilizer had pushed Faith's body to the limit. She would remain comatose for the present.

Clark knelt beside the prostrate girl. "It looks like Webb was on the money."

He pulled a set of handcuffs from his coat and snapped them on Faith's wrists.

Wilson shook his head. "With what we've seen, you really think that's gonna cut it?" He stepped over to the limo's open boot and peered in. "Okay, we're in business. It looks like the big dope came prepared." He pulled out a wide roll of heavy-duty duct tape.

"Help me take off her dress," said Clark.

"What the hell for?"

"I need to use something to clean off those blood smears in the limo. Besides, the duct tape will work better on bare skin."

Wilson took hold of Faith's arms and pulled her halfway up so that Clark could remove her dress. He allowed her body to slump back onto the ground.

"You sure you haven't done this before?"

"Funny man," said Clark. "Now, let's get this bitch contained before we both end up like Samurai Jack over there."

The men taped Faith's wrists together first before moving to her ankles. Then they cocooned the unconscious girl in a tight web of tape from neck to feet.

"If this doesn't work, nothing will," said Wilson and stood up.

Clark chuckled. "I'd love to watch that little prick trying to cut her out of this lot."

"Not our problem," said Wilson. "You gonna go back for the car?"

"Give me a sec. There's something I think we should do first," said Clark.

He picked up the discarded katana and walked over to the dead man, slicing through the remains of Lotho's neck.

"Are you out of your fucking mind?" exclaimed Wilson.

"Out of my fucking mind? We got a man over here who cut the head off a teenage girl. Then he got his throat ripped out by a vampire, and you're asking if I'm outta my mind? Jesus, Nate, get a grip already!"

He stooped over, wiped the blade of the katana off on Lotho's coat, and sheathed the weapon. "Okay, I'll be back in five."

"You're keeping the sword?" asked Wilson incredulously. "It's a murder weapon for Christ's sake!"

"It's got my fingerprints all over it, Nate. What do you think?" said Clark "I'll get rid of it someplace else. Right now, why don't you keep an eye on vampire girl, and I'll go get our car."

He started off back down the road.

Clark pulled up behind the limo a short while later and left the headlights on to ensure they wouldn't miss anything during their clean-up. He popped the boot and got out. He walked round to the back of the car and reached into a box in the boot and retrieved two pairs of latex gloves. Then he walked over to Wilson and held out a pair.

"We're dumping her in the boot?" asked Wilson, taking the gloves. He pulled them on.

"Do you want her in the back seat?" said Clark, pulling on the gloves. He bent down and took hold of Faith's ankles.

"That's a good point," said Wilson, sliding his hands under her armpits. "By the way, how come I get the end with the teeth?"

Clark smiled. "Luck of the draw, I guess. You ready? One, two..."

The two men lifted the comatose girl and carried her over to the sedan. They set her on her side in the boot's cramped confines. Clark closed the boot then walked round to the driver's side of the vehicle. He picked up Faith's discarded dress then reached in through the open window with one hand and pulled the lever to activate the front windscreen's water jets to soak the dress. He tore it into two roughly equal parts and handed one to Wilson.

"You clean one side, and I'll do the other."

The two men returned to the limo and quickly set about cleaning the blood smears from the plate glass.

"Good enough to pass a cursory inspection," muttered Clark. "Now, let's get rid of the bodies."

The men got out of the limo and walked over to the bodies on the plastic sheet.

"Fuck me," muttered Wilson, prodding Meredith's rapidly desiccating corpse with his shoe. The dried muscle and skin tissue rent easily under the applied pressure. He lifted his foot and pressed down hard. Desiccated tissue and bone crumbled and snapped like kindling beneath the heel of his shoe.

"This is like something straight outta *The X Files*."

"Well, Agent Scully, you better move your sweet ass because the night's not getting any younger and we got two bodies to get rid of," said Clark.

"Where'd you plan on dumping them?" asked Wilson.

"Besides the duct tape, the big dude also brought along a shovel."

Clark reached into the open boot to retrieve a long-handled shovel.

"Something tells me the man would've prepared beforehand. That means there'll be a pre-dug hole somewhere near here. All we gotta do is find the hole, wrap the bodies in the ground sheet, drag them over there, push them in, and fill the hole up."

"And the limo? We leave it here?"

"Why not?"

They located the prepared hole twenty minutes later. Then, after what seemed an eternity of sweating and cursing but was in fact only forty-five minutes, the pair dragged the ground sheet with its gruesome cargo to the hole and buried the bodies of Lotho and Meredith. They walked back to the limo and closed both doors and boot before returning to their own vehicle.

Clark tossed the shovel onto the back seat of the sedan as they got in.

"You gonna phone him now?" he asked and started the car.

"Have to," replied Wilson reaching for his cell. "He still hasn't told us where he wants the girl."

"Twenty-five thousand, Nate. Twenty-five fucking thousand. Aren't you glad you changed your mind?"

"Don't go counting your chickens, Allan. The little fucker hasn't paid us yet."

"Oh, he will, Nate. He will."

Clark looked back and reversed the sedan a short distance before turning the car round to face the way they'd come. He pulled away slowly. A short distance later, he accelerated, and the car leapt forward, kicking up gravel and dust in its wake. Each passing mile took Faith further from her other life and closer to a new and uncertain future.

◊ ◊ ◊

It was still dark when Anastasiya pulled up behind the abandoned limo. She turned off the sports car's engine and, sensing no reason for caution, got out. The night air was crisp. The stars glittered dimly against the black fabric of the sky—glass chips scattered carelessly by an unseen hand. She peered into the forest on either side of the gravel road. It was eerily quiet. She walked over to the limo.

The scent of the two men who had been there earlier still hung in the air, but there was also the stench of death. A screech owl hooted in the distance. She turned and began following the route taken by the men. A light breeze rustled the leaves as she walked through the brooding forest. Her senses lead her unerringly to her faithful servant. She knelt and took a handful of the freshly turned soil. Lotho and Meredith were here.

Lotho, the man who'd served her faithfully for more than fifty years. Ex legionnaire, a warrior, and veteran of countless wars. Cursed by a Bedouin crone in the arid wastes of the Tassili n'ajjer to die by the hand of a Si'lat—the succubus of death. He'd finally met his Si'lat years later, feeding on the underworld boss he'd been hired to protect. He'd fallen to his knees expecting death. But she had not killed him. She had offered him life and with it the privilege of serving a living god. Now he was dead, murdered by contemptible thieves.

"Farwell, my faithful servant. You did not deserve this death," she said, allowing the sand to run through her fingers.

She stood up and looked around. Had Faith survived? Her instinct told her she had. There'd be no answers in the abandoned car, but she decided to check anyway. She turned and headed back to the road.

Anastasiya opened the passenger door of the limo. Her keen senses picked up the small traces of dried blood the agents had failed to remove. She noted the girl's high heels strewn on the floor of the passenger compartment and the torn leather upholstery. Lotho had managed to activate the gas canisters. She walked to the back and opened the boot. It was empty. At what stage, she wondered, had the men interrupted him? Had he killed Meredith by then or had the men killed her in the ensuing fight? What concerned her more was the realization that this had not been a random occurrence.

The men had followed the limo to this place. Did this mean they knew about her? Did they know about the school? As much as she hated the idea, she knew she'd have to acknowledge the possibility. Who were these men? Law enforcement? She immediately rejected the idea. The police would have raided the school before now. Besides, these men had taken the trouble to bury the bodies and clean the plate glass in the limo. This meant they were as eager as she to avoid detection by the authorities.

The logical conclusion was that these men must work for an individual or organization that had discovered her existence. Had the men observing the school been following instructions when they tailed Lotho and the girls? Had his actions forced them to intervene and rescue Faith? The alternative was something far more sinister. The men had been instructed to kidnap the girls. What did they hope to achieve by studying them? The discovery of a new species? A biological weapon? How would they do this? Vivisection? Her stomach tensed at the thought. How long before they came for the rest of them?

The urge to cut and run welled up inside her. She closed the limo's passenger door, walked back to her sports car, and slid into the driver's seat. It was now a matter of turning the ignition and driving away from it all. She'd done it before. But not like this, she reminded herself. She had never abandoned her followers. Nor would she this time.

Anastasiya gripped the steering wheel with a renewed determination. She would return to the school and her acolytes. She would inform them that Faith and Meredith had been sent with Lotho on a camping trip. Given the enmity between the two, the girls would assume she had arranged it to force them to resolve their differences. Any concern the girls might have had for their friends would be dispelled. It would also provide her time to organize their relocation and a new cover—perhaps a drug rehabilitation clinic or spa.

All this would have to be arranged within the next week. Time was a luxury she could no longer afford.

33

Anastasiya had commenced the morning class by informing them of Faith and Meredith's unscheduled camping trip to the Sierra Nevadas. She glanced at the clock on the back wall. She'd chosen to maintain the usual routine despite all which needed to be done. Even though her acolytes appeared to accept her explanation, she understood cancelling her class might raise doubts. It was far better to lose an hour or two than risk making the girls suspicious. She reached over and opened the large book on the raised book stand to reveal a typical Renaissance painting. It depicted a young boy bound upon an altar. A man, obviously the boy's father, stood alongside, a dagger in one hand and his eyes looking to heaven. She turned to the class.

"Human sacrifice was practiced by many ancient cultures, either to appease their gods for some imagined sin or as a way of invoking their favor in a new enterprise, be it ensuring victory in war or a good harvest. What then can we conclude from this? Is it that human beings are a naturally bloodthirsty species? Or that they enjoy the act of killing? No, it is that humans recognize the existence of something greater than themselves in this world. Whether humans are religious or not, this need to worship, to submit to an omnipotent power, is engrained in their psyche. Humans want to relinquish responsibility for their lives because they are weak. They prefer the easier alternative of propitiating some imagined god with the blood of others than taking control of their own destiny. That is the path of the weak. You were chosen to walk a different path."

Anastasiya paused to allow the implication of her words to be understood.

"You were chosen to...." She stopped and turned to the window.

The girls looked quizzically at Anastasiya and then they also heard the noise. It was the sound of a thousand angry bees, faint at first but growing louder every second. The girls looked around at each other, unsure of what they should do. It was Judith who stood up and walked over to peer through the window.

"What do you see, girl?" enquired Anastasiya, carefully maintaining her outward calm.

"I don't know, ma'am. A bunch of drones, I think. Above the trees. But they seem... They seem to be headed straight this way."

She turned and looked at Anastasiya.

"Go back to your seats!" snapped Anastasiya to the others before moving towards the window. "Are you sure?"

"Yes, ma'am, I think they're..."

She watched the drones reduce altitude. The flight of six levelled off then suddenly picked up speed as they headed straight at her.

Judith screamed and threw up her arms to shield her face.

The lead drone shattered the window and exploded with an ear-splitting crack, spraying the room's interior with a hundred steel ball bearings that tore through furnishings and flesh with equal ferocity. The next drone followed within seconds of the first, hurtling through the shattered window to explode above the wounded acolytes. The vampire girls' screams of pain and terror were obliterated by the quick succession of explosions as the remaining four drones delivered their murderous cargo with deadly efficiency.

Then, as suddenly, it was over, an eerie quiet settling over the ruined remains of the room. Anastasiya pulled herself upright, blood streaming from a dozen ugly wounds. She looked around in a daze, her mind struggling to comprehend the carnage about her.

Judith was no more, her body shredded almost beyond recognition by the first blast. Mia was motionless amongst the splintered chairs, her shattered limbs beyond the virus's healing skill. Jen clawed her way along the blood-soaked floor dragging her smashed leg behind her. With a detached interest, Anastasiya noted that the virus had begun regenerating the girl's shredded bone and muscle tissue. Here and there, the surviving acolytes stirred, the virus working frenetically to heal their horrific wounds. Anastasiya lurched to her feet and limped over to the wounded Jen. She knelt beside the girl and placed a hand on her shoulder.

"Come, let me help you," she said.

"I don't understand," said Jen, looking up at Anastasiya in bewilderment.

"You must remain calm. Your body will heal itself," said Anastasiya, helping the girl upright.

"But who would do this?" cried Jen, struggling to contain her panic as she saw the ruined bodies of her fellow acolytes.

"Does it matter? Understand only that you have survived and will be stronger for it," said Anastasiya, taking Jen's hand in hers.

"Do you believe that?"

"Yes, everything will..."

Jen's head exploded under the impact of the high velocity round, spraying Anastasiya with blood and brain. The next two rounds fired in quick succession sent her sprawling to the floor. She turned to see a man with an assault rifle advancing across the mansion's lawns.

The weapon cracked again, and a round ricocheted off the wall behind Anastasiya. She hugged the floor to avoid the relentless volley of fire and crawled frantically towards the doorway. She grunted in pain as a bullet smashed into her thigh, and then with a desperate lunge, she hurled herself through the open doorway to the relative safety of the hallway beyond. She pulled herself up against the wall and heard the rifle's staccato report and a girl cry out. He was executing them!

It took all her willpower to move further down the hall away from the room where the gunman continued his deadly work. Anastasiya knew the only way to survive now was to lure him to a place where she could fight him on her terms. The assault rifle cracked again, and a part of her died as another of her girls met a brutal end. She pushed her body on, her strength and determination returning with every step as the virus continued to heal her wounds.

◊ ◊ ◊

Goran raised the assault rifle to his shoulder and fired, killing the last of the wounded acolytes with a head shot. He looked about at the bloody carnage with grim satisfaction. The drones had performed beyond his expectations, and his follow-up assault had been almost perfect. Almost. Goran eyed the open doorway warily.

He realized pursuing the vampire queen would be dangerous, but he had no choice. His brother's murder demanded it. He trained the assault rifle on the doorway and advanced cautiously. As he neared the open doorway, Goran lobbed a primed grenade into the passage beyond and stepped back against the wall. The grenade exploded with a loud bang, and then he moved through the doorway and found nothing. He looked down the gloomy hallway that stretched before him. There were bloody smears along the wall and floor. Was this her way of luring him further into her lair, or was she in fact wounded? It was no matter, he decided. The police would have been alerted by now, which meant time was running out. Only one thing remained. He must find her and eliminate her. He started down the hallway.

The blood trail led further into the mansion. The seconds ticked by, but he found no vampire queen. He kept moving, peering cautiously round corners and doorways as he went. The trail continued. He turned left down a corridor that led towards the back of the mansion. The blood spatters were lessening, he noted. Was she bleeding out, or was something else at play? She wasn't human. Did that mean she could self-heal? He stopped to reevaluate.

The corridor led to a glass door up ahead. He could see the lush green of the tropical plants housed in the conservatory beyond. He could also see the bloody handprint in the middle of the door's glass paneling. Was she attempting to lure him into a trap?

He snapped open the handle strap of the fighting knife at his shoulder before aiming the assault rifle at the door. He fired a quick burst. The door disintegrated in a spray of glass, and he followed up by lobbing another primed grenade through the jagged opening. There was a reassuring thud as the grenade exploded.

Goran wasted no time. He sprinted through the twisted remains of the door and sprayed the conservatory's interior with a liberal burst from his assault rifle before stopping to look around. Thick tropical foliage and colorful exotic flowers dominated the interior, all but hiding a view of the outside world through the conservatory's glass-paneled walls. The air was thick and claustrophobic. He moved cautiously up to the edge of the large pond in the center. The water reflected the dappled shades of green foliage that grew around its edge but gave no hint to the secrets beneath its opaque surface.

Jets of water spraying from three fountains located at one end rose then fell lazily to strike the water's surface with a noisy spatter. Giant lily pads moved gently back and forth on the ripples issuing from the steady splash of water. The perfectly tranquil setting made the deadly hunt in progress almost surreal.

As he looked for an obvious way to cross, he observed that each fountain was in the shape of a woman's head. Replicas of the vampire queen, perhaps? His eyes moved across the water's surface to search the thick jungle on the far side of the pond. There! It had to be. Slightly to the left—a hint of blue fabric amidst the green.

He lifted the assault rifle, took aim, and fired. The burst of fire cut through leaf and stalk like a scythe, leaving nothing but splintered wreckage in its wake. He fired another burst for good measure then waited. Nothing moved.

He knew he needed to be sure. He inserted a fresh magazine clip into his assault rifle before stepping into the thigh-high murky water of the pond. The lily pads' long root tendrils brushed against his legs as he moved carefully towards the far side, his rifle at the ready. Anastasiya struck when he was midway across, launching herself from the pond's murky bottom, where she'd waited patiently. Her attack knocked the assault rifle from Goran's hands and cracked three of his ribs. He fell back under the water drawing his fighting knife as he did. She charged forward as he resurfaced, swinging his knife in a wicked arc, which she barely avoided. The vampire queen and hired killer circled each other warily.

"Worthless man! How you will scream when I slowly drain your life blood," snarled Anastasiya.

She bared her fangs with a hiss. Her blue dress had been discarded earlier. The heavy fabric would only slow her in the water. She moved around the waiting man, a half-naked fury streaked with blood and gore, her lithe muscled body coiled to strike.

"Demon whore!" spat Goran. "You will die for what you did."

Anastasiya lunged at her opponent, but her attack was slowed by the combination of her terrible wounds and the clinging root tendrils beneath the water. He evaded the lunge and countered with a thrust that sliced into her side. Determined to deny her opponent the satisfaction, Anastasiya refused to cry out. She gritted her teeth and moved back beyond the knife's reach.

"What do you wait for, bitch? Come, fall onto my knife and join the others," taunted Goran.

Enraged, Anastasiya charged again only to be rewarded with a deep cut to her thigh. She grunted in pain and shuffled back away from her smiling opponent. She looked into Goran's eyes and saw a man who did not fear death. This made him more dangerous.

Anastasiya knew she did not want to die, and the realization cut her to the quick. What God was afraid of death? How had she allowed herself to become so weak? She felt a wave of self-loathing, and her spirit faltered. The hit man sensed her self-doubt and seized the initiative. He darted forward, feinting with the knife in his right hand then quickly shifting the blade to his left and thrusting at the vampire's exposed midriff. In the instant Anastasiya felt the blade pierce her flesh she understood.

I must embrace death.

The vampire queen bore down on the blade, driving it in her to the hilt. Her body convulsed as the knife pierced her heart, but she pressed on, locking her arms about Goran and pulling him to her. Anastasiya felt her life force ebb even as the virus began working feverishly to mend the ruptured organ. She had mere moments.

"Time to die!" she snarled and sank her fangs deep into Goran's neck.

He let go of the knife as he attempted to prize the vampire loose. The struggling pair lurched about in the foaming water, human and inhuman locked in a macabre tango. Anastasiya fed voraciously as the hit man fought desperately to break free. With each passing second, he grew weaker and she stronger as his life blood surged through her veins.

In a last frantic effort, he grabbed the knife handle with both hands and thrust it up hard, twisting the blade as he did. The violent action caused both to lose their footing, and they plunged beneath the water. The pond seethed and bubbled as the violent struggle continued beneath its surface, and then it was over.

The agitated water became calm, its mirrored surface reflecting the world back at itself once more. An eerie silence filled the conservatory. Then Anastasiya surfaced, rising slowly from the water like a goddess of the underworld, Goran's severed head in her right hand. She lifted the head to look into its sightless eyes.

"Worthless bastard! Fool to think you could destroy me. How I wish you could have suffered more," she said then tossed the head carelessly into the foliage.

She remained in the water and reflected for a moment. He had come close to killing her, closer than she cared to admit. Yet she had passed through the fire and emerged stronger. But at what cost? The sound of police sirens fractured the silence and cut through her thoughts. There would be no time to leave now, she realized. They were too close. She'd go to her hidden underground rooms and wait. Then she would escape when the opportunity presented itself, either this night or the next.

Anastasiya stepped out of the pond as the sound of sirens grew ever louder. She looked around her precious sanctuary one final time then turned and walked resolutely from her old life.

34

Webb looked through the one-way glass at the girl secured to the operating table. It had been a frenetic thirty-six hours since she had been delivered to him. He felt at once exhausted and elated. After so many frustrating months, he finally had his living specimen. An initial analysis of the blood he'd taken from her earlier had confirmed his bacteriophage theory. But isolating the virus was only the beginning.

He still needed to analyze the viral genome and then, more importantly, determine how the girl's own body had reacted to the initial bacterial infection. He suspected the virus was the agent of that change, and this raised another question—how did a phage that should only infect bacteria manage to alter the human host's cells?

It was obvious the bacterial infection triggered the dormant phage hidden within its own DNA, but what then? How had it subsequently entered the host's cells? Was it a chance mutation? Maybe it fused with another virus already present in the host? Or perhaps it truly was alien. A phage and animal virus rolled into one. Capable of evolving to suit the situation. What made this girl special? Why had she survived the infection when others had not? To what extent had the virus altered her physiology? He had many questions and yet so little time. The man who'd provided him the fancy lab he stood in expected results.

The mysterious Mr Chen, or the organization he represented at least, was becoming impatient. Webb realized the situation was entirely of his own making. He had demanded a lot of money and made some big promises. Now he must deliver.

Webb's iPhone buzzed. He retrieved it from his pocket and looked down at the number. He cursed then let it ring a few more times before answering.

"Hello, Mr Chen. I've been expecting your call."

Chen ignored the greeting and got straight to the point: "You have indicated you have a live subject?"

"Yes."

"I presume you have taken samples and commenced testing?"

"Yes, I've started."

"And?"

"As you're probably aware, Mr Chen, the process cannot be rushed. The virus DNA structure will need to be analyzed. I also suspect the virus has altered the subject's own DNA. This will require further analysis itself. Then, of course, I will need to study the subject to ascertain the effect of any physiological changes. As you can see, it might be a while before I have anything substantial."

"That depends on how you apply yourself to your work, Doctor," said Chen. "I expect you will submit daily progress reports."

Webb blinked. "Daily?"

"Our investment in this project has been substantial. Do you not agree, Doctor?"

"Yes."

"Then you would agree strict monitoring of progress is essential?"

"Yes, Mr Chen, but..."

"Good, I'm glad we are in agreement."

Webb gritted his teeth. "Yes, Mr Chen."

"Of course, I would also like to see the subject for myself. This Friday, 9 p.m. I assume you have no objection?"

"No, Mr Chen."

"Until Friday then, Dr Webb. Goodbye."

"Goodbye, Mr Chen," replied Webb, feeling the weight of the master's yoke upon his shoulders.

He looked at the girl again, his eyes following the contours of her half-naked body. She was quite exquisite. He wondered again how it would be to touch her intimately. Mr White and Mr Black had brought her to him trussed up like a turkey. For an extra five thousand, they had cut her free and secured her to the table. Webb had waited for them to leave before getting to work. She'd awoken the moment he'd started to draw blood from her. The fear in her large doe-like eyes had aroused him, and it had taken all his self-control not to take her then. He had left the room immediately. Now, standing in the darkened outer room watching her, he felt an overwhelming sense of self-loathing. Was he not better than that?

He walked over to the lab door, took a deep breath, and entered.

The girl turned her head and watched silently as he walked over to the table where he kept his instruments.

"Please, why am I here? What are you going to do to me?" she asked.

Startled, Webb dropped the scalpel he was holding. He turned to look at her but did not answer.

"The men who kidnapped me—whatever they told you, it's all lies. They think I'm something that I'm not. I'm just a girl."

"I think we both know that's a lie," said Webb, walking over to a small refrigerator. He retrieved a vial and held it up to her. "Blood, on the other hand, never lies, and yours has a very interesting story to tell."

"I don't know what you're talking about. Let me go, please," said Faith, squirming in her steel restraints.

"You know I can't do that now," said Webb, replacing the vial in the refrigerator. "Besides, I've plenty more tests to run on you."

"The school I go to, they'll be looking for me. They've probably called the police by now. You'll be in a lot of trouble when they find me. Let me go. I promise I won't say a thing."

"The school?" said Webb. "The same school that wanted you dead?"

"What do you mean?"

"The big man with the sword. If the men working for me hadn't stopped him, you would be nothing but a headless corpse now."

"The men working for you, how do you know they're telling you the truth?"

"I really don't care either way. But the fact you haven't asked about the man who tried to kill you or the other girl he murdered tells me more than you care to admit. Your mistress obviously wanted to be rid of the both of you. I think I've done her a favor, don't you?"

"You son of a bitch!" screamed Faith. Her body arched as she strained against the unyielding steel holding her to the table.

"Your struggles are quite useless. Those manacles have been designed to restrain a five-hundred-pound gorilla."

"You think the countess won't come looking? When Lotho doesn't return, she'll go to the forest."

"And find what? An empty limousine? The bodies were buried away from there. She wouldn't have known where to look."

"You don't know her. She'll find them and will know you took me. She will search for me, and when she finds me, you'll wish you were dead. You can count on it."

Webb smiled. "Perhaps I should have mentioned this earlier. Your mistress is dead."

"What?"

"Yes. It appears someone took a dislike to your so-called countess. They blew up part of the school and killed a whole lot of your friends in the process."

"You're lying!"

"Oh, I'm afraid not."

"I don't believe you!"

"You want proof?"

Webb left the room and returned a few moments later with his iPad.

"Here it is. This morning's news," he said and began reading aloud. "School bombed. Students murdered in horror attack."

He raised the iPad up to allow Faith to read the headline for herself. A photo of the bomb-scarred mansion accompanied the article. She fought back her tears as she read the report. The place she'd wanted to escape for so long had been destroyed, and with it her only hope of salvation. She sank beneath a wave of helpless despair. Down she plunged into the black pit of misery. To think her life should end this way—a lab rat strapped to a table, doomed to a slow and agonizing death. She turned her head away from Webb.

"So, you see, you're here to stay. Besides, where else could you go now?" said Webb.

"Leave me alone," said Faith.

"I have a remote control for the restraints, so if you require the toilet, let me know. I wouldn't want you to suffer any undue discomfort," he said, pointing to a small portable toilet in the corner of the lab. "Oh, and in case you get any ideas, I can flood the room with nerve gas anytime I need."

Faith did not respond. How she wanted to scream out that his precious science experiment was doomed. It was only a matter of time before her body started to disintegrate without Anastasiya's blood.

"I hope we understand each other," said Webb.

Faith continued to look away from him.

"I'll take that as a yes," he said and walked back to the table.

He proceeded to place a winged infusion set, some blood culture bottles and other related items onto a trolley. Satisfied he had everything he required, he wheeled the trolley over to Faith. He prepared the sampling kit before placing a tourniquet about her arm and pulling it tight. Once he'd found a vein, he sterilized his hands with an antibacterial gel and pulled on a pair of latex gloves.

"This won't take a moment," he said, cleaning her arm with an alcohol swab.

He picked up the infusion set and started to push the needle into her arm. She lunged at him then, her fangs bared with a hiss. The needle gouged deep into her arm as he stumbled backward. But the restraints held firm, and all she could do was growl ineffectually at him.

"Jesus!" he said, his hands shaking. "You little bitch! Look what you made me do."

She glared at him, blood trickling onto the table from her wound. Webb stood back from the table and composed himself. He took another swab from the trolley and stepped closer to her again.

"It'll do you no good, you know," he said, cleaning the blood from her wound. "The quicker you cooperate, the quicker this will all be over."

He paused. The deep gash in Faith's arm had started to heal, flesh fusing neatly under the virus's healing spell.

He smiled. "Oh my word, you are full of surprises."

"Fuck you!"

"I think," he said, retrieving a scalpel from the trolley, "you should learn to be a little more cooperative."

He drew the blade across her thigh, slicing deep into her flesh, and she cried out.

"You still have a pain response. That is interesting."

"You're an animal!"

"We're all animals, my dear. But some animals happen to be in a more advantageous position."

Intrigued, he watched as the subcutaneous layer began bonding followed by the outer dermal layers. Faith cried out as he cut her leg again, deeper this time to slice through the muscle tissue.

She screamed in pain. "You motherfucker!"

"You know, this reminds me of a Greek myth my father once told me as a child," said Webb, watching the muscle tissue knit together. "Do you know any Greek myths?"

She glared at him, tears streaming down her flushed cheeks.

"No, I don't suppose you would. The Titans were immortal giants. Some say they were the first gods. They were overthrown by the Olympians—the new gods. Fire was kept on Mount Olympus. The Titan, Prometheus, stole a single spark and gave it to man that they might be raised above all the other animals. Zeus, king of the gods, was angered by this and punished Prometheus. He had him chained to a rock so that an eagle could rip through his abdomen and tear out his liver. But Prometheus was immortal, and each night his body would regenerate. And the following day, the eagle would return to devour it again. And again and again, day after day, for all eternity. Think of the agony."

He pressed the scalpel against her bare thigh once more.

"You sick fuck, let me go!"

He cut, and she screamed again. "Would you like to test which fails first—your capacity for pain or my willingness to inflict it?"

He raised the scalpel again.

"No, please stop!"

"Good, I'm glad you understand," he said, placing the scalpel back on the trolley.

He proceeded to wipe away the excess blood from her thigh, watching as the wound healed itself.

"I wonder if you realize how extraordinary a creature you are," he said.

She turned her face away from him.

"If you don't, you soon will. Together, we will explore your special gifts."

He picked up a new needle from the trolley and inserted it into her arm. As he watched her blood fill the first bottle, his mind began exploring the unique opportunities her alien physiology might offer.

35

Three days had passed since the attack. The police car parked out front of the school was a testament to the public interest, which remained high despite the lack of anything new to report. Goran's murderous assault had caused a sensation in the press, but it was the National Security Agency investigating the crime that now controlled the narrative. The official story was that a woman-hating gun nut had attacked the school and killed the head mistress and her students.

Identification had been complicated by the condition of their bodies, and an appeal had been made for relatives to come forward. No one appeared to know if any had.

Agency investigators on the ground knew slightly more. A car located near the scene had been searched and a driver's license discovered. A cross check with Interpol had identified Goran Millovic as the probable gunman. This together with the lack of any school records or information on the headmistress had raised suspicions of a drug-related gangland hit. The identity of the female students remained a mystery.

Initial medical examination of the curiously withered corpses had revealed little. The pathologist had suggested chemical attack, and so the remains had been sent to a lab specializing in chemical warfare for further testing. The authorities were sufficiently concerned for Washington to assign a special unit to investigate the case.

It was past midnight when a concealed door in the library swung inward and Anastasiya emerged from her subterranean refuge. She was dressed in black. A small backpack slung over her shoulder carried her false ID, credit cards and some cash. Even though there was little chance of her underground labyrinth being discovered, she'd cleaned it of incriminating evidence. She stepped into the room, and the door sealed itself behind her, blending seamlessly with the bookshelf.

"Ms Strajinski, I presume?" said a voice from the dark.

Anastasiya turned to face a man seated in a chair in the corner of the room. There was just enough ambient light to make him out.

"Good evening, Detective Jablonski," she said.

"I knew if I waited long enough you'd show up. Didn't figure you were right under our noses the whole time."

"What do you want, Detective?"

Jablonski switched on his flashlight aiming its beam at her face. "I want some answers."

"Such as?" asked Anastasiya, squinting into the light.

"What did you have to do with Jack Holland's death?"

"My school was attacked, my students brutally murdered, and you ask me what I had to do with your partner's death," she growled her eyes flashing like a tigress in the light.

"You didn't answer the question."

She shrugged and dropped her backpack to the floor. "Until this moment, I did not know he was dead. Why do you think I had anything to do with his murder? He was murdered, I presume?"

"Not exactly."

"Not exactly. Either he was or he was not," she said and took a step towards him.

Jablonski drew his pistol. "Not so fast, lady."

"I pose no threat, Detective, I assure you," she said raising her hands palms outward to show she had no concealed weapon.

"Maybe you do, maybe you don't. Let's say I'd prefer you stay put. And to answer your question, he died in an auto accident. At least that's the official line. But they found a quantity of cash in the burned-out wreck, and that got me thinking."

Anastasiya lowered her hands. "Thinking? About what, Detective?"

"He was investigating you. Then a hit man with ties to the mob does a number on this place, and I put two and two together."

"And what did you get?"

"Not a whole lot that adds up. No records of your so-called pupils. No invoices, no bills to parents, and no records on you either. It's like this place never existed. It's like you never existed. But we've got six dead women. We've got a big mansion in a fancy neighborhood. And we've got the body of a heavily armed killer. So I'll tell you what I think."

"Please do," said Anastasiya, taking another step forward.

"Lady, you move again, and I'm gonna put a slug in ya."

"Detective, I am woman, and I am unarmed. What risk could I possibly pose to you?"

"You tell me."

"I'd much rather hear your theory first."

"The way I see it, what you have here is some kinda exclusive whorehouse for your Russian mob boss friends. We've got no records on the girls, and with all the security you got around here I figure we're looking at sex trafficking. They're probably Eastern European, shipped in against their will from whatever shithole town they called home."

"An interesting story, Detective, but what does Jack Holland have to do with all of this?" She took another step forward, shifting her weight onto the balls of her feet as she did.

"That's what I want you to tell me."

"Shall I tell you what this place is, Detective?"

"That would be a good place to start."

"I'm not used to having a gun pointed at me. Before I begin, I ask that you put it down or at least point it away from me."

Jablonski placed his pistol within reach on the armrest of the chair. "Happy now?"

"Yes!"

Anastasiya moved with frightening speed, clearing the remaining distance between her and Jablonski in a heartbeat. She leapt upon the man, flipping the chair over with her on top of him, the flashlight sent flying from his grasp. It spun across the floor, illuminating their uneven struggle like a disco strobe light. Anastasiya's left hand gripped the wrist of his gun hand as the vice-like fingers of her right closed around his throat choking him. She squeezed her left hand and heard his wrist snap like kindling. He grunted in pain and dropped the gun.

"This is not a whorehouse, Detective. It is a sanctuary. It is a place where we can be ourselves, a place away from the rest of you."

Anastasiya smiled to reveal her long, pointed canines. Jablonski's eyes widened in horror, and he attempted to speak but could not until she loosened her grip about his throat.

"What the fuck are you?" he croaked.

"I am a god, Detective."

"I don't believe in gods."

"And yet I exist. I am older than you could ever imagine. I have seen more than you will in three lifetimes. I will be here long after you lie forgotten, cold in the ground."

"What do you want from me?"

"I want you to look after something for me."

"What?"

"The painting."

"It's real, isn't it?"

"You decide, Detective."

"What if I say no? Are you gonna kill me then?"

"But you won't say no. Your love of art won't allow you to. And your life will finally mean something. You will be the caretaker of a true masterpiece."

"What if I talked? What if I reported what I know?"

"A vampire god? Who would believe you? No, Detective, you will not talk. You will take the painting and leave. And some day I will return for it."

She saw in his eyes the truth of her words, and she released her grip on him.

"How many more policemen are there out there?" she asked.

"The two in the car at the gate," said Jablonski. "They owe me a favor, so they let me stake out the place. They thought I was crazy, but they let me do it anyways."

"Goodbye, Detective Jablonski. Perhaps we will meet again."

Anastasiya stood up. She picked up her rucksack and turned to look at the Klimt painting one last time. Her eyes traced the line of pale bodies drifting aimlessly through the seeming void, powerless and alone. She looked into the eyes of the mysterious female at the bottom of the painting. The woman stared back mockingly from behind her black veil. What did the woman see—a failed god or someone being dragged along helplessly by the current of destiny?

She walked from the room, leaving Jablonski to tend to his broken wrist.

A lone figure in black scaled the large stone perimeter wall surrounding the mansion's grounds a half hour later. Anastasiya reached the top of the wall and paused to look back at the place that had been her home for the past fifty years. Life had been good here. Perhaps that had been the problem. It had caused her to become complacent. But it was too late for regrets. She exhaled slowly and let go of it all. She turned away, dropped silently to the street below, and walked silently into the night.

36

Faith closed her eyes. Her head ached from the lab's harsh fluorescent lights Webb insisted stay on around the clock. Whether intentional or not, she felt disorientated. Was it Thursday or Friday? She could no longer tell. Time stood still. She shifted her body to get comfortable, or as comfortable as her restraints would allow. Worse was the constant gnawing hunger that threatened to push her to the edge of sanity. Webb had mockingly offered her his takeaway meals, knowing she could not eat.

It was blood she craved. Warm, sweet, delicious blood. How long would it be before she starved to death? Days? Weeks? She'd also not had Anastasiya's blood for at least that long, yet the virus had not attacked her. Why? She knew the answer deep down. She didn't need, probably had never needed, Anastasiya's blood to survive. Even now she found it difficult to accept, though in hindsight it appeared obvious. Her enhanced abilities had allowed her to challenge Anastasiya. Had the alien virus intended that she replace her?

There was no way of knowing that now. She was the last of them. But for how long? What would Webb do with her once he had everything he needed? Would he leave her to rot on this table by simply closing the door and walking away? Or would he hand her over to someone else so they could continue experimenting? She couldn't tell which frightened her more—the virus slowly eating its way through her or being strapped to a table like some modern-day Prometheus, doomed to suffer cruel experimentation for an eternity.

The door to the lab opened, and Webb stepped into the room. He was followed by three Asian men dressed in plain dark business suits. The two more physically imposing men took up station at the door whilst the remaining man accompanied Webb. He was tall and lean with a thin cruel face and carried himself with the self-assured air of somebody used to being in authority. The pair approached the table. The thin-faced man regarded Faith speculatively. His cold black eyes sent a chill through her.

"You've stated in your report that her cell tissue regenerates," said the man.

"Yes, Mr Chen, I have conducted a few experiments in that regard," said Webb.

"Show me."

"What, now?"

"I'd like to see for myself. Show me now."

"Yes, of course," said Webb pulling a nearby trolley close.

He chose a scalpel from the neatly arrayed stainless-steel instruments and casually cut into Faith's leg. She gritted her teeth against the pain. She would not give them the satisfaction of seeing her distress. Webb wiped the blood away with the flourish of an amateur magician revealing his latest trick. A fascinated Chen watched as the wound began to heal itself.

"Yes, I see. Very interesting," he said. "Tell me, have you ascertained the extent of this regeneration, Doctor?"

"Excuse me?"

"How well does she heal herself, Doctor? Would she be able to regrow a limb if it were removed, for example?"

"Well, I haven't... I mean... Is that really necessary?" said Webb, looking bemused.

Faith could see Webb was appalled by the idea. She also knew him well enough by now to realize compassion played no part in his response. It was the thought of seeing his favorite new toy defaced that upset him.

"All unknowns should be considered, Doctor. I would have thought that to be standard practice in any research," said Chen. "It is of no matter. I will have our scientists run the necessary tests when she is moved to our facility."

"Moved?" exclaimed Webb. "What do you mean?"

Chen offered a condescending smile. "Come now, Doctor, surely you did not think we would entrust you with such an important find. Besides, I think our own scientists are more than capable of continuing your research."

"But you can't!" protested Webb. "What about our agreement?"

"Not an agreement, Doctor, a contract. That contract is now cancelled."

"Cancelled? What do you mean? You can't do that. Not now! Not when I've still so much to do."

"That is no longer your concern, Doctor. Your recent indiscretion is what decided it."

"Indiscretion?"

"Two in fact—Special Agent Wilson and Clark. I believe you knew them as Mr White and Mr Black?"

"I didn't know that. I assure you, Mr Chen. I wouldn't have hired them had I known that."

"That is because you're an amateur. Of course, the two men have now been eliminated."

"What? You killed them?"

"Purely a matter of ensuring there are no loose ends, Doctor. Would you not agree?" said Chen, turning to the two men at the door and nodding.

"No, wait!" stammered Webb as the men advanced. "I'm sorry. I didn't know. You must believe me!"

"Oh, I do believe you. But as I've already said, there can be no loose ends. Goodbye, Doctor Webb, China appreciates your small contribution."

Chen stepped away as the men moved in. One produced a pistol from his coat. Steel instruments clattered to the concrete floor as Webb stumbled backwards, overturning the trolley as he fell against the table where Faith was. He righted himself and turned to look at her with an expression of disbelief. His killers were almost upon him. He shoved his hand in his coat pocket and pressed the panic button. Faith's restraints sprang open with a metallic click. She attacked without a moment's hesitation. In less time than Chen could scream, Webb's would-be killers were dead, and Faith had pinned the terrified Chinese agent to the cold concrete floor. Her face, hands, and arms were streaked red with blood.

"I'm more than a piece of meat, you ignorant fuck!" she hissed.

Her hands closed about his throat. Chen's eyes were wide with terror. He clawed frantically at her arms but could not loosen her grip about his throat.

"If I ripped your head off, would it grow back, I wonder?" she said, tightening her grip around his throat to choke off his frantic pleas. "What do you think, Doc?"

She looked over to where Webb cowered, but he didn't answer.

"Too bad we don't have time to find out. Guess I'll have to drain you instead."

She bared her fangs in a mirthless grin and fell upon her victim. Webb watched in horrified fascination as she fed voraciously. Chen's body arched, the heels of his shoes scarring the concrete floor as he struggled futilely to throw off the vampire latched to his throat. He slowly weakened, and then it was over.

Faith wiped the blood from her chin as she looked up from his corpse. Webb remained crouched near the table staring at her with a mixture of fear and awe. She moved towards him on all fours with the sensual power of a predator, drunk with blood lust. He tried to move but found his limbs would not respond. The vampire stopped in front of him, her face inches from his. The metallic scent of blood was heavy on her breath. She looked hard into his eyes.

"And what am I going to do with you huh, Doc?" she said huskily.

"Don't you see? I helped you," said Webb "I saved you."

"No, Doc, you didn't save me," she said, slowly straddling him. She placed her hands on his shoulders and pressed his back firmly against the table leg. Then she leaned forward and whispered into his ear, "No one can save me."

He managed a single strangled squeal as she sank her fangs deep into his neck and fed again. She was surprised at how little resistance he offered. It was almost as though he was relieved to accept his fate. She took her time, drinking slowly, inexorably draining every drop from him. Once she'd sated herself, she stood up and let his corpse sag to the floor.

She looked about slowly—first at the mutilated bodyguards then at Chen and finally Webb. It took her a moment to comprehend what she'd done. She walked over to the sink unit, turned on the faucet, and began washing the blood off her body. Once she'd finished, she turned and walked across to where a white lab coat hung from a rack, carefully avoiding the expanding pools of blood leaking from the dead bodyguards. She reached up, took the coat, and slipped it on. She paused to contemplate her situation.

It was obvious she could not remain hiding there. Chen's superiors were sure to investigate his absence. Besides them, who else knew of this place? Either way, someone was sure to appear sooner or later. Staying would inevitably mean killing, dying, or both, and right now she was too mad at everyone to die.

The only alternative was to run. But where to? And once there, what would she do? How was she to survive, living in the shadows for an eternity as Anastasiya had done? She thought of Jen's excitement at the idea of living forever. Poor innocent Jen. Dead. The rest of them, dead. Living forever! She laughed out loud at the thought. Hiding from humanity forever like Anastasiya. Denying your existence. No, her life would mean something. She thought about what Webb had said about the virus and its effect on human DNA. Something about each human infection being an occurrence, and that given enough iterations of that occurrence a new type of human might be created. Perhaps one that didn't require human blood to survive? It was a thought. She smiled at the idea of starting her own revolution. Maybe it was time to give humanity the boot up the ass it needed. Her hands curled into fists.

Why the fuck not?

She walked over to Webb's corpse, knelt, and went through his pockets until she found a set of car keys. She looked down at his watch and noted the time. It was still day. She would wait till night. There would be fewer people about then.

The skin on Webb's hands was translucent, and his veins had started turning black. She looked at his face. He was turning. Sometime from now his corpse would reanimate itself as some shuffling undead thing, driven by the virus to feed on human flesh.

She'd only seen it twice before and had no idea how long the process would take. She looked across at Chen's corpse. He too was changing. It seemed appropriate—the two men trapped in this room by their own greed, unable to satisfy their hunger, doomed to die a second time as the virus slowly consumed them. She exited the room. She had no desire to watch the horror unfold. In a few hours, it would be night, and she'd leave and begin her new life. A new destiny beckoned.

37

Anastasiya stood looking out the window of her exclusive penthouse apartment. Located on New York's Upper East Side, it had an excellent view of Central Park, which now was blanketed under a white shroud of snow. Her gaze drifted over the leafless trees, their gnarled branches reaching up like crooked skeletal fingers to claw at the cold winter sky. There was, she decided, a stark beauty to it all.

She turned, walked back to the low couch that stood in the center of her sparsely furnished lounge, and sat down. The Zen-like minimalist decor of the apartment was a purposeful attempt to move away from the baroque antique of her previous life. She turned on the large flatscreen TV set into the wall opposite and began idly flicking through the countless channels. There appeared to be nothing on offer but a monotonous variety of reality-based drivel. Reality TV, the pinnacle of human achievement. She settled on CNN.

In truth, her present living arrangement was less than ideal. There was the doorman who observed her every coming and going, fellow residents who attempted idle conversation in the elevator, and of course the nosey neighbors from the floor below. Enticing men or women to her bed was easy. Getting them up to her apartment unnoticed was another matter entirely. Finally, there was the problem of disposing of her victims' corpses. It was such a tedious task. She pictured herself kneeling on the plastic sheet, arms, face, and hair coated with the dust of each desiccated corpse as she crushed them into fragments.

So much for being a goddess!

At least she could console herself with the knowledge that her present situation was a temporary one. Even now the law firm of Whitcomb Newton & Moore were negotiating the purchase of a property in upstate New York. The mansion was situated on ten acres of forestland and would provide the cover and privacy she needed to start again. Anastasiya gazed idly at the TV as her thoughts picked over the various possibilities afforded by this new beginning.

A figure suddenly lurched into view on the TV and wrenched her from her thoughts. She watched the contorted creature stagger towards a group of diners in a restaurant. The images had the shaky out-of-focus appearance of being footage from someone's cell phone.

A man out of frame laughed. "What's this guy's problem?"

People could be heard laughing nervously.

"It's not Halloween yet, buddy!" shouted another voice off screen.

A man, probably the manager, stepped into view. He walked up to the strange figure.

"Can I help you?" he asked.

The moaning creature turned and lunged at the surprised man, who stumbled back and fell. The creature was upon him before he could recover, sinking its teeth into his neck. There were terrified screams, and the video frame jerked back and forth as people scrambled away from the shocking scene before them. The image froze and was replaced by the newsreader who continued with the report.

"This station has chosen not to broadcast the remaining footage due to its disturbing content. As we've reported, two people have been killed and three injured in the vicious attack that occurred in American Falls, Idaho. According to some eyewitnesses, the attacker reportedly began eating his victims. Police called to the scene were forced to shoot at the man when he attacked them. Eyewitnesses say multiple shots were fired at the attacker before he was stopped. The man died of his injuries at the scene. It is not clear whether he had been under the influence of narcotics at the time of the attack. Three injured people have been taken to a local hospital for treatment and are said to be in a serious but stable condition. In a further development, a source close to the investigation has indicated that a team from the CDC is being sent to the town to investigate. We'll be crossing live to Bob Jarvis in American Falls a little later in the program for further updates. In other news..."

Anastasiya stared at the TV but no longer cared to listen to the newsreader. Faith was alive! Somehow, she'd escaped from whoever had taken her and now, like some modern-day Pandora, appeared intent on releasing her plague on all humanity.

Córko moja, jesteś taka nieprzewidywalna!

She understood why Faith was doing this. The girl was angry, as she herself had been those many years ago. But this world was very different than the one in which she'd found herself nearly two hundred years before, and the danger of being discovered was much greater.

There were two options—either allow Faith to vent her anger and hope nothing came back to threaten her own existence or hunt her down, confront her, and finally put the matter to rest.

There would be challenges ahead, no matter which path she chose, but what was life without a challenge?

SHAUN GRIFFIN
240

END BOOK TWO

SHAUN GRIFFIN
242

THE STORY WILL BE CONCLUDED
IN BOOK THREE
OF THE AMERICAN NOIR TRILOGY

Faith has unleashed the vampire virus upon America. Infection guarantees death to all but the few who bond with it—the new vampires. As panic spreads the government scrambles to eliminate the mutating virus. But two men, billionaire Xavier Masters and Senator Drake, recognise its potential—both in the promise of immortality and creating a super soldier. All they need is to find the one who started it all.

Guilt ridden by what she has done, Faith vows to destroy her vampire creations even if it means venturing into the military controlled quarantine zones. When Faith rescues Hannah, a young girl infected by one of her creations, she becomes the target of Xavier's deadly team of mercenaries. Aided by another vampire they close in on her trail. But another threat looms—Anastasiya, her maker, hunts her too.

As the climactic battle nears, Faith must decide: is she truly a monster or the key to humanity's survival? Find out in the final instalment of the American Noir Trilogy – Hera's Lament.

HERA'S
LAMENT

Shaun Griffin is a structural engineer currently working in Australia. He and his wife live in a small coastal town where they share a house with their spoiled pet Cavoodle. The children having moved out to follow their own careers, Shaun divides his spare time writing, reading history, collecting comics and in the gym.

HERA'S SCREAM
REVENGE. BETRAYAL. DEATH.
BOOK TWO OF THE AMERICAN NOIR TRILOGY

written by SHAUN GRIFFIN
cover by JASON LETTS

ISBN 978-0-6481701-6-7 (Paperback)

www.ingramcontent.com/pod-product-compliance
Lightning Source LLC
Chambersburg PA
CBHW060148180626
46813CB00007B/2676